BABYLON 5™

THE SHADOW WITHIN

By
Jeanne Cavelos

Based on the series by
J. Michael Straczynski

BALLANTINE BOOKS • NEW YORK

A Del Rey® Book
Published by The Ballantine Publishing Group

www.delreydigital.com

ISBN 0-345-45218-6

Manufactured in the United States of America

First Ballantine Books Edition: December 2002

OPM 10 9 8 7 6 5 4 3 2 1

To my mother

Acknowledgments

I'd like to thank all the people who read this book in manuscript form, gave me helpful feedback, and spotted a number of real whoppers: Laurie Shanahan, Allen Wilkins, Chris Aylott, Joe Garza, Margo Cavelos, Patricia A. Jackson, John Donigan, John Brooks, Michelle Zellich, and William (Pete) Pettit. Thanks also to my panel of *Babylon 5* experts: lurker Steven Grimm, nitpicker Phil Farrand, Michael A. Burstein, and Nomi Burstein. I received wonderful information (in response to what must have seemed some very odd questions) from Dr. Bob Goodby of the University of New Hampshire's Archaeology Department, Dr. Eugene Boudette, the New Hampshire state geologist, and Dr. Paul Viscuso of Cornell University. I also must thank, of course, Joe Straczynski, for creating such a rich and compelling universe, Harlan Ellison for his support, and Beth Toussaint, Melissa Gilbert, Bruce Boxleitner, and Ed Wasser for their inspiration. At Dell, thanks to Leslie Schnur, for believing in me, and to Jacquie Miller, my editor, for always being there. For her encouragement and advice, I want to thank Lori Perkins. And on the home front, thanks to my husband, Michael Flint, for telling me all about Confederate Colonel Emory Fiske Best of the 23rd Georgia Volunteer Infantry. And finally, thanks to Igmoe, my iguana, whose daily bouts of Igmoe-psychosis made the writing of this book a lively and unpredictable experience.

November 2256

Time present and time past
Are both perhaps present in time future,
And time future contained in time past.
—T. S. ELIOT

CHAPTER 1

ANNA Sheridan rested her elbows on her desk and her chin on her nested fists, studying the artifact that lay before her. It was about five inches long, three wide at its widest point, and about three inches high. The front end, as she had come to think of it, rounded in a gentle curve, looking almost like a head, while the back end tapered to a point, almost like a tail. The surface of the object, with an odd elastic property like skin, was a mottled grayish color. The various shades of gray, rather than merging into each other as they did in living creatures, were separated in small block segments, giving the surface a mechanical appearance. The shape of the object had the feel of something organic, living, though her tests had shown her that it was a mixture of the biological and the mechanical. This object, the mouse as she called it, was the first example of true biomechanical technology ever discovered.

She tried not to think about that too much, tried to limit those embarrassing daydreams about accepting the Nobel prize to a quickie after lunch. The discovery was no good unless she could figure out how the technology worked, unless she could figure out how to work the technology. She'd run every test and scan she could think of, and while they had

yielded incredible information, they'd left her no
closer to understanding the purpose of this device or
the method by which it was operated. She'd tried
every method she could think of to activate it, to
wake it up, from old-fashioned poking to subtle alterations to its environment, but it remained inert.

She took the mouse in her hand, feeling the slight
warmth of it against her palm. Its skin felt like that of
Dr. Chang's hairless pet cat. There was a slight smell
to it, too, like the anchovies she loved and John hated,
though more subtle and faint. She could almost feel the
life of it in her hand, as if she were holding a sleeping
mouse. She admired the simplicity, the smoothness of
its outer shape, the complex, intricate skeleton she
knew was within. She visualized its heart beating quietly, steadily at its core, the brain waves' repeating
oscillation within. She imagined the electrons flowing
through the superconducting metal.

She noticed then that the shades of gray on the back
of the mouse were shifting. She put her hand under the
desk light. The surface of the mouse was changing
shades in block segments, one small rectangle of skin
now a light gray, then a charcoal, then a medium gray.
Overall the pattern gave the sense of lines of charcoal
proceeding slowly down the mouse's back. The device
seemed activated.

It was so beautiful, so elegant. Neurons fired, circuits responded, patterns emerged. And to this beat it
carried out its function, living, breathing, its functioning a song, a march in lockstep, unified in purpose,
focused, uplifting. It was the machine, and the machine was the universe. It towered dark in the vault of
the sky, ageless, mighty, a perfect mechanism, never
tiring, never slowing. Perfect grace, perfect control,
form and function integrated into the circuitry of the

unbroken loop, the iteration, the closed universe, in which was written on the neural pathways and in the dark microscopic voids its purpose, circulating like a shadow through the heart of the machine. Her life belonged to the machine. She loved the machine.

Anna dropped the mouse onto her desk and jumped out of her chair. Something had happened. The shifting of the gray blocks slowed, stopped. What had she been thinking? Alien thoughts. The mouse's thoughts. The mouse had been communicating its thoughts to her. The mouse, the loyal tool, had been communicating its love of its job. And it had nearly overwhelmed her in the process.

Anna backed away from the desk, her heart pounding. The mouse sat quietly in the circle of light from her desk lamp. Holding the mouse and concentrating on it had somehow activated it. How could she have lost herself so easily? For a few moments, she had forgotten who she was, what she was, even *that* she was. She had been absorbed by alien thoughts, enthralled by the machine. The machine had taken over her mind.

Her fear slowly dissipated as she realized what a breakthrough she had made. She had activated a device utilizing a totally unknown technology that had lain dormant for over a thousand years. But what, exactly, had activated it, and how could she study it if any contact overwhelmed her?

Her hand tapping against her leg, Anna crossed the lab to the window, shooting glances back at the mouse. Outside, it had begun to snow, the thick flakes driving against the windows of Geneva City Hospital across the wide boulevard. Three floors down, the morning traffic was now in full swing. She'd missed it, coming in early after a night of restless sleep to study the mouse. It was potentially the greatest find she'd ever made, but if she couldn't discover how it worked, the find would be meaningless.

Three months ago, she'd returned from a dig for Interplanetary Expeditions (IPX) on Theta Omega 2, a planet near the rim of known space. Under Dr. Chang, the mission commander and her old instructor at the University of Chicago, they'd unearthed the remains of a race who called themselves the J/Lai, an offshoot of the Brakiri. Although the artifacts and the culture they implied had been fascinating, IPX had been mainly interested in a particular crystalline stone that the J/Lai had used as an energy source. Once she and the other archaeologists had determined that the J/Lai used this stone for energy, the information was handed over to the engineers. She and the others on the science team of the expedition were left batting cleanup, at least in the minds of the IPX executives.

Their interest in archaeology was perfectly summed up in the corporate slogan, "Exploring the past to create a better future," as long as the better future was better for IPX. Or as one of her colleagues, Favorito, liked to paraphrase, "Exploiting the past to create a better profit margin." If they couldn't use it, swap it, or sell it, they didn't care about it. But when it came to mounting major expeditions to distant planets, they were the only game in town. As she'd justified her growing involvement with IPX to her husband, John, "It's all right to deal with the devil, as long as you do it freelance."

And so the executives' attention turned elsewhere, which was fine with Anna. She could fill out the end of her contract with IPX in peace. Then she planned to return to MIT for a year, where her baggy sweaters, khaki pants, and irregularly combed hair wouldn't be so out of place. She would teach for a while and get back into the in-depth research that allowed her to immerse herself in a long-dead alien culture.

Most people didn't understand her desire to know how alien cultures had thought and lived. John tried, though he was undeniably a man of the present. Her parents appreciated the profitability of discovering ancient alien technologies. But most nonarchaeologists didn't understand that in the practice of her profession she traveled in space and time and body, unlocked ancient secrets, gained communion with races staggeringly different from her own, and examined how all these different races tried to answer the same questions, to cope with the same problems: *where did we come from, where are we going, and what significance can my life possibly have?* Maybe, someday, she'd find the answers for herself.

Her specialty was tools, the favorite of most archaeologists, and she'd been working up her report on the tools of the J/Lai culture two days ago when she'd realized that there was one pallet of artifacts she'd failed to examine. In the computer, the pallet was designated "Miscellaneous," which to archaeologists meant items too small to be identified or those deemed of no significance. These were usually natural, unmodified objects that happened to be located at an archaeological site. In a dig on Earth, for example, rocks or acorns that had not been used by humans and had not been modified by them would be included in "miscellaneous."

But she was a perfectionist—didn't like to leave any stone unturned as Chang liked to joke—archaeologists' humor—and so went down to the warehouse to examine the pallet. Most of the items did look like "miscellaneous," though after scrutinizing each piece she found ten she wanted to pull for further study. Three, in particular, intrigued her.

Back in her lab, she studied the three. They looked almost like dried-out corn husks, two quite shriveled, the third one less so. They at first appeared similar to a plant on Theta Omega 2, which was probably how they had gotten into "miscellaneous," though on further examination the error of that identification became clear. The more she studied them, the more animallike they seemed. The outer layer was thin and fragile, almost like a butterfly's cocoon, with a slightly iridescent quality. She decided to run a few more tests before handing the objects over to Churlstein, the physical anthropologist from the expedition.

Her first scan came back with incongruous results: the objects inside the husks appeared to have simultaneously biological and mechanical characteristics. She repeated the scan and got the same results. Anna studied the nonsensical readouts for a long time, her mind racing through possibilities. The J/Lai had nothing like this. It was far more advanced than anything they had; far more advanced than anything anyone had. An RNA screen revealed that the mitochondrial RNA of the objects didn't match that of the microorganisms on Theta Omega 2. The objects came from a different planet, a different culture. Forcing herself to sit still and breathe deeply, she ran one final scan, to reveal hard structures within the husks. The two shriveled husks revealed what looked like quasi-skeletal remains, broken and jumbled. The third husk revealed a complex, elegant skeleton, one with a bizarre structure and an unusual variety in bone density and width. In all the skeletons from all the planets she had seen, she'd never seen anything that looked like this. Its intricate, bizarre pattern gave her the sense of something crafted, artificial. And it looked perfectly intact.

This was when she ran, yelling and waving her test results, down the hall to Dr. Chang.

He'd been as excited as she was, and she saw a quickness in his step, a sharpness to his gestures that she hadn't seen since he'd left the university and started working full-time for IPX about ten years ago: *Time to cash in on all those laurels I've accumulated,* he'd joked at the time.

Yesterday she'd opened the three cocoons, apparently protective or preservative envelopes of some kind, uncovering in the two shriveled cocoons the quasi-skeletal remains, and in the remaining cocoon the mouse. With Chang and occasionally others looking on, she'd run a battery of tests. The results often generated more questions than answers. Late into the night after Chang had gone, she'd continued to examine the mouse. She wondered whether it should be considered a biomechanical device or a biomechanical species. Tests had shown it had a pulse and a rudimentary circulatory system. She had also detected low-level electrical activity suggesting a quasi brain wave, though the brain waves had a perfect, uniform cyclical structure. No known creature had a simple, perfectly cyclical brain-wave pattern; the steady frequency and amplitude were more characteristic of electronics. In addition, the electrical pattern was propagated throughout the entire object, as through a classical electronic device, rather than being limited to a certain area. While certain components contained organic compounds, others were forged from an unfamiliar superconducting metal. A complex array of microprocessors clung to sections of the skeleton like barnacles. The mouse's energy source was a mystery.

Why would an advanced species create something like this? If it was a tool of some kind, she'd been unable to discern its workings. There were no obvious controls or mechanisms. She didn't know what it might do. When working with the artifacts of a specific culture, she always tried to create a part of her mind that thought like the alien. Bit by bit she added information—how they obtained food, how they created shelter—until in some limited way she could re-create the way they saw things, the way they lived. That was her method: study the artifacts left behind, deduce the culture of those who had left them, reconstitute their behavior, recapture their thoughts. But in this case, she had only three artifacts from which to deduce an entire culture. It was like trying to deduce the contents of a dark room from what she could see in the beam of a stationary pinpoint light. And if she didn't come up with results soon, she knew IPX would hand the mouse over to someone else. Her planned three-week vacation/anniversary celebration starting tomorrow only added to the pressure.

Anna turned away from the window. The mouse sat still in the circle of light cast by the lamp, a point of calm in the center of the maelstrom she called her lab. In the last two days, it had deteriorated from cluttered to barely controlled chaos. Test results were scattered over her desk and lab table, where the three isocases holding the quasi-skeletal remains and the mouse's cocoon sat waiting for her insights. The counter along the left wall was covered with testing equipment she had borrowed from other labs, several comp-pads, only one of which was hers, and reference books she'd pulled down from the bookcase beside the door. Along the right wall was the isolab and the console controlling it, her personal computer hanging over the edge of the console alongside a scattering of unlabeled data crystals. Hardly the corporate image Chang so often reminded her they wanted to present. But she knew where everything was, and she got results. Usually. But for some reason, after her big breakthrough, here she was delaying. The thoughts of the mouse, so clear and so powerful, had shaken her. Losing her self, even for a few moments, was terrifying. And she sensed that the mouse had only been brought to a minimal level of activity, awakening only for a few moments. What would it do when fully activated?

She returned to her desk. If her touch had activated the mouse, then she'd re-create the environment of her touch until she found the factor that had activated it. She took two of the printouts on her desk, used one to nudge the mouse onto the other. Then picking that printout up from either side, she carried the mouse into the isolab and sealed it inside.

With the mouse now isolated, Anna sat at the isolab console, where she could observe the artifact through the window and manipulate the environment within. She re-created the temperature of her hand. She re-created the chemical salinity and oils on her palm. She re-created the pulse of her blood, the faint electromagnetic field of her body. All to no effect. The coloring on the mouse remained unchanged.

She raised the temperature another ten degrees, far beyond what it would have been in her hand. Waited. No change.

Chang's heavy footsteps sounded behind her. "I got your message. Any luck?" He sounded like a different person from yesterday, as if the growing pragmatism and caution of the last ten years had suddenly been doubled over night. The enthusiasm in his voice yesterday had been replaced by his corporate poker-neutral tone.

With a practiced push of her foot, Anna swung around in her chair, turning away from the isolab window and console.

Dr. Chang had looked almost the same for as long as she'd known him: fine flyaway grayish white hair, a short, compact build, around his eyes and mouth the rugged wrinkles of someone who spent a lot of time outdoors. Her favorite part of him was his hands, covered with the calluses that were the badges of honor of field archaeologists, yet graceful in their movement. Her own hands were callused—it was an occupational hazard—but it would take years before they looked like Dr. Chang's. The main change in him over the years had been a slight widening of his midsection and a radical change in clothes when he joined the corporate environment of IPX. She still found it odd to see him in a tailored suit and tasseled loafers. He seemed to belong in rugged outdoor gear. Yet today he looked drained, a slump in his chest and a slackness to his mouth as if he'd lost touch with his body.

She thought she'd cheer him up. "I activated the mouse this morning somehow, when I was holding it."

"You did?" he said, the question sounding more like a statement. "What happened?" He leaned forward to look at the mouse down on the floor of the isolab.

"Is something wrong?" she asked.

"What? No." He straightened. "I didn't get much sleep last night."

Anna smiled. "Me neither. So I came in early, and when I was holding the mouse, the color patterns on it started to shift."

He sat down beside her at the console, enthusiasm warming his voice. "Incredible, Anna. So what are you doing now?"

"I was trying to re-create the environment of my hand, to isolate the factor that activated it. But nothing's working." She brought up the variables she'd been manipulating on the monitor. Chang's eyes seemed to glide over them.

"None of these variables had the same effect as your touch."

"No."

He turned to her. "You're holding something back."

Anna's hand tapped against her leg. Through the isolab window the object rested, quiet as a sleeping mouse. "This morning when I was holding it, when the patterns started to move, I felt something. I felt it thinking. It communicated to me telepathically."

"So you think maybe it's operated telepathically." With his thumbnail he scraped at a callus on his index finger.

"I'm no telepath, but I think that maybe by holding it, and by focusing my attention on it, I may have brought it to some minimal level of activity." Now that she'd come out with the theory she'd been avoiding since her contact with the mouse, it seemed inevitable, and the next step was clear. "A telepath may be able to fully activate it."

Chang's tone turned neutral. "You want to bring a telepath in on this?"

"I don't see any other way. We've brought in various experts before. Hell, I'm a freelancer, along with half of the people in this building."

Chang glanced over his shoulder into the hall.

"When you discovered that mouse, you turned this place upside down. There's a lot of interest in it."

Anna shrugged. "Of course there is."

"You have to proceed carefully."

She sighed. "Politics, I know."

"You shouldn't dismiss politics so quickly. Politics are often a stronger force than the truth." He paused, his weatherworn face again seeming drained. "I can't authorize it. I know what they want. They want absolute secrecy. They're even more paranoid than normal."

"But a telepath would have to keep this confidential."

Chang nodded, his gaze drifting back to the mouse. "Have you tried affecting it mentally, from a distance?"

"No. I don't see how I could."

"Try it for me. Just to see."

She turned to him, twisting her lips. "I'm going to feel stupid."

"Worse things have happened."

She took a deep breath, let it out. The mouse lay still, sleeping. She focused on the patterns frozen on its surface, the supple skin, the complex structure of bone, the oscillating current of brain, the heart she knew beat within. *Move, damn it, move. Wake up. Time to wake up. Do something. Dance a jig. Sing a song. The machine says it's time to wake up!* Nothing.

She turned back to Chang. "I do feel stupid."

"We had to try."

She ran her hands up under her shoulder-length hair and grabbed her scalp. She wasn't about to give up. This puzzle was solvable, and she'd discovered the key. "I don't need your authorization, you know. To bring in a telepath."

Chang nodded. "But if you tell me about it, I have to forbid it."

"What if I don't tell you about it?"

Chang looked over his shoulder again. "I've been directed to get daily reports from you on your progress."

"They *are* interested." She released her head. "What if you come for your daily report at"—she checked her watch—"six o'clock?"

Chang smiled. "Four."

Anna made what John called her monkey face, gritting her teeth and pulling her lips back. "Five?"

Chang stood. "Dr. Sheridan, I'll expect your report at five o'clock."

"And I'll be pleased to give it to you, Dr. Chang." She had the computer retrieving business listings for telepaths before he'd left the room.

CHAPTER 2

TERRENCE Hilliard, certified telepath, arrived at three o'clock. He was a tall, slim black man who wore a fashionable olive-green suit and, of course, black gloves. He presented his credentials, certifying him P5. All the telepaths she had met were slim, Anna mused. She wondered if it was part of their training.

"Thanks for coming on such short notice."

"Not a problem," Terrence said. "I had a cancellation this morning, and you fit right in." He had a lovely voice, deep, with a lilting, Irish accent.

She took him to the isolab window and showed him the mouse inside, explaining her experience with it. "I'm hoping that it may have been designed to be controlled telepathically. Or at least that some telepathic contact may activate its own internal mechanisms."

"This is quite unusual," Terrence said. "I've never attempted telepathic contact with an object before."

"You probably think I'm crazy, right?"

Terrence smiled, and it was the kind of smile that lit up his face, the kind of smile John had. God, she missed him. In eighteen hours she'd be on her way to see him, and for three weeks she hoped never to see the outside of the hotel room.

"You could fill a thimble with what I know about

archaeology. But I have to say, I don't think I'm going to be able to sense anything, let alone be able to order it 'round to fetch your slippers.''

They both laughed, and Anna had him sit beside her in front of the isolab window. She set the isolab scanners to record. "Is there anything you need?" she asked.

"I assume you want to keep it isolated? This would be easier with physical contact."

"I'd like to try it this way first. If there are any changes in the object, we can get a clear record. If it doesn't work, then we can try physical contact."

"Very well. Just give me a few moments quiet, please." He folded his hands, and his face grew serious.

Anna studied the isolab readout. The scanners were detecting no change. The mouse sat, stubborn, silent. Then the gray began to flow over its skin, not like before, in a halting, block by block progression, but in a wave of darkness pulsing down its body from head to tail, again and again, faster and faster, like a heartbeat. Anna jumped up, bit back a yelp, sat down again. The mouse's temperature was beginning to rise. The wave had now engulfed the mouse, so that its entire skin seemed to lighten and darken at once, pulsing. It glowed with a gray, shadowy light. Even its shape seemed to be pulsing, growing larger and smaller, as if it were panting. The frequency and amplitude of the brain waves increased. The temperature of the mouse shot up. "Terrence! It's superheating!"

The pressure in the room changed. Anna's ears popped, and with a flash of light and a shriek that shredded the fabric of the air, she was scooped up out of her chair on a geyser of hot air and tossed back over her desk to the floor.

Her ears rang. She shook her head and climbed to her feet, holding the desk for support. Her knees were shaking. "Shit!" The mouse had exploded.

The lights in the isolab had been blown out, as had the window, yet she could see in the remaining light that little of the mouse survived. Fragments of skin and bone and glops of quasi-organic matter were splattered over the inside of the isolab. There went her Nobel. There went her reputation. There went the only example of biomechanical technology. But most of all, there went her opportunity to understand this thing, this semicreature that had fascinated her and presented her with the chance to learn so much. Her pinpoint light into the darkness of this unknown culture had blown out. She should have gone slower, should have started with only a moment of telepathic contact. She could be impatient, and she had been. Now she knew how John felt when he "screwed the pooch." It felt like crap.

She noticed that Terrence wasn't moving. He'd been knocked straight over and was still in the chair, on the floor. She climbed over the desk toward him, noticing shiny streaks on his face. Blood. Fragments of the window had pierced his cheeks and neck. He was saying something, but she couldn't hear. She realized an alarm was blaring. She pushed aside her own empty chair and knelt beside him. "Terrence!"

His wounds didn't appear severe, but he seemed dazed. His eyes danced without focus, and his lips continued to move. She grabbed his shoulders and leaned in close. "Terrence, what is it? Are you hurt?" She brought her ear to his lips. They whispered over her skin as his deep voice flowed out.

"I am the machine. I am the machine. I am the machine."

She jerked back, and then the door to her lab burst open, knocking aside the bookcase that had fallen against it. Churlstein shoved his wide body through the opening. "Sheridan! Are you okay?"

She could barely hear him over the damn alarm. She pointed to Terrence. "He needs help," she screamed. "We need to get him out." Churlstein waded through the mess with his characteristic waddle, several others slipping through the door behind him.

Terrence's lips continued to move. If only they would stop. God, what had she done to him?

Churlstein's round, moonlike face pushed its way into her field of vision. He helped her pull Terrence up, and they dragged him out into the hallway, into the onlookers.

"We've got to get him to a doctor," Anna shouted. Lines of blood from the cuts on Terrence's face had now run down to his moving lips.

"We'll go next door," Churlstein said, dragging Terrence, and also Anna, down the corridor. His large bulk swayed from side to side as he moved.

At first Anna didn't understand where they were going. Then she remembered. Geneva City Hospital.

As they left the IPX building and the alarm behind, Terrence's words emerged beneath the sounds of the traffic, repeating, repeating.

With Churlstein she dragged Terrence across the boulevard into the emergency room and stammered out that Terrence had been in an explosion. They took him into a curtained cubicle.

"What happened?" Churlstein asked.

She found she had to sit down. There were a couple of chairs in a wide spot in the hallway.

"What was that telepath doing in the lab?" Churlstein sat beside her, the side of his body pushing into hers. His face wore its usual wrinkled frustration. "The mouse was destroyed, wasn't it? I saw the iso-lab."

"Not now, Churlstein, okay?" She scratched her neck, was surprised to see blood on her hand. Her hand was shaking. She willed it to stop, but it didn't. She rested her forearms in her lap. Found they continued to shake there.

She'd been able to break her contact with the mouse this morning because she *hadn't* been a telepath, because the contact had been weak. The strong telepathic contact had somehow locked Terrence into the machine, locked him and it together in some sort of feedback loop, which he was still unable to escape.

"Dr. Sheridan."

Anna had the sense that time had passed, though she didn't know how much. A woman stood in front of her dressed all in black, like a block of shadow under the harsh lighting. Her body radiated a sense of confidence and strength, from her balanced, shoulder-width stance, to the hands on her hips, to the thick muscles obvious in her shoulders beneath the tailored suit. The Psi Corps insignia was fastened to her lapel. Her dirty-blond hair was pulled back in a tight bun, a small scar on her left cheek in the half-circular shape of the letter D. She looked more like a soldier than a telepath. The only telepaths Anna knew who gave off a similar military feeling were Psi Cops, and she didn't wear the uniform of a Psi Cop. Besides, Psi Cops tracked down rogue telepaths; they didn't minister to sick ones.

"I'm Dr. Sheridan."

"My name is Donne. From Psi Corps." When Donne spoke, her jaw barely moved, as if it had been wired shut. Her face seemed clenched, sullen. "You are to give me full access to all information and materials relating to the injury of Terrence Hilliard and the J/Lai expedition.'' She took out a paper from her breast pocket and handed it over to Anna.

Anna unfolded the paper with trembling hands, found she couldn't focus on its words. "How did you know we were here?"

"I need to examine Mr. Hilliard," Donne said. "And I want you to come with me."

Churlstein stood with Anna, tentatively grabbing her elbow as if he would help her along, when Donne turned on him. "I will talk to Dr. Sheridan alone."

"I'll see you back at the office," Anna said, starting toward the cubicle with Donne. She turned back and noticed Churlstein staring after them, his round face wrinkled in frustration. "Tell them not to touch anything at the lab," Anna said. "I want to record it all before it's cleaned up."

As they approached the curtained-off cubicle, the sound of the doctors, the nurses, the equipment, the bustle, all seemed to fade under the whisper of Terrence's voice. Donne followed behind, as if Anna were some prisoner who might try to escape. Anna pulled the curtain aside, and the words enveloped her. He lay still in the bed, quiescent, reminding Anna of the mouse. Only his lips moved, in a dull, careless way, lines of spittle running down his chin, and his eyes, searching—for something.

"I am the machine. I am the machine."

Beside Terrence's bed stood a doctor, studying the readout on a monitor. "His physical injuries are superficial. I've treated them. But his mental condition . . . I've never seen anything like it." He pointed to the monitor. "His brain waves show a rigid, perfectly cyclical pattern, totally unlike human brain waves. Yet there is no physiological reason for this abnormality. There is no damage from the explosion to the skull or brain that could possibly be responsible. Is there anything more you can tell me about what happened?''

"Thank you, Doctor," Donne said. "Psi Corps will transfer him shortly to one of our facilities. See that he is accompanied by a complete report of your findings."

The doctor hesitated. "Yes, of course. You'll need to complete some paperwork to release the patient." Then he left, the curtain billowing behind him.

"I am the machine. I am the machine."

Donne approached Terrence, her eyes narrowing with what might have been fear. "Tell me everything you know."

Anna told her, Donne constantly interrupting with questions. It was obvious Donne knew nothing about archaeology, and very little about any of the other sciences. At the end, Donne seemed no more satisfied than when Anna had begun. "So you have no idea what planet this 'mouse' originally came from?"

"No."

"And you have no other 'mice' to study?"

"No. Only the quasi-bones I told you about, and the remaining fragments of the mouse."

"I need a fragment for study, as well as some of the bones. And I need all your notes and test results."

"You'll have to go through IPX for that. They own everything." Anna took a step closer to Terrence. "I want to help any way I can."

Donne turned her harsh, clenched face on Anna. "You *will* help any way you can." She pointed to the monitor. "These brain waves are the same that you observed from the mouse?"

"I am the machine. I am the machine."

"It's a similar, perfectly cyclical pattern," Anna said. "Originally the brain waves of the mouse had a lower amplitude and frequency. But as Terrence made contact, I saw them both shoot up to about these levels. It's as if Terrence reflected the mouse's patterns and reinforced them." Terrence's gloves had been removed, revealing slightly paler skin, pruny fingertips. Anna laid her hand over his. She had stopped shaking. "Can't you bring him out of this telepathically?"

"Thank you for your suggestion, Dr. Sheridan. That will be all." Her tone could have frozen helium.

"Will you let me know how he does?"

"He's in the hands of the corps now. That's all you need to know."

Anna twisted her lips, fighting the sudden pressure of tears. "How did you get here so quickly?"

"I ask the questions; I don't answer them. I'm not the one who turned a telepath's brain to jelly."

And in the silence, the whisper of Terrence's lips. "I am the machine. I am the machine."

Terrence's eyes continued to dart sightlessly around the room. He didn't see her. He didn't see anything. Anna squeezed his hand and left. She had to go back to the lab, had to record the debris pattern of the explosion, pass it to the engineers to calculate the force of the detonation. She had to collect the fragments. She looked at her watch, suddenly remembered her vacation and John. In fifteen hours she was supposed to be on a transport to see him and celebrate their anniversary. How could she leave now? After all that had happened. She looked at her watch again. In an hour, she was supposed to be having dinner with Liz.

She walked into her lab, distracted, reaching her desk before she realized that all signs of the blast had been cleaned away. It didn't even look like her lab, it

was so clean. All furniture and equipment had been
restored or replaced, except for the equipment she'd
borrowed from other labs, which had simply been removed. All the glass and mouse fragments had been
swept up. All her books had been restored to her bookcase, out of order. All her reports and test results were
gone. Her personal computer was centered neatly on
her desk. The only evidence of the explosion was the
missing isolab window, which would probably take
days to replace.

"You're late for our meeting."

Anna jumped. Dr. Chang was standing in the doorway behind her. "I'm sorry. I forgot all about it." She
looked at her watch again.

"Are you all right? You have blood on your neck."

She touched the area she'd been scratching. "It's
nothing." He remained in the doorway. "I know I've
screwed up."

"According to them"—Chang flashed his eyes sky-
ward, toward the executives—"we both did. But truth-
fully, no one could have known what would happen.
And your theory was right. The mechanism was telepathically controlled. I don't think anyone else would
have figured that out. At least not so quickly."

"I know we don't have a lot left to work with, but I
don't want to give up. Maybe by studying the fragments I can figure out something that might help that
telepath to recover."

"I've been asked to take over the testing," he said
in his neutral tone.

A thousand objections ran through Anna's mind,
but she didn't feel she had the right to utter any of
them. She sat.

"I know you're the best person for this job."
Chang came inside, closed the door behind him. "I

meant what I said. But believe me, it's better you're out of this. Nobody's going to come out on top of this thing. I wish I could pass it to someone else." His thumb scraped at the callus on his index finger. "This has nothing to do with archaeology anymore, and everything to do with power."

She sighed. "Why does everything have to be so political?"

"Because man is a political being."

The corner of her mouth went up. "Did they calculate how strong the blast was?"

"The equivalent of a half-second burst from a pulse cannon." He raised a hand before she could ask another question. "I need copies of your notes and records so far."

She nodded and opened up her computer, downloading the files onto a data crystal. Chang knew she kept all her preliminary notes on her own system. He even knew her password. He could easily have retrieved them if he'd wanted to, even confiscated her computer so she wouldn't have access to the information. He was purposely allowing her to keep her files, to have continued access.

She laid the crystal in his callused palm. "I think I should cancel my vacation. I don't feel right about going away now."

The wrinkles around his eyes deepened. "Your vacation. I completely forgot about it. You know what a great people person I am." This was an old joke, about a criticism she'd written on a teacher evaluation years and years ago.

"I don't think I should leave now."

He took her hand. "Yes, you should. That's exactly what you should do. Give things some time to cool off here. Get away from all this craziness. When you come back . . . we'll see what happens.'' He released her hand.

She knew he was holding a lot back, that he was under pressures she could only guess about. But she trusted his advice. She nodded. "I'll see you in three weeks."

He opened the hall door. "Get some rest."

She smiled. "I hope not." At his hesitation, she wished she hadn't said that.

After Chang had left, Anna gathered together her belongings. She closed up her computer and slid it into her carryall. On her desk, neatly centered in the space where her computer had sat, was a long, flat, shriveled piece of mouse. She picked it up and whispered, "Thank you, Chang."

Although the edges were crusty and dried, the center remained soft and elastic. There was a slight dampness on the underside, and she turned it over to find a black, tarry substance. Stealing a glance out into the hall, Anna found a small container for the fragment and packed it quickly into her carryall.

She wished her vacation had begun yesterday. But it hadn't, and now Terrence had been hurt, and there was nothing she could do about it. She could at least get some work done on the transport, though. The vacation wouldn't be quite the romantic escape she'd hoped for, not with all this hanging over her head, but maybe John could distract her for a while. It had been a long time.

She left IPX behind for what she hoped would be three very distracting weeks.

CHAPTER 3

"Sorry I'm late." Anna slid into the chair opposite Liz Sheridan and ordered some wine to get rid of the waiter.

"It's okay. I haven't been here long," Liz said.

They both smiled. "Liar," Anna said.

They both knew Liz was compulsively early. They'd known each other since undergraduate days, long before Anna had met Liz's unbelievably sweet brother John, fallen in love, and married him.

Anna gazed absently across the restaurant, Terrence's words whispering through her mind in an unending loop. She wondered if he'd been transferred to the Psi Corps facility yet, wondered if they would be able to free him from the feedback loop.

"You're going to love the food here," Liz said.

Anna nodded. The restaurant was one of Liz's "finds" and allegedly fulfilled all her criteria: tables far enough away from each other for some privacy, relaxing music, a warm ambience—in this case created by a Swiss Chalet motif—and food good enough to eat.

"Ready for your big anniversary bash?" Liz asked.

"Any more ready and I'd burst." Anna tried to smile, but her face wouldn't cooperate.

"What's wrong?"

Anna's fist went to her mouth. "I screwed up at work. I can't talk about it."

"You need to get out of that corporate environment. You're freelance. Get out of there and get back to teaching."

"Maybe you're right."

Liz raised her chin, her earrings swaying. "I know I'm right. Now as of tonight you are officially on vacation. I want you to put all that stuff in the vault and lock it away for three weeks. Think about having some fun. You guys haven't been together for how long?"

Anna took a long sip of her wine, thinking back. "The last time we saw each other for more than three days at once was over a year ago. August, before school started. I don't think I'll even know what to do when I see him."

Liz smiled. She had the face of a pixie, with a small, pointed chin, high cheekbones, and huge deep eyes. "Allow me to jog your memory." She brought a box out from under the table and presented it to Anna. "Happy anniversary."

"Oh you didn't. Not again."

Liz waved her objections away. "Allow me my sick fun. I only have one best friend. And one sister-in-law."

Anna leaned across the table. "I'm not opening it here."

Liz raised her hands. "That's fine. Open it when you see Johnny. It's as much for him as it is for you."

Anna sighed. "What would I do without you?"

Liz shrugged. "Go naked?"

"As Dr. Chang would say, 'Worse things have happened.'" They giggled a while, and Anna drank more wine, trying to relax. There was nothing she could do now. She needed to be with John, to feel his arms enfolding her, the warmth of his body, the rumble of his voice, the vitality of his presence.

No matter how long they spent away from each other, her love for him never faded. She felt she truly had found the love they talked about in poems and in ancient alien inscriptions. A universal love. A love without end, a love without borders.

She couldn't wait to see him.

John Sheridan wondered if his wife, Anna, was thinking of him right now. He'd noticed that in the years they'd been together, they'd begun to talk alike, and even to think alike—a quality he'd noticed long ago in his parents and grown to love. He couldn't wait to see her.

Less than an hour to Station Prime. Another hour to button up the ship, begin leave rotation, hand things over to the technicians. Twenty minutes by shuttle from space dock to the station, twenty more to the hotel, and he would be with her.

Unfortunately, that was in two hours and forty minutes, not now. He barked out the words. "Are you aware of the proper procedure for bringing the laser cannons to battle alert status, Lieutenant Spano?"

"Yes, sir."

"Recite the procedure, Lieutenant."

"Request confirmation of battle alert status from command. On confirmation, the defense grid is activated. Baffles are lowered. Settings are initialized and confirmed. Activators are put on standby. Tracking system is upgraded to targeting mode. Optics are brought on line. Primary ignition is triggered. Laser—"

"Lieutenant." John took a step closer to Spano, his

voice rising. "What will happen if primary ignition is triggered with tube hatches open?"

"The laser would fail to fire, sir."

"That may explain why procedure dictates a check of the tube hatches before primary ignition is triggered."

Lieutenant Spano held his silence, remaining stiffly at attention in his Earthforce uniform, his hands clenched at his sides. His skin had flushed a deep red, visible even through his blond buzz cut, and his wide nostrils flared with each hard breath. He was a twenty-eight-year-old veteran of the Earth-Minbari War with a huge chip on his shoulder. Although John had not had much direct contact with him since taking command of the *Agamemnon*, he already knew that Spano didn't like being told anything by anybody. Earthforce was the last place he belonged. He seemed a walking embodiment of anger. The muscles in his neck stood out like cables, and his eyes had an opaque, flat quality that was disquieting.

John could feel his own face growing just as red as Spano's. This crew had more than its share of slackers, and nothing he did seemed to have any effect. "Procedures are created for a reason, Lieutenant, the reason for this one being to ensure the safety of every soldier aboard this vessel. As a weapons officer, I expect you to know the procedures relating to laser cannons backward and forward, upside down, in your sleep, surrounded by enemy ships, and with my face in your face." He stopped, exasperated, then paced a few steps down the line. The four weapons officers stood shoulder to shoulder at attention, the sixteen gunners formed in two ranks behind them, filling the weapons bay. "How long have you been a weapons officer, Spano?"

"Five years."

"Five years and you don't know the procedure."
Spano looked ready to burst. John had no idea what
was going on in his mind. After almost one month as
captain of the *Agamemnon*, one of the most powerful
ships in the fleet, John had made no progress toward
melding this crew into a team. He'd run more drills in
the last month than he could count, and several sections continued to perform inadequately. Weapons was
one. Not good for a destroyer. He'd had the weapons
chief speak to the crew under his command. No effect.
He'd had his first officer speak to the weapons chief.
No effect. So now here he was. So much for delega-
tion. He knew he shouldn't encourage excuse-making,
but maybe it would help to know what was on Spano's
mind. Maybe then John could begin to make some
headway here. "You have something to say, Lieutenant?"

"Sir." It sounded like a curse. "We always leave
the tube hatches closed. There's no need to check
them. The four of us have been working together for a
long time, and we know how to handle things."

"And that makes you think you can disregard procedure?"

"Sir, Captain Best never found our work less than
satisfactory."

John's patience reached its limit. "And what if one
of your fellow weapons officers was servicing the tube
when we went to battle alert, or if a gunner was doing
maintenance, or one of the weapons officers was sick
and had been replaced—then would you remember to
follow procedure?" John looked down the line, making eye contact with each one of them. "Every captain
has his own way of running a ship." And Captain
Best's was, by all the evidence, one of the shoddiest in

the fleet. "My way is not Captain Best's way. A ship can only operate efficiently if every member of the crew does his job. I want things done by the book, and I want orders followed to the letter. Is that clear?"

"Yes, sir," Spano said.

It was days like this John wished he'd become a professional baseball player. His link chimed. He responded with relief. "Sheridan. Go."

"Captain, we just received a message from General Lochschmanan." John recognized the voice of his first officer, Corchoran. "He advises us that he will conduct an inspection of the ship upon our arrival at Station Prime."

John stared down at the link on the back of his hand. As usual, command had impeccable timing. The *Agamemnon* would be arriving at Station Prime within the hour. And they'd been scheduled for shore leave. "Understood, Commander."

He faced the four weapons officers and the ranks of gunners behind them. "I told you all that you would start with me with a clean slate. What happened before doesn't matter to me, but what happens now *does*. I'll be damned if I'm going to expect anything less than the best from you. And that means we're going to run these drills until we get them right, if that means drilling from now until doomsday. Carry on."

They remained at attention as he left the weapons bay. John headed back to the command deck. Why did the last day before a leave always turn out like this?

He'd been so excited to get the command of the *Agamemnon*, an Omega-class destroyer with a crew of one hundred and sixty. It was a big step up from his first command, the *Galatea*, a heavy cruiser with a crew of 102. Yet since taking command, he'd been unable to get the crew into fighting shape.

It had taken John a few weeks of matching names to faces to realize that the service records for each crew member and the crew member himself often had little in common. It seemed the previous captain, Best, had played favorites. Big time. Certain members of the crew, like Spano, who seemed poorly motivated and borderline negligent, had exemplary records, commendations, and recommendations for promotion. Others, who were diligent and competent, had never had a promotion under Best, their records filled with reports of incompetence and dereliction of duty. Several of them had lodged complaints over their evaluations, but the complaints had been dismissed.

And so one week ago he had instituted his "clean slate" policy, explaining in a speech to the crew that he would disregard everything that they had done in the past and judge them only by what they did under his command. This worked well with those who had been undervalued by Best. Their enthusiasm and performance showed marked improvement. But those who had been favored by Best, for the most part, reacted poorly, growing even more sullen and uncooperative. A few of them were making efforts to improve, but too few. He was left with at least ten percent of the crew whom he could not count on to perform. And while a few of them could be transferred, and a few would probably have to be court-martialed, that still left him with a huge problem.

As he entered the command deck of the *Agamemnon*, he was reminded again of why he was here. The command deck was a thing of beauty. More space, more control and information easy at hand, more power and flexibility available, a clear line of sight to all officers, not impeded by bulkheads or banks of equipment, and a huge observation screen, which revealed the lulling red currents of hyperspace. It made him proud to be a part of Earthforce.

Commander Corchoran saw him and stepped down from the command chair. "We're thirty minutes from the jump gate, Captain."

"Thank you." John sat. His throat was dry from yelling.

"How did the drill go?" Corchoran's face always seemed to have a dark cloud hanging over it. His salt-and-pepper hair, cropped close, clung to his head, and his dark, pronounced brows overshadowed his deep-set eyes. An odd slackness to his cheeks gave him a constantly glum look.

"Not well. I don't want to transfer these problems into someone else's lap, but I'm having a hard time coming up with another solution."

"Perhaps I could talk to the crew again. Who was giving you trouble?"

Corchoran had been on the *Agamemnon* throughout Best's tenure, had, in fact, transferred with Best and about thirty of Best's handpicked men from the *Athena*, Best's previous command. John had been happy to accept Corchoran with his strong record as first officer, and though he'd come to realize that record was meaningless, Corchoran had nevertheless lived up to it. He knew everything about the ship and her crew, and he'd been the source of some valuable information since John had come aboard, though it did seem to John that he had trouble enforcing discipline. That was why John had been forced to take action himself this morning. "No, thanks. I need to form my own relationships with the crew, and they need to learn to accept my way of doing things. But I do get the sense that some of them resent the hell out of me, and I'd dearly like to know why.''

Corchoran took a step closer and lowered his voice. "If you don't mind my saying so, Captain, I think a number of the crew may envy your war record. Those of us who served with Captain Best on the *Athena* came away from the war with an undeserved stain on our reputations. Some of us have moved on, but others, I think, might resent your presence.''

John wondered which group Corchoran included himself in. He was eight years older than John, and though that was not an unreasonable age for the rank of commander, it had been four years since his last promotion. If he did resent John, there had been no sign of it. Perhaps Corchoran resented Captain Best, for screwing the pooch so badly a few months ago that even his political connections couldn't save this command for him. Best had attempted to make the jump to hyperspace with an engine port open, causing a dangerous instability in the jump engines that had spat them out in the same spot an hour in the future, nearly on top of another Earthforce vessel. The investigation had stopped short of preferring any charges, but Captain Best had been "promoted" to a desk job, leaving all his favorites behind.

At least Corchoran was being honest about Captain Best's reputation, a quality John valued highly. He must have found the rumors of Captain Best's cowardice at the Battle of the Line eight years ago embarrassing at best. "Thank you for your frankness. Now, about this inspection. Inform each of the section chiefs. Make sure they're prepared. I want this inspection to go by the numbers, no surprises. Tell them to make sure their crew is alert, not daydreaming about what they're going to do on leave. If we don't pass this inspection, there won't be any leave.''

And that, John thought, was a possibility he didn't even want to consider.

CHAPTER 4

ANNA could barely keep a straight face as the bellhop showed her through the Honeymoon Suite of the Imperial Hotel on Station Prime, orbiting Centauri Prime. She'd thought booking the suite would be romantic. But she was afraid the Centauri idea of romance was not quite the same as hers. The walls were draped in purple velvets and gold cords, with suggestive paintings of scampering Centauri in ornate gold frames centered under mood lights. Gold sculptures of what might have been various Centauri gods and other shiny knickknacks covered nearly every available surface. The style of the engravings and ornaments was somewhat Romanesque, but the Centauri had gone where no Roman had gone before. Subtlety was not part of their style. The rug was made of a long, hairy fur—dyed purple, of course—that seemed to cling to her shoes. The bed was elliptical and huge, bigger in itself than an entire hotel room in New York. The bellhop showed her the bed's control panel, which wasn't much different from the cockpit of the starfury John had once snuck her into.

The bathroom had some odd appliances, for the styling of the male Centauri's hair, her bellhop explained, and a huge golden bathtub that seemed to be in the shape of a six-tentacled octopus-type creature. The bellhop explained how the tub could be filled with a variety of liquid substances while Anna nodded her head gravely. She thanked him and showed him to the door, as soon as he left bursting out into laughter and making a running leap at the bed. She landed with an incredible bounce, the springs—or whatever they were—sending her nearly into the ceiling. Anna threw out her arms for balance, riding the declining bounces with bursts of laughter until the bed at last became still. She decided not to try the bathroom until John showed up. She knew a lot more about dead civilizations than living ones.

Out the window Centauri Prime came into view as the station rotated above it. The blue water and tan-colored land masses, strewn with wispy clouds, reminded her of Earth.

The communication console rang out a short, grandiose flourish. Anna ran over to answer it. The controls were similar to those she was used to, and she quickly saw how it worked. She accepted audio and visual.

"Hi there."

It was John. He had his military face on, which meant a tensing of the brows, a tautness to the cheeks, and a slight downturn to the lips.

Seeing him instantly made her smile, and her expression was mirrored in his. The smile lit up his face. For a few moments they simply took each other in.

"How was your trip?" he asked.

"Well, if your sister hadn't gotten me drunk the night before I left, it would have been better. But after the first day it was fine." She slipped into the plush purple seat beside the console. "How about you? Are you here? How's the ship?"

"Yes, we're in space dock. They say it's only forty minutes to the hotel. The *Agamemnon* is incredible. You can hardly feel the transition into hyperspace. This ship can do things you wouldn't believe. The maneuverability, for a ship this size, is incredible." His hand closed into a fist as if to capture his excitement, his voice rising like a boy with a new toy. "There are a lot of new systems to learn, but I'm working on it. I'm going to learn every inch of this ship inside and out."

"I have something here that requires an equally thorough study, Captain."

John's mouth hesitated in mid-response as the meaning of the words caught up with him. "I would be happy to help you in that endeavor, Doctor." He looked down at something. "I'm afraid I'm going to be a little late, though. I'm having a surprise inspection."

"I thought I was giving that to you."

"You're next. How's the room?"

"I've been trying out the bed," she said. "It has a number of special features."

He laughed. "Sounds like you don't even need me."

She gave him her husky voice. "Oh, but I do."

"I'll call you if I'm not going to make it by tonight. I love you." Although they always ended their calls this way, there was nothing automatic or perfunctory in the statement. He meant it every time he said it. As did she.

"I love you."

He disconnected, and she felt a silly smile on her face. Okay, so now what did she do? She could tour the station, but she was tired, and she didn't really feel like dealing with people, not after three days in the close quarters of a transport. She found herself digging the container with the mouse fragment out of her carryall. Liz had told her to forget about work. Well, she'd forget about it when John showed up.

She removed the stiff fragment, laid it on the communications console. The anchovy smell had gotten stronger, and the piece had dried somewhat since she'd looked at it last. The edges felt crusty, sharp and artificial, almost like plastic, while the central area still looked almost like skin, though now stiff and dry. The color was now a uniform shade of charcoal. She wished she had her equipment with her, so she could take some readings. But surely Chang was running every test in the book on the fragments in his possession.

Hesitantly, with a shadow of the fear she'd felt when she'd connected with the mouse, she picked up the fragment and stroked it with her index finger, focusing her attention on it. She couldn't imagine that it was still operative. But without any equipment, there was little else she could try.

The coloring of the piece remained constant. She sensed no heat from it, no life. She wondered what its true purpose had been. It could have been designed to explode, but she sensed that the explosion had been an accident, caused by the unstable feedback loop. The device seemed overly sophisticated for a bomb.

She remembered the intensity of the mouse's thoughts, the clarity, the focus, the beat. She received faint echoes of this now, halting, intermittent, interspersed with a blankness like static. And out of the blankness came the fresh scent of a bed of shavings, nuzzled into deep and warm, and of the cool darkness of stone all around. Then it was the machine all around, close and vital, beautiful, a perfect instrument painted in shadow, and then too close, too vital, currents racing in circulation, tightening like wires, the pain, the brilliant lockstep pain, rising in intensity, and then the shriek. It was only a tiny echo of what it had been in the lab, but it reminded her of the shriek she had heard then, the shriek that had been lost in everything that had followed. The shriek of something terrible being born. And dying.

The communication console's grandiose flourish was sounding again and again. She put the fragment back in the container, put it out of view of the monitor. "Hello?"

Dr. Chang sat in his office, his face stiff, unreadable. "Sorry to bother you on your vacation."

"No bother. John's been delayed. I'm just sitting here twiddling my thumbs."

"I have some exciting news." He was speaking in his neutral tone. "One of IPX's probes, out near the rim, has found something on a planet called Alpha Omega 3. The ruins of an ancient civilization no one has ever encountered before. The ruins cover over thirty percent of the planet's surface, and they're totally unlike those of any culture we know. Preliminary dating indicates the ruins are over one thousand years old. And there are indications of advanced technology."

Anna shook her head. "This is huge. Why aren't you dancing on your desk?"

Chang glanced away, took a deep breath. "Sorry. It's only ten o'clock, and it's already been a long day. The biggest discovery since the Krich, they're saying."

Her mind was racing. Being the first in a thousand years to walk in the ancient halls of a lost, advanced race, uncovering their implements, re-creating how they lived, how they thought, unlocking their secrets—

it was the ultimate rush. "The biggest discovery of our lifetimes."

His face loosened into a smile. "And I saved the best part."

"What!"

"Initial RNA screens indicate that the protein fingerprint of the planet's microorganisms matches that of your mouse. This could be its home."

Anna jumped to her feet and began circling the communications console. "This is incredible. The chances have to be a billion to one. They're planning an expedition?"

Chang nodded.

"God, I would give anything to be on that ship. Who's mission commander?"

"I am."

She stopped. "They don't want me to go, do they?"

"It's not a matter of what they want. Or what I want. I need you to go. As science officer, second in command under me."

"They've okayed it?"

"They've okayed it."

"This is incredible. The chance to confirm a find like this, and to be the first ones to study it . . . As soon as I get back I'll start helping with the prep work and drawing up some preliminary lists of equipment."

"The expedition launches in ten days."

She thought she must have misunderstood. "When?"

"Ten days from now. We're using the *Icarus* out of Station Prime. I'm leaving on a transport in an hour."

Anna rubbed her finger against the top of the console. "That's impossible. There's no way you can prep an expedition in less than two months. How can they possibly—"

"When the bosses say jump, we jump."

But she knew it wasn't possible. Even if there was pressure to rush, which wouldn't be smart. After all, as exciting as this find was, the ruins weren't going anywhere. IPX had to have been prepping this mission for some time. Perhaps they'd only told Chang about it now. Or perhaps he'd only told her about it now. She wondered if the rush had anything to do with the explosion of the mouse.

"I'd need you to start prep work for me right away. Your vacation would be shot."

"I understand." She'd get more from Chang in person. He was telling her all he could for now.

"Does that mean you accept the position?"

She made her monkey face, as if deliberating. "Of course I accept! How could I pass up an opportunity to be a part of history?"

Chang nodded, and she could have sworn his chest slumped. "I thought it was an offer you couldn't refuse." He held up a data crystal. "I'll transmit the specs to you for follow-up. The crew is set, but I need you to give the equipment manifest a thorough going-over and coordinate with Captain Hidalgo of the *Icarus*. I'll give a mission briefing as soon as I arrive."

Anna nodded. "Thank you for including me. I won't let you down."

Chang's final comment could have been taken as a compliment, though it somehow sounded more like a warning. "If I didn't need you, Sheridan, I wouldn't bring you."

Whoever had written the inspection manual had been a sadist, at least as far as John was concerned. The inspection began in the zero-gravity sections at the aft end of the ship—the cargo bay, aft laser cannons, en-

gines—then down through the zero-gravity center of
the ship, following the central laser tube and electronics connections, into the zero-gravity sections in the
fore end of the ship—the fighter bay and the fore laser
cannons—and then into the rotating gravity section
near the center of the ship—the crew quarters, ship's
stores, life support, mess, security, brig, command
deck, engineering, and finished in the weapons bay.
As General Lochschmanan completed his tour of each
section, finding everything satisfactory, John nodded
tightly, thinking of the weapons bay still to come.

The weapons bay was actually a misnomer. In an
advanced Omega Class ship like the *Agamemnon*, the
weapons bay was a fairly small room, about twenty by
twenty feet, under normal watch conditions manned by
one weapons officer and four gunners. Their main duties under those conditions were maintenance of the
weapons bay systems, the central laser tube, and the
four laser cannons; periodic checks; drills; and naval
gazing. During battle or battle alert conditions, or during an inspection, of course, the full complement of
weapons officers and gunners was present.

The weapons bay did not contain the four laser cannons themselves; they were mounted two and two at
the fore and aft ends of the ship. Instead the weapons
bay contained the hardware for the targeting system,
which could be accessed here or on the command
deck; the weapons diagnostic system, which gave detailed information about the condition and functioning
of each component of the system; the weapons control
system, through which the cannons and the tube were
kept at the proper level of readiness and fine adjustments to their functioning were made; and the appara-
tus for the manual targeting system.

John doubted the manual targeting system aboard

the *Agamemnon* had ever been used outside of drills or battle simulations. The four hemispheric man-sized cages looked horribly antiquated beside the sleek, advanced controls that surrounded them. But they provided a method for manual, holographic targeting in case of emergency, with one weapons officer handling one cannon inside each targeter.

As the inspection progressed, the general discovered several infractions, in the mess of all places, gear not stowed properly, and in life support. His aide, a short, grave-looking woman, made notations on a comp-pad. Then the general led the way into the weapons bay, John and Commander Corchoran following.

Lochschmanan was the skinniest general John knew, but he carried himself with a deliberateness and authority that demanded respect. Each movement was crisp, each word enunciated. His uniform was immaculate. The weapons officers and gunners snapped to attention, the gunners in tight ranks in the center of the room, the weapons officers beside their various stations. The general approached the targeting system, beside which Lieutenant Watley stood, checking that the system had been left in standby mode and that it was in working order. Beside the general, Watley looked unkempt, her jacket wrinkled, her stetbar unpolished.

The general moved on to the weapons control system, shadowed by his aide and John. Spano and Lieutenant Ross, the weapons chief, stood nearby. John reviewed the correct settings for nonalert conditions: defense grid deactivated, baffles raised, tube hatches closed, activators off, optics off line. Lochschmanan bent closer to the console. His head turned toward John. "Captain."

He'd found something. "Yes, sir."

Lochschmanan pointed to the console, and the aide typed a note into her comp-pad. The optics had been left on line. John's jaw clenched. Optics on line when they were so near a space station was a serious error. The optics were a series of mirrors that regulated the flow of photons within the central tube and out to the four laser cannons. If there was a fire or explosion aboard the ship, with optics on line the laser cannons could accidentally fire. The general continued his inspection. Spano and Ross kept their eyes front.

Failing the inspection was more than an embarrassment to John and more than a black mark on his record: it was a breach of faith. Earthforce had put their faith in him, giving him command of one of their most powerful ships, trusting him to have the ability to run it efficiently and effectively. And he was failing them. He'd never doubted his own abilities—as a pilot, as a fighter, as a tactician, as a leader. But now something wasn't working. Under Captain Best's command, Earthforce discipline and commitment had broken down, and he didn't know how to fix them.

They ended the inspection in John's office, a small room with a desk and chairs attached to his quarters. John had managed to unpack most of his belongings: on a shelf mementos from various worlds he had visited; fastened to the walls photos of the wedding, Anna and Liz, his parents, and a large photograph of the Lone Cypress; secured to his desk his lamp and the snow globe of the Nantucket lighthouse he and Anna had fallen in love with on their honeymoon. But he still didn't feel at home, as he had aboard the *Galatea*.

The four of them—Lochschmanan, his aide, John, and Corchoran—all remained standing. Lochschmanan seemed perpetually to be at attention.

"You have failed the inspection, Captain. Minor

infractions in the mess and life support, and a major violation in the weapons bay." Lochschmanan spoke with the same deliberateness with which he carried himself. "That is unacceptable, and a disgrace to Earthforce."

"Yes, sir." Nothing could make John feel any worse than he already did.

"We put you in command of the *Agamemnon* because we thought you could handle the increased responsibility. We thought you were worthy of her. If you can't get your crew to function competently under these calm conditions, how can you ever expect them to react well in a crisis?" The general paused, glancing at Corchoran, and clasped his hands behind his back. "I know you inherited a number of problems here, John, but we cannot afford to have the *Agamemnon* out of service. We need her back in fighting shape now. Consider this a test of your leadership abilities. If you can't be an effective leader, then your command will always be inferior. We need a strong leader in charge of the *Agamemnon*. Prove to me that we have one. In the meantime, I want you running this crew day and night until they get it right. If you need a limited number of transfers, I'll give them to you. Just get results."

"Yes, sir. Thank you, sir."

Lochschmanan's hands returned to his sides. "The technicians should be over shortly to begin the systems upgrade. Make sure you give them full access."

"General, may I ask the nature of the upgrade?"

"You're being outfitted with a new stealth technology. I'll be back tomorrow to check on their progress, and I'll give you a full briefing at that time."

"Yes, sir."

Lochschmanan nodded and made a smart turn out the door, followed by his grave-looking aide.

John took a deep breath, determining to accomplish what the general had asked. He turned to Corchoran. "I want you to set up a drill schedule. I want it hard and I want it heavy." His hand punctuated each instruction with a short, chopping motion. "And I want to conduct daily inspections. Each section chief will make a special daily progress report directly to you."

"Yes, sir," Corchoran said, his face seeming gloomier than ever beneath his pronounced brows. "Just for the record, does this mean you're canceling leave?"

"Yes, it means we're canceling leave. You don't fail inspection and then go on leave. Now I want this schedule put into effect immediately. And let me know when the techs come on board."

Corchoran nodded. "I'm sorry we let you down, sir."

John let out a breath, shook his head. "I'm afraid we've all let Earthforce down. And I'm not going to let that happen again."

"Yes, sir," Corchoran said, and left.

John sat down behind his desk. It was ironic. During wartime, the crew either functioned correctly or they died. Motivation wasn't an issue. In peace, the motivations were subtler: promotion, pride, a paycheck. But Captain Best had twisted all that, promoting those who didn't deserve it, holding back those who did. John would do whatever it took to get them into shape, if it meant drilling for a week, a month, a year—

Oh hell. Anna. She'd kill him.

The com system was on the wall behind his desk. He put through a call to Anna at the Imperial Hotel.

He checked the time. She might have gone out to dinner. But she hadn't.

She looked as beautiful as she ever had, her shoulder-length hair a disorganized mass around her head, her smile, which arose when she saw him, emanating warmth. But there was more than warmth to her. She had a certain presence, a vitality and an intelligence that was totally Anna. That energy and insatiable desire for knowledge was what made her such a great archaeologist. She loved digging up the past, loved solving a mystery. She never gave up on anything and, luckily for John, that included him. "Is it time to open Liz's present?" she asked.

He laughed. "Not another one."

"You've seemed to like them in the past."

John felt his smile slipping. "I can't make it, Anna."

She became immediately serious. "What's wrong?"

He rubbed his forehead. "I had to cancel leave. We failed the inspection. We had a serious violation. Lochschmanan is giving me a chance to bring the crew up to par, but he's not happy. I'm not sure whether they'd take the command away from me or not."

Anna sat. "Listen, they're not going to do that. Earthforce believes in you. That's why they gave you command of the *Agamemnon*. You told me how screwed up the crew is. The previous captain was in there for years. You can't fix that overnight."

"I know, but I feel like they've put their faith in me, and I've let them down."

"All this inspection shows is that you have a problem. So now you go and fix it." He loved the way she angled her chin when she was making a point. "I know you can do that. No one was hurt, right?"

It was an odd question. "No, of course not."

"So then nothing irreversible has happened. You can still fix it. You've always said that you have to know your crew. So if there's a problem, you find out why. Then you deal with it, with your usual tact. Very simple."

He smiled. "Maybe you can solve my other problem. I have this wonderful woman I'm supposed to meet."

Anna propped her foot on the edge of the chair and wrapped her arms around her leg. "If she's so wonderful she'll understand."

John sighed. "I'm sorry I can't make it."

"No. Listen, this wouldn't have worked—"

Someone knocked at John's door. He shook his head. "I have to go. I'm sorry. I love you."

"I love you. I'll call tomorrow and see how you're doing."

John nodded, and they absorbed each other silently for another moment before he ended the communication.

CHAPTER 5

Aₙₙₐ stepped onto the brightly lit tube, wishing for sunglasses. She hadn't been able to get much sleep in that huge bed last night, though experimenting with the settings had made for an educational evening.

Practiced as she was with Geneva mass transit, she was able to maneuver her way ahead of the other boarding passengers to an empty seat. An overweight Centauri jammed into the seat on her right, and she now noticed a powerful smell coming from the dock-worker on her left. Sometimes she wished she could spend all of her time among dead civilizations.

Station Prime was basically a revolving ring, with two diametric passages running at right angles to each other connecting opposite sides of the ring and a central landing bay for small to moderate-sized ships. Different tube routes ran around the circumference of the ring or cut through the diametric passages. Anna was simply riding around the circumference for this journey, since her destination was less than halfway around the ring.

She'd been so excited about the expedition last night with no one to talk to that she'd sent a message to Liz. The communications console offered plenty of frills, of course, including various virtual backgrounds that her body could be inserted into for different messages. She wasted some time playing with them, finally settling on a relatively conservative tropical sunrise scene. She even combed her hair. Sharing the news with Liz made it seem somehow more real.

She felt bad for not telling John about the expedition. He'd looked so guilty when he'd told her he had to cancel the vacation. But it hadn't been the right time. He was worried about his career, and she knew how much that meant to him. It drove her crazy to see him in pain. She'd like to take every malcontent on the *Agamemnon* and rip his head off. What were they doing in Earthforce anyway if they didn't want to follow orders? This kind of trouble challenged John's whole philosophy. His relationship with Earthforce wasn't like hers with IPX. She knew that in working for the corporation she was dealing with the devil. She didn't expect them to do anything that wasn't profit motivated. But John believed in Earthforce, believed in it so hard and with such passion that to find flaws in it hurt him at his spiritual center. Serving Earth—and so consequently serving Earthforce—was his purpose in life. He felt called to it. Finding that the one he served was not worthy of service would, she thought, destroy him. She prayed that Earthforce would be worthy of him.

She opened her computer to take her mind off John and began to review the specs sent by Dr. Chang once again. The expedition to Alpha Omega 3 would last for six months: approximately one month in transit in each direction, and four months for study and excavation of the site. The *Icarus*, owned by IPX and commanded by Captain Hidalgo, had a crew and science support staff of one hundred and thirty. The facilities on the *Icarus* seemed to be more sophisticated than those on previ-

ous ships she'd taken. The support staff seemed well
trained in the operation of heavy equipment like crawlers, dozers, drills, sonic probes, and resonance
imagers as well as in the more delicate washes and
separation techniques.

When she'd first looked at the equipment manifest,
she'd thought they must have made a mistake. It read
like her ultimate wish list of toys and tools for a dig. A
few items she hadn't even heard of. She couldn't believe they could afford all this and stay on budget, so
she jumped to the budget analysis. The expedition had
a budget over four times that of any other expedition
she'd been on. Chang was right. There was too much
interest in this.

The archaeological team numbered ten. Since Anna
had gone on most of her expeditions with Dr. Chang,
and Chang, a creature of habit, liked using the same
people again and again, Anna expected to see the usual
suspects. Doctors Churlstein, Favorito, Razor, and
Scott she all knew fairly well. Two other archaeologists, Petrovich and Standish, she'd met around the
office but had never worked with before. They worked
under a different mission supervisor, not Galovich, as
Chang and Anna did. This troubled her. It seemed so
unlike Chang. Perhaps Chang's normal team prefer-
ences were tied up with other projects and couldn't get
free. But then there was the capper. A member of the
archaeological team who was neither a Ph.D. nor an
archaeologist nor an employee of IPX. *Ms. Donne,* the
personnel roster read, *of Psi Corps.* How had she
muscled her way onto the expedition? It was unprecedented. She knew absolutely nothing about archaeology. Now Anna understood why Chang had
seemed so ill at ease. IPX had granted Donne a place
on board. The pressure from Psi Corps must have been

terrific. It must be related to Terrence: Psi Corps concerned about the effect of the mouse; IPX launching an expedition to the planet that might be the home of the technology that created the mouse. Everything was starting to come together now.

The expedition would be under a microscope. It all had to do with power, as Chang had said. Perhaps Petrovich and Standish were there to keep watch over Chang himself.

And then there was the final member of the archaeological team, on loan from Earthforce. Earthforce employees contracted out to IPX had occasionally accompanied expeditions, but IPX preferred to bring in Earthforce personnel after they had something to sell and had calculated an asking price. The few expeditions Anna had heard about them participating in were usually follow-up missions, after the preliminary archaeology had been done and a tentative deal struck with Earthforce.

At least this Earthforce contract employee had a Ph.D. in archaeology, with a specialty in archaeolinguistics. They needed a linguist on the expedition. She looked through the file on him that Chang had included. It didn't contain much information. The Ph.D. was earned at a mediocre college, and then he'd gone straight to work for the government. No teaching, no research. Anna knew a good part of her feeling was snobbery, but she tended, along with most of her colleagues, to look down on scientists who did not stay grounded in academia, particularly scientists who worked for the government. Dr. Chang was the only scientist she knew who worked full-time in a corporate environment and kept his scientific edge. According to the file, this archaeolinguist had taken a leave of absence from his job about six months ago, and had only been reactivated for this expedition. The whole situation seemed suspect. Chang, left to his own devices, would never have chosen this man for his linguist. Anna doubted he could translate the Book of G'Quan, never mind the writings of a totally new, unknown culture.

There wasn't much more to the file, except his current address, oddly enough, on Station Prime.

From the tube stop, the address was a five-minute walk, as he'd described. She'd told him she wanted to review what equipment he needed, though what she actually wanted was the chance to size him up before they all got on a ship together headed for the rim. The neighborhood was somewhat shabby, according to Centauri standards, the halls rather narrow and modest, with a lack of decorative ornament. She found the address and rang. The door opened, and she entered.

A compact man came out of the darkness toward her. "Dr. Sheridan."

"Dr. Morden?" She held out her hand, a bit uneasy. "A pleasure to meet you."

He shook her hand, and his palm was soft and smooth, not like an archaeologist's at all. The door closed behind her, cutting off the main source of light.

"Lights," he said, turning away as the overheads came on. "I'm sorry. Is it two o'clock already? I'm afraid I lost track of time."

"I'm sorry. Were you resting? I can come back later."

He turned back to face her, a pasted smile revealing a row of perfect white teeth. "No, don't be silly. Please stay. Have a seat. Can I make you some tea?" His voice was as smooth as his palms.

"No, I'm fine." Anna sat on the couch. It was velour, with a high back, in the Centauri style. All of the furniture looked Centauri, if rather inexpensive and unornamented. The apartment had a rather generic quality, a lack of personal effects, except for some shelves of artifacts against one wall. It was a look Anna recognized, since her freelancing required her to move about once a year. The furniture came with the apartment.

"You're sure?"

She nodded, and Morden sat in an armchair opposite her, folding his hands quietly together. The smile was still there. Everything about him bespoke control. He sat neatly, carefully, arms against his body, legs together. He wore a dark suit, freshly pressed and creased. His dark hair was styled cleanly back, no split ends or stray hairs like her own indefinable style. He was definitely an exception from the typical scraggly archaeologist.

"I guess we're going to be shipping out together soon," she said.

He nodded. "Yes."

"I brought the equipment manifest." She opened her computer, called up the screen. "I wanted to make sure you have everything you need." She handed it over to him.

He scanned down it, the smile remaining carefully in place. "Wow. I wouldn't have dreamed of asking for so much. I don't even know what half of this stuff is."

"So there's nothing you need me to add?" Her ruse now seemed painfully apparent, but there was nothing to do but play it out.

He returned the computer. "No. I have a few of my own things I'll bring along, but that's it." His eyes drifted away from her, to a point over her left shoulder.

"Is this your first expedition with IPX?" she asked.

His dark eyes came back to her. "No, I've been involved in two others, though not recently. You people at IPX do some wonderful work."

"I just freelance for them. But I agree. They're about the only ones who can launch a major expedition these days."

"You're probably wondering why I work for Earthforce."

"No—I didn't—well, how do you like it? What division is it you work for?"

"New Technologies, which as you know are sometimes very old technologies. We don't launch any major expeditions; we leave that to IPX. But we do come into possession of some fascinating artifacts, which I have the opportunity to study. Unfortunately, I can't talk about most of them. You know the government."

"My husband is a captain in Earthforce." She was starting to wonder how long that smile could last. Surely his mouth had to get tired.

"Oh. Your husband." His eyes drifted away again.

"Is that how you know Dr. Chang? Through your previous work with IPX?"

"We've never met actually. I'm looking forward to it."

"I was wondering how he picked you for the expedition."

"I'm afraid I don't know. I'm sort of out of the loop here. My superiors just called and asked if I'd be willing to go. Of course I said yes. It's a wonderful opportunity."

She wondered how she would ever find out his credentials, or ever break through that smile of his. "You have some interesting artifacts here." She stood and went over to the shelves.

He followed. "Oh, well, miscellaneous leftovers mainly, but they remind me where I've been." He stood neatly as well, hands still clasped in front of him.

She found a number of semicommon pieces, among them an Anfran love stone. The round black volcanic glass was smooth except for a tiny inscription on the back, the name of the Anfran star god, who regulated matters of love. The stone was meant to be worn as a necklace, with the name of the god worn against the chest, never showing. The stone was believed to carry the good wishes of loved ones. "You've been to Anfras? I did my doctoral thesis on their culture."

Morden nodded.

"I thought their love incantation was the most romantic thing in the world. I used to recite it to my husband. 'The love that knows no borders.'"

His smile seemed to crack then. "I'm familiar with the line. I'm afraid you mistranslate. The correct meaning is, 'The love that abides no borders.' You can see my article in *Archaeology Quarterly*."

She wondered if he could be right, if she and others could have mistranslated it. Maybe he did know what he was doing. She'd have to check into it. She sifted through the other artifacts. "I was surprised to find that you were living right here on the station. How do you like it?"

He picked up the love stone. "It's liveable. I had to get away from Earth."

She smiled. "Why, are you wanted?"

His smile grew in intensity for a horrible moment, then it fractured and fell away. She could see his features attempting to regroup. "You probably saw it on the news." Then his face became still: controlled, fragile, waiting for an answer.

"No—not that I know of."

"My wife and daughter were killed in the terrorist bombing of the Io jump gate last May."

Anna wished his eyes would drift away from hers now. They had fastened onto her, as if daring her to respond. She didn't know what to say. She'd come here determined to uncover his deceptions or incompetence. She'd never imagined she would find something like this. It was just like Chang to leave something personal and critical out of the file. "I'm sorry. I was on a dig last spring. I heard about what happened, but I never watched any of the feeds."

He nodded. "Many people still recognize me. I guess I was screaming or something. I don't remember."

"I'm so sorry for bringing this up."

He smiled, and this was a slight, tired, lop-sided smile that passed quickly. "It's not like I wouldn't think of them otherwise." He handed her the love stone. "I gave that to my wife, as a wedding present. I read her the incantation. We agreed we would abide no borders." He stopped. "I'm going to make that tea."

"That sounds wonderful," Anna said.

The kitchen was in a nook at one end of the living room, and Anna sat on a stool at the counter as he prepared the tea. As she looked again around the apartment, she realized he'd just been marking time here for the last six months, unable to resume his life.

"Their ship was just entering the jump gate when it blew," he said, his back to her, his voice slightly musical. "Of course I should have been with them. They found debris, but not enough to account for the whole ship. They said some of it must have been drawn through into hyperspace. They said no one could have survived. I know they're right. Half of a blown-up ship in hyperspace. But sometimes I wonder if they could be alive. And then I wonder what it would be like, floating through hyperspace, lost, alone. Sarah would be six now.''

He turned to her with the tea, and Anna was surprised to see his face carrying that same still, controlled expression. She remembered a quote from her favorite author, John Steinbeck: *There are some among us who live in rooms of experience that we can never enter.*

''How do you cross a border like that?'' he asked.

''I don't know.'' She was wondering what she would do if John ever died. It was a constant danger in his career. Yet she couldn't imagine it. ''I don't think it's so much that you cross the border as that your love transcends the border. Wherever they are, they must know you love them. That love can comfort them. Just as their love can comfort you.'' The words seemed so empty. She felt like a bad pop psychologist.

''I'm afraid our interpretations, as well as our translations, differ, Dr. Sheridan.'' Morden drank his tea, all in one long draft, and set down his mug, the smile back on his face, though in diluted form.

''You can just call me Sheridan,'' Anna said. ''We like to go by last names in our group. It distinguishes us from the IPX execs, who like to use first names as if they're your best friends.''

''Then you can call me Morden. Let's get back to the expedition. Is there anything I can do to help prepare?''

Anna gave him a few jobs, and they talked some more about the expedition. By the time Anna left, she had decided to make Dr. Morden her secondary project. She would help him begin to move on with his life by the time they returned from the rim.

* * *

John stood in the entrance to the weapons bay. Just inside, to his right, the status monitor displayed battle alert. Another day, another dozen drills. But he'd decided to take the direct approach this time.

Lieutenant Watley was the weapons officer on duty, assisted by four gunners whose names John was still trying to keep straight. When the ship's status had changed to battle alert, John had started his timer. At ten seconds, Watley had put down her book and called up to the command deck for confirmation of the battle alert. After receiving confirmation, at thirty-two seconds she'd begun making the appropriate adjustments to the weapons control system.

At fifty-three seconds Ensign Timmons, the youngest weapons officer and the only one who hadn't been brought from the *Athena* by Best, pushed his way past John in his haste to get to his post. As he stumbled into the room and saw whom he had shoved, Timmons came up short, his mouth gaping. "I'm sorry, sir. I didn't realize. I was just. I didn't know."

John raised a hand. "It's all right, Timmons. It's your job to get to your station as quickly as you can under alert conditions. I appreciate your—enthusiasm. Carry on."

Timmons gave a gap-toothed grin. His hair was pressed flat against one side of his head, probably from sleep. "Thank you, sir." He rushed to the targeting system.

Watley had now realized John was here and was going about her duties with a greater show of concern. John repositioned himself inside the doorway to the bay.

At one minute, ten seconds, gunners started rushing into the bay.

At one minute, forty seconds, Lieutenant Ross arrived. The weapons chief wasn't setting much of an example. He didn't appear to be out of breath or unkempt. There was a hesitation in his gait when he saw John, but then he continued to the weapons diagnostic system. He asked the other officers their status, double-checked their settings, directed the gunners. Thirty-five years old, Ross was a mountain of a man, six foot six and burly, who walked with a swagger and boomed his orders in a strong, intimidating voice. Yet something in the set of his muscular frame, in the quick snaps of his head at any change, in the occasional halt of his hand in the middle of a gesture, conveyed unease. His features were sharp, delicate, an odd contrast to his burly build. Ross confirmed the tube hatches were closed, then had Watley bring optics on line and trigger primary ignition.

At two minutes, twenty-two seconds, the last two gunners arrived, apparently in no rush.

At three minutes, three seconds, Spano strolled in. "I was right in the middle of a very hot letter from home. Can't we time these things more—" Spano stopped when he saw John. "Captain." That word didn't sound a whole lot nicer than *sir*. Spano's opaque, flat eyes radiated contempt.

John held up the timer. "I'm sorry to have inconvenienced you, Lieutenant."

Spano continued to his station, beside Watley at the weapons control system, where he reset several controls. Spano made no effort to hide his bad attitude. His tone was insubordinate, his actions careless, lackadaisical.

Ross got on the link to the command deck. "Weapons bay battle-ready."

"Stand by weapons bay," Corchoran responded.

John stopped the timer. "Three minutes forty-one seconds to battle-ready status. Timmons, how long does the manual say you have from the initiation of a battle alert to reach battle-ready status?"

"Two minutes, Captain."

"Two minutes. And yet you took three minutes and forty-one seconds. Three minutes and forty-one seconds during which an enemy ship could be blasting us out of the sky. Lieutenant Ross, what would you suggest caused the delay? Were there unforeseen hardships, such as damage to the ship due to a sneak attack?"

"No, sir," Ross boomed.

"Lieutenant Spano, what adversities kept you from reaching your post for three minutes and three seconds? I'd like to make the path as smooth for you as possible."

Spano shot a glance at Ross, said nothing.

"Spano!"

Spano's nostrils flared. "I didn't hurry, sir, because I knew it was a drill, sir. And we're all pretty sick of drills, sir. We know there's really no point to it all. Everyone in the galaxy is our friend now, right? Whether we like it or not. It'll be a cold day in hell before we'll be using any of this equipment. We're just Earth's friendly envoys now. All we have to do is grin and keep our fingers off the trigger."

"I'm surprised that someone who's been to war," John said, "would be so anxious to return to it."

Spano let out a laugh. "You're a hero. What do you need with another war?"

Why was that always so important to everyone he met? The damned war had ended eight years ago. He'd done what he'd had to do, nothing more. "Whether you imagine the alert is a drill or not"—and he walked from one of them to the next, making eye contact with each—"your duty is to get to your station as quickly as possible and bring us to battle-ready status. If any of you are incapable of fulfilling your duties, then I can relieve you of them." He stopped in front of Ross. "I want results. And I want them now. Lieutenant Ross, are you capable of making your section perform up to standards?"

"I'll try my best, sir," Ross boomed. John could see the resistance in the hard line of his mouth.

"And is your best better than what I saw here to-day?"

He could see Ross puzzling out how to answer that one. The line of his mouth thinned. "Permission to speak freely, sir."

"All right. Get it off your chest, and then let's get on with it."

"Sir, I think a number of the crew in the weapons section feel you're coming down hard on them because you feel your combat record is superior to theirs. You destroyed the *Black Star*, and we served under Captain Best, allegedly the coward of the Battle of the Line."

"That's ridiculous," John said, immediately regretting his words. *Tact*, Anna always reminded him.

"That's right," Spano said. "It is ridiculous. He's no hero. Spreading mines and then sending out a fake distress signal aren't a hero's methods."

Spano had no discipline whatsoever. He shouldn't have lasted a minute in Earthforce. Obviously Captain Best had let him get away with all sorts of inappropriate behavior, perhaps even encouraged it. John should have charged Spano with insubordination, should have made him face a court-martial. Chances were he'd have to do that, not only to Spano, but to Ross, Watley, several of the gunners, and several of the crew in other sections. But he felt, first, that he had to give them a chance to reform, or perhaps, as the general had suggested, to transfer. These weren't new recruits. They had spent years and years in Earthforce. They were behaving as they had been taught to behave.

Earthforce should have taught Spano what it meant to be an officer. Earthforce, in the person of Captain Best, had failed him. Politics and influence had put Best in command and allowed him to damage the officers under him. Now Earthforce, in the person of John Sheridan, was responsible. If Spano, Ross, and the others could adapt, he wanted to give them that opportunity. They had to learn what it meant to wear the uniform of Earthforce. And he had to learn what behaviors Captain Best had rewarded in his crew.

"I meant it when I said we would all start here with a clean slate. No charges were ever made against Captain Best. And I certainly hold none of you responsible for any actions that he may or may not have taken." He made a chopping motion with his hand, his voice rising. "I'm coming down hard on you because your section's performance is unacceptable—and deteriorating. And you don't seem to care. This uniform means something to me. Serving Earthforce means something to me. Doing my best every time out. Running this ship to the best of my abilities. Not giving up, no matter how tired, or frustrated, or bored I might be. Devoting myself to something more important than me, a larger cause. And I intend to make sure *everyone* on this ship upholds those standards."

Spano's face had flushed red. "You think you can teach us how to handle laser cannons when we've been doing it for years. Maybe you'd be better off teaching us how to handle mines. We know how to handle laser cannons."

"Lieutenant Spano," John said, his voice darkening, "you are insubordinate. You are confined to quarters until further notice, effective immediately."

With a flare of his nostrils Spano snapped to attention and marched out.

"The rest of you, except for Lieutenant Ross, are dismissed." John waited until the gunners and other officers had left. Ross straightened the mountain of his body in preparation for an assault.

Spano needed discipline, hard and fast. But Ross was a different story. Something was eating at Ross, something that had been eating at him for a long time. Having been in the military for so long, John could sense it through his regulation posture, through his sharp, strictly composed features, through the loud boom in his voice.

John positioned himself right in Ross's eyeline. "Lieutenant, I understand that living in the shadow of the rumors about Captain Best's performance at the Battle of the Line may not have been very pleasant for you and the crew. It seems to have put a giant chip on everyone's shoulder. But the resistance I'm sensing has a deeper base than that. It goes far beyond just those officers who served with Captain Best on the *Athena*. As I've become familiar with the various members of the crew and reviewed their records, I've found that my evaluation of just about every crew member is in direct opposition to Captain Best's. What is your opinion of Captain Best's methods of crew evaluation?"

The sharp line of Ross's mouth shifted as he hesitated.

"I'm asking for your frank opinion, Lieutenant."

"Captain Best had his own personal criteria, Captain."

"And as weapons chief, did you often find yourself in agreement with his evaluations?"

"Sometimes, sir. Sometimes I felt Captain Best must have had more information than I did."

John's voice rose. "More information on the weapons crew and how they carried out their jobs than you, their immediate superior, did?"

Ross averted his eyes. "Captain Best was a real hands-on commander, sir."

This was getting him nowhere. Ross was stonewalling. John took a step closer, drawing Ross's eyes back to him. "My sense is that Captain Best did not have more information—not about the crew's performance of their duties, anyway. He seemed to reward some of the sloppiest, laziest crew members and to punish some of the most efficient. Which leads me to believe he did have his own personal criteria in evaluating his crew, criteria that have nothing to do with those laid down by Earthforce. Would you agree, Lieutenant?"

"I'm not sure what you mean, sir." Ross's burly frame shifted, the sharp line of his mouth hardening. John felt he was very close to a breakthrough with Ross. Spano could spout off all day and John didn't think he'd learn any more than he already had. It was all surface flash. But Ross's troubles ran deep, and if he could break through to them, find out what was eating at him, perhaps he could forge a link. Ross had been resisting his authority indirectly until now, performing poorly, unwilling to initiate a direct confrontation. If there was a direct confrontation, perhaps the issues could be resolved and the need for resistance would disappear.

"I mean that I have to look at all my highest ranking officers and ask *why?* What did they do for Captain

Best to get promoted?'' He extended a hand. ''Let's look at you as an example. You started out with Captain Best nine years ago as an ensign third class. Now, here you are a lieutenant and the weapons chief. When I look at the state of your section, Ross, and at your own behavior—your negligence, your resistance, your failure to follow procedure, your poor motivation—I wonder what criteria Captain Best was using when he recommended you time and again for promotion.'' John tilted his head. ''What criteria do you feel he judged you by?''

John saw the decision happen on Ross's face, the catastrophic decision to throw a punch at his superior officer. Ross's sharp features twisted, and then his right shoulder dropped as his huge right hand closed into a fist, his elbow drawing back like a piston. This wasn't the kind of breakthrough John had been hoping for. As he raised an arm in defense, Ross's windup fizzled, his aborted punch shooting down in a jagged arch to his opposite hip. Ross's head had jerked nervously from John to the doorway.

''Captain?'' General Lochschmanan said. His aide was with him.

John lowered his arm. ''We—were just running a drill, General. What can I do for you?''

''A drill.''

John's link chimed. ''Excuse me, sir.'' John brought the link near his mouth. ''Sheridan. Go.''

''Captain,'' Corchoran said, ''you have an incoming call from your wife.''

John glanced at the general. ''Tell her I'll call back. I'm busy.'' Relaying a personal communication to him during battle alert was a clear violation of procedure. Corchoran should have known better.

"Take the call, Captain," Lochschmanan said.
"I'd like to talk with the lieutenant about this drill."

John hesitated, then realized he had no choice.
"Yes, sir." He spoke into the link. "Put the call
through to the weapons bay com station." John went
over to the com station near the door, snatching a nervous glance over his shoulder at the stiff back of the
general.

"Hey, handsome."

He turned, saw Anna in the hotel room.

"What's wrong?"

"I can't talk now." The general was consulting
with his aide.

"I just felt so bad about how guilty you looked yesterday . . . " The general was turning to Ross now,
was saying something. " . . . decided to accept a
position as science officer on an expedition with Dr.
Chang to the rim. It's a six-month assignment."

He turned back to her. "You're going away?"

"It's a great opportunity. I'll be back before you
know it."

He felt as if he'd driven her off. "I'm sorry things
didn't work out."

"It's okay. Just bad timing." Ross was responding
to the general now, his booming words obscured by
Anna's.

"Listen—can we talk about this some other time?
I've got the general here, and I'm in the middle of a
crisis."

"Yes. Sorry. I'll send you the expedition specs."

"Great." Ross, standing tight-lipped before the
general, made eye contact with John. "I've got to
go." He terminated the communication and rejoined
the general.

"Perhaps you'd like to explain this drill, Captain

Sheridan,'' Lochschmanan said, enunciating deliberately. ''I can't seem to get a clear answer from your officer.''

John clasped his hands behind his back. He wanted to keep this between him and Ross, for now, anyway. ''It was a standard battle-alert drill, sir.'' Throughout the general's silence, John maintained a pleasant expression.

''I see,'' he said at last. ''I've checked on the progress of your upgrades. The technicians should be completed with their upgrade of the ship's systems in three days. I expect at that time that your crew will be capable of performing some training maneuvers.''

''Yes, sir.'' Three days to get this mess called the *Agamemnon* straightened out. He'd heard they had a job available freezing hell over.

''No trouble at home, is there?''

John closed his eyes for a moment. Lochschmanan was a spit-and-polish general. Having Anna's call come through while they were under a battle alert looked about as unprofessional as you could get. ''No, sir.''

''Glad to hear it. Accompany me to the engine room, would you? I'll brief you on the upgrades.''

John turned to Ross. ''We'll finish our discussion later, Lieutenant.''

''Yes, sir,'' Ross boomed.

It was then, as John left the weapons bay with the general, as he wished that Corchoran had never relayed Anna's call, as he wished that Anna had chosen some other time to call, that he realized: he'd forgotten to tell her he loved her.

Well, he'd do it next time.

CHAPTER 6

It was late afternoon and nearly time for their mission briefing when Anna found Dr. Chang aboard the *Icarus*. His transport had arrived early, so she'd missed him at customs, instead running into Favorito and Razor, the self-appointed party gods of the big dig. They were obsessed with planning a Gigmosian New Year's Eve bash, allegedly a re-creation of the actual Gigmosian ceremony, with a statue of the Gigmosian tree goddess of the new year, authentic fermented Petraki, nose horns, and ceremonial dewlaps.

Favorito and Razor had spent so much time together in confined spaces that they had actually begun to look alike. Although Favorito was white and Razor was black, they were both balding, the fringe of hair remaining to them tied back in a ponytail; they both wore reading glasses perched up on their foreheads, sported scraggly beards often sprinkled with crumbs, and wore comp-pads hanging from their belts. They were nerds, but they were archaeological nerds, and that made them kin. Their relationships seemed to pick up right where they'd left off, with old jokes and insults exchanged. It felt good to relax a little. She showed them to the Imperial Hotel, where they would spend the next eight days in tacky opulence before moving into the austere, cramped quarters of the *Icarus*. Compared to the hotel, the *Icarus* might even look good.

While she waited for them to get settled in, she called up the index of *Archaeology Quarterly* and read Morden's article. While tight in focus, examining only the Anfras love incantation, it was the most brilliant piece of linguistic work she'd ever come across. He was right: it was "the love that abides no borders."

She'd always thought the incantation had meant that, in knowing no borders, love could transcend any impediment. But now, in abiding no borders, the incantation suggested that love should stand for no impediment. It was a more aggressive philosophy, and it demanded more action from its adherents. She wondered if she had allowed impediments to come between her and John. She didn't believe so; she had never believed their careers and their time apart had been impediments. Yet it had been over a year since they'd spent an extended amount of time with each other. And now it would be at least another six months. If she had really wanted to see him, she should have moved heaven and earth to see him. The thought troubled her. Yet it was nothing compared to what Morden had to face. His wife and daughter were dead. That impediment he could not overcome.

By the time she'd gotten Favorito and Razor loaded into the tube and down to the *Icarus*, which was docked in the central landing bay of Station Prime, only a few minutes remained before the mission briefing. She found Dr. Chang on the command deck in discussion with Captain Hidalgo. Chang turned as she approached. He'd changed into his expedition khakis and boots.

"It looks like you've done an excellent job working

with Captain Hidalgo to prep the ship." Chang seemed energetic. Perhaps escaping corporate headquarters and his tasseled loafers had raised his spirits.

"The captain has been very helpful," Anna said. In truth, Hidalgo, a short, wiry man, had answered her questions, but he was hardly forthcoming. His philosophy, when it came to archaeologists, anyway, seemed to be to speak only when spoken to. A philosophy to which he continued to adhere. "Over fifty percent of our equipment is loaded," Anna said, "and the rest is arriving over the next few days. The ship's systems are all being prepped for the journey. Everything should be ready with two days to spare. Are we still on schedule, Captain Hidalgo?"

"Yes, Doctor." Hidalgo gave the impression that all doctors had blended together long ago in his mind, into one great nameless Doctor. She doubted he knew her name.

"Dr. Chang," she said, "I was wondering if I could talk to you for a moment before the mission briefing."

Chang nodded. "Excuse us, Captain." He headed toward the conference room, Anna following a step behind in the narrow passage. "I know what you're going to say."

"I don't think you do," Anna said. "I think Petrovich and Standish are here to keep an eye on you, make sure you maintain IPX's priorities."

He shot her a sharp smile. "Very good, Sheridan. You're almost ready to swim with the sharks."

"Ms. Donne I know is bad news, and I resent the fact that she's taking a slot we needed for an archaeologist. But I think Dr. Morden may be an asset. I don't know how he got on the team or what his agenda is, but he certainly knows his stuff. What's your take on him?"

"I haven't even met the man. But if I were you, on this trip I would trust no one. You care about people, Sheridan, and on this trip caring is a liability. The only one I trust is you."

"I trust you," Anna said.

"Well, maybe you shouldn't," Chang said. "I invited you into this madness." On that they entered the conference room, and the conversation of the archaeologists inside graded into silence. "If everyone will collect their coffee and donuts and take a seat, we will begin."

The conference room was little more than a cube, barely big enough for the rectangular table, a com station against one wall and a data-processing station and view screen against another. But it was nicer than the facilities they'd had on any other trip.

Chang stood at the head of the table, and sitting to his right looking up at him, Anna felt some of the old awe that had faded over the years. Chang was like the old lecturer she knew back at the University of Chicago, his gestures sharp, his voice vibrant, compelling. He knew this was the find of a lifetime, as they all did. Politics couldn't change that. And once the news of their discovery got out, it would become bigger than politics, beyond its influence. Listening to him lay out the expedition, she felt the excitement building inside her. Her career, it seemed, had built to this moment, to the discovery of a totally unknown race, a totally unknown technology.

After an overview of the mission specs, Chang went around the table and introduced each team member. Beside Anna sat the old friends Favorito, Razor, and Scott, Razor holding his hands up, modellike, to high-

light Scott's new short hair, she yanking his ponytail in
return. At the foot of the table sat Donne, her face
clenched, determined, to her right Morden, a careful
smile on his face, his fingers steepled on the tabletop,
beside him Petrovich and Standish, trying a little too
hard in Anna's mind to look as if they belonged, and
opposite Anna to Chang's left sat Churlstein. It was
always important to him to sit near the head of the
table, as if he was afraid he would be forgotten otherwise. He nodded at everything Chang said, and as he
did his eyes swept down the table, insuring that everyone was in support of their leader.

Chang made no attempt to explain the presence of
Donne or Morden. He simply introduced them, said
what organizations they were from, and moved on. No
one seemed surprised—they'd probably heard the
make-up of the team days ago through the grapevine—
except Donne at the introduction of Morden. Though
her expression didn't change, her head swiveled in his
direction, and their eyes met over Morden's secure
smile. He almost seemed pleased at her reaction.

After the introductions, Chang began to review the
data transmitted by the probe, data that had been con-
spicuously absent from the mission specs Anna had
received.

"The majority of the surface appears to be made up
of two kinds of rock. The mountains, which are extensive, have been formed from igneous rock, while the
plains are covered by deposits of sedimentary rock.
Sand and dust eroded from these two types of rock
have formed eolian deposits in various sheltered areas.

"The atmosphere carries a radioactive residue, the
decay patterns of which suggest its decay began approximately one thousand years ago. The nature of the
radioactivity—which I leave to the physicists"—the

group laughed here, as physicists were generally despised—"is indicative of an artificial source, suggesting a war may have been fought on the planet at that time. No life has been detected above the microscopic level, which may be a result from that war. But the atmosphere is extremely dry, which would aid in the preservation of any organic remains.

"Weather patterns appear violent. Dust storms covering one-quarter of the planet's surface are nearly constant. Some constituent of the dust is causing sporadic disruption in our communications with the probe and some image distortion. But I think you'll find the results quite impressive."

With a touch he activated the viewscreen on the wall behind him. A static-distorted image appeared of rocky terrain stretching toward sharp distant mountains. The atmosphere was a reddish brown, the same color as the rock, clouded by intermittent gusts of dust. The landscape appeared harsh, desolate. As the probe panned to the left, a tall thin finger of stone appeared in the foreground, covered with vague runes. As the probe continued to turn, more pillars were revealed, at varying distances. They stretched as far as the eye could see.

"Surviving structures include numerous inscribed pillars, obviously not natural formations, ranging from one hundred to one hundred fifty yards high. These pillars are spaced at a constant distance of 2.43 miles from each other, and are spread over the entire area the probe has scanned thus far. They are made of the native sedimentary rock. Other structures"—he pointed to a scattering of large, worn hexagonal blocks of stone that had just come into the foreground— "made of the same rock existed in this area, though they did not survive while the pillars did. A fascinating paradox. In the background, you'll notice the mountain profile contains some spiky anomalies that suggest artificial constructs. The probe has not visited that area yet.

"The most exciting find was discovered at the base of the tallest pillar scanned thus far." A new image appeared on the screen, more static-distorted than the previous ones. The probe panned down the length of a huge pillar perhaps twenty yards away. At its base an ovoid object sat in shadow, only its silhouette visible. "The egg, as I've been calling it, is approximately ten yards high, fifteen yards long." About the size of a house, Anna thought. "While the visual is unclear, preliminary scans indicate that the egg is riddled with numerous indentations and tunnels, almost, perhaps, like a piece of Piridian sculpture." He flipped through a series of scans then, which revealed a twisting, intricate structure honeycombing the object. Anna wished he would go slower and cover the data in more depth. She saw similarities to the mouse, though this object was much more complex.

"These irregularities indicate a color mottling on the surface of the object that appears almost runic in structure. These mottling patterns continue within the holes and tunnels. They may form lettering of some kind, though how they were created is unclear. While we initially assumed the egg was carved from the same sedimentary rock as the pillars, test results were inconclusive. Some indicated that the egg had an electronic component; others showed biological characteristics. A resonance scan then revealed the most fascinating aspect of the egg." He switched to a new visual, which Anna recognized with excitement. "It has a heartbeat. This is when I made the connection to Sheridan's mouse, which I'll let her discuss in a few minutes. RNA screens confirmed that the protein fingerprint of the planet matched that of the mouse.''

Anna had no idea they'd found something of this significance. This biomechanical organism was incredibly more complex than the mouse. And it appeared in excellent condition. If they already knew about one surviving biomechanical device on the planet, there would most likely be others. She wondered what its function might be. The other scientists were whispering to each other, totally amazed at what they had seen. Morden turned her way, his smile now replaced by a more subtle expression of genuine curiosity. Donne's face had gone blank, her mouth tilted at a forgotten angle.

"The probe, as you know," Chang continued, "is running a preprogrammed pattern of investigation and testing. We may change general directives for the probe at this point, but my sense is that it would be premature—no matter how much I want more testing on that egg. We only found the egg because the probe was carrying out its preprogrammed pattern, which is designed for optimum use of time and energy. I'm afraid that by interfering we may miss an equally exciting find. Once we're about a week and a half into our journey, we'll be close enough that we can take direct control of the probe. Doing so sooner than that, because of the distances involved, would create a dangerous time delay between our directives and the probe's responses. Most of you have experienced smaller time delays and know that they can easily lead to accidents and the destruction of the probe. So we're just going to have to wait until then.

"You now have access to all the data, which are updated on a real-time basis. I want you to study them and get me your recommendations for our most efficient use of the probe." Chang sat. "Now I'll have Dr. Sheridan tell you about her experience with the mouse."

Anna described her discovery of the mouse, the characteristics she had observed, and the conclusion she had drawn that it was a biomechanical device of some kind. She tried to convey the sensations she had received from the mouse, and how those had led to her decision to bring in a telepath. At that point, Dr. Chang interrupted.

"The telepathic contact seemingly triggered the mouse to explode," Chang said, his words aimed at Donne. "That's all we know at this point. I've made test results on the mouse available to you also, and there are a few surviving fragments I'm keeping under lock and key if you'd like to have additional tests run. If there are no questions—"

"Excuse me," Morden said, with his fixed smile. "I wanted to ask Sheridan about this mouse."

Chang began picking at the callus on his index finger.

It was obvious that Morden knew Chang was covering up something, and he was circling in on it. "You say you felt you were in some sort of telepathic contact with it. Do you think if you had concentrated harder, or sustained your contact with it, that you could have triggered the explosion?"

Anna chose her words carefully. "I really don't know. But my instinct tells me that my contact with the mouse was of a much lesser intensity than that of the telepath. It felt almost like my own mind wandering, like dreaming that I'm hearing someone else's thoughts in a dream. Not like what I've read the telepathic experience is like at all."

"Only Ms. Donne could tell us that, I suppose."

Anna realized then that Morden's smile was sometimes genuine, sometimes not. The trick was figuring out which and when.

The room fell into an awkward silence.

"Dr. Chang," Ms. Donne said, "will you be focusing the expedition on this egg?"

"It would be premature to make a commitment like that. Yet at this point it does seem a find of major importance."

"Is there more data on it?"

Chang tilted his head curiously. "Yes, the probe's records are available for downloading, if you'd care to study them." After a hesitation, he picked up where he had left off. "We have only eight days until launch. There's a lot to do. Study the data and get your recommendations to Sheridan. Coordinate through her."

There was some impassioned speculation as the team broke up. Anna managed to excuse herself and caught up with Donne about twenty feet down the narrow passage. "I wanted to officially welcome you to the team. I wasn't aware of your archaeological expertise."

Donne gave a tight, humorless smile, the skin wrinkling under the small D-shaped scar on her cheek. "I'm not on your team, Dr. Sheridan. At least give me some credit for admitting that, unlike that sleaze Morden. If I were you, I'd be keeping your eyes on him."

"Thanks for the advice." Donne must be great at her job, Anna thought, whatever it was. Her personality certainly didn't win her any brownie points. "So what can we expect you to contribute to this expedition?"

"If there's any technology uncovered that poses a threat to telepaths, I'm here to make sure Psi Corps knows about it. Without me on site, we'd never hear about it. You mundanes at IPX would have the whole thing packaged, marketed, and sold to the highest bidder—most likely Morden—and we wouldn't find out about it until telepaths' brains started turning to jelly.''

Anna's fist came to her mouth. "How is Terrence?"

"Mr. Hilliard is the way Mr. Hilliard will be for the rest of his life. Mr. Hilliard is jelly." Donne continued down the passage.

Anna had been hoping that they'd been able to break Terrence out of it. Somewhere inside she had even believed it. It seemed impossible that in a few moments the mouse could have so trapped his mind.

She brought her fist away from her mouth, opening it to reveal the pattern of calluses that had grown up over years of digs. Climbing in and out of pits, up and down from cliffs, detecting the subtle edges of a buried object, digging carefully into tiny recesses, sensing weaknesses, fractures. No matter how advanced the tools, there was no substitute for touch, for the sensitivity and delicacy of control of the hand. She'd paid little notice to the injuries to her hands, well willing to trade a little skin and a little sensitivity for the thrill of discovery. She'd even come to see them as badges of knowledge and expertise.

A callus was the body's response to repeated injury and irritation. She wondered if the memory of Terrence, over time, would create a new callus, one that would lessen her sensitivity. She didn't know whether to hope for that or not. Perhaps it had already begun. She had surrendered him with relief to Psi Corps. Her overriding concern had been for her standing at IPX and her continued access to the mouse fragments. And now she'd let Chang and Donne cover up what had happened to him. It was as if he hadn't even existed.

She ran her fingers over her palm. The injuries of the past created a hard, protective layer, on the hand or on the soul. As an archaeologist her job was to uncover the past, to remove the protective layer, to reveal the wound. She believed inherently in the value of the past, and in its presence in and influence on the present. People were in many senses controlled by the past, even though they might not know it. The wound, even through its covering, influenced them. Yet could there be no lessening of pain over time, no escape from injuries and passions, mistakes and humiliations? Could there be no healing without a loss of sensitivity, of memory? She never wanted to forget Terrence. She never wanted to forget what she had done to him. But if she felt her guilt as intensely as she had felt it when the accident had first happened, she wouldn't be able to function. Without a callus, what was the alternative? An open wound.

"Hi." Morden had come down the hall from the conference room. His hands were folded in front of him, his posture still neat, controlled, but his smile seemed more relaxed. "That was some briefing. I can't believe what they've found."

She twisted her lips. "You seemed to enjoy baiting Ms. Donne."

"I don't like Psi Corps. I don't know why she's here. I don't know what she's covering up. And I don't trust her to respect our privacy. While that may make the long trip a little more interesting, I think I'd prefer it if she'd blurt out everything and we'd all end up sitting around playing poker."

"She says you're the one keeping secrets."

Morden nodded. "And now the games begin. And

we haven't even left the station yet. Want to catch some dinner?''

Anna decided this would be a good time to start on her secondary project. And if she got Morden to confide in her any more, all the better. "I'd love to.''

"Have a seat,'' John said.

Ross, Spano, and Watley sat in the chairs on the opposite side of his desk. The small office was crowded with them.

John rested one arm on the desktop, his fingertips grazing the snow globe. "Things got out of control yesterday. I feel I've cut each of you some slack, though you may not agree with me. But I will not tolerate that kind of behavior, or that kind of performance on a drill, again.

"I'm offering each of you the same proposition I've offered to several of your crewmates. If any of you would like a transfer, I will get it for you, no questions asked. If you decide to stay, I will tolerate no less than one hundred percent from you. I've made my expectations clear. I want every person on board this ship to give his all. If you stay and I continue to find your performance unsatisfactory, you will be brought up on charges.

"Commander Corchoran said that some of you may feel you have an undeserved stain on your reputations.'' He held up a finger. "What counts is not what other people think of you, but what you are and what you do. You are responsible only for yourself. What's important is not convincing them of your integrity, but convincing yourself: maintaining your integrity when you're alone, when no one will know but you. So you can look in the mirror at the end of the day and think, I did my best, I did my duty.''

Ross's sharp mouth had compressed into a line, Spano's eyebrows were lifted in contempt, and Watley seemed to be staring into space. John clasped his hands together and leaned forward, trying by sheer force of will to reach them.

"Decisions we've made in the past have shaped what we are today. Experiences we've had in the past shape our expectations of the present. Those patterns are difficult to change. But things are changing here on the *Agamemnon*. To deny that is to deny your future. I would like you to change with them, and I believe you can. But if you don't want to, then I advise you to take the transfer. The change that is happening here will not be denied. I will not allow you to stand in the way of it."

He closed his hand into a fist. "I expect to receive your decisions before the *Agamemnon* is deployed."

"Yes, sir," they replied in near-unison.

"Lieutenant Spano, you will remain confined to quarters for an additional forty-eight hours."

"Yes, *sir*," Spano replied.

They sat, stiff and still, waiting to be dismissed. He didn't think he'd gotten through to any of them. But he didn't know what more to say. Perhaps they couldn't change, or wouldn't change. Perhaps Best had spoiled them. But somehow the war seemed to stand between them, as if, eight years past, it still reverberated on the present, never allowing them to forget, dominating their lives even now, carrying them into the future. How could he fight the past?

"Dismissed," he said.

December 2256

"Deep is the well of the past.
Should one not call it unfathomable?"
—THOMAS MANN

CHAPTER 7

O<small>N</small> the conference room view screen, Anna saw the ring of Station Prime begin to shrink as the *Icarus* pulled away from it toward the jump gate. In a few minutes they would make their first in a series of jumps that would, in a month's time, bring them to the rim of known space. Among the larger ships surrounding the station, the *Agamemnon* was nowhere in sight. She went to the com station against the wall and tried once again to reach John. She had to use Chang's access code to make the call; he'd told her that IPX, to maintain security, had ordered that all communications go through him. The way he'd explained it, Anna wasn't sure if this was a new corporate policy or a special procedure for this expedition. But Chang trusted her not to abuse his code.

It was ironic that today, December third, was their seventh anniversary, the day she and John had planned to spend together to celebrate their love for each other. She wanted to spend the whole day in his warm arms peeling him oranges and reading him silly mistranslated love incantations. But she'd made her decision, and he'd been unable to get away anyway. Borders. She told herself they had years and years of anniversaries to look forward to.

The com system gave her the same response she'd been getting for over a week: "The Earthforce ship you are trying to reach is currently out of contact. Please try again later."

"Still trying to reach your husband?" Donne was standing in the doorway, her muscular body, covered in black, like a block of shadow.

Anna had thought the whole team was up on the observation deck. "Yes, no luck."

"I was wondering if you would conduct an experiment for me."

This was new. Donne seeking cooperation. "What's the experiment?"

Donne came inside. She revealed a small box in her gloved hand. "Your company granted me a fragment of the mouse. We've done extensive tests on it, but none of the results reveal the telepathic nature of the object. We, of course, don't want to endanger any other telepaths by having them attempt to make contact with the object. I'd like to see if you still detect any telepathic activity in the fragment."

They, of course, wouldn't mind it if Anna's brain turned to jelly, though she knew it wouldn't. But she couldn't tell Donne about the experience she'd had with her own fragment at the hotel; she wasn't supposed to have had access to the mouse at that point. "Sure, I'll try."

Donne hesitated. "You have no telepathic abilities, correct?"

"None whatsoever."

Donne handed her the box. The unexpected weight almost fell out of her hand. "What's this made of?"

"Lead," Donne said, and pulled out a chair. Her face relaxed slightly.

Anna sat beside her. She opened the small fastening

on the box, took out the fragment. She took satisfaction in the fact that the fragment Donne had was significantly smaller than the one she had. Anna closed her hand around the fragment, concentrated on it. The experience was similar to the one she'd had at the Imperial Hotel, though now she studied the impressions more intently.

"Sheridan." Morden was shaking her shoulder.

"What is it?" Anna asked.

"We were just getting concerned." He was tight-lipped, grim. He moved away. Chang was also in the room, and Churlstein. Anna felt rather self-conscious. She extended the fragment toward Donne.

"It's still active at some—"

"Back in the box, please," Donne said. Her normal way of speaking, with little movement of her jaw, was exaggerated, as if she were clenching her teeth. She didn't want to touch the thing.

"Of course." Anna allowed herself a slight hesitation, enjoying Donne's discomfort, then returned the fragment to the box. "There was a faint echo of the pulsing, the heartbeat I heard before. But it was intermittent, and in the blank spots I got this feel of static, and on the other side of that there was this weird animal sense of a nest . . . burrowing into shavings, something warm in a dark place, stone all around. And then it was different, the machine was all around, and it was beautiful, and it hurt." She felt foolish. The words couldn't convey what she had seen, what she had felt. "The animal. I think it's what the mouse was, once."

"You mean an evolutionary memory?" Churlstein asked. "You think this device evolved naturally out of a real animal? That's ridiculous."

Anna ran her hands up under her hair, grabbed her

scalp, feeling fuzzy, frustrated. "That's not what I mean. I'm not sure what I mean."

Chang said, "Perhaps the DNA used to create the device was adapted from that of a living creature. Perhaps that is some imprinted instinct you sensed. Our knowledge of how these devices are created is nil. It's too early to discount any possibility." He directed those words at Churlstein.

"So it might still pose a threat," Donne said, "even at this stage."

"I suppose so," Anna said.

Donne reluctantly took up the box. "Thank you for your cooperation, Dr. Sheridan. I think if we work together, we'll be able to unlock the secrets of these devices, which would be in all our best interests. If we can't understand something as simple as this mouse, how will we ever understand the egg?"

As she left, Morden sat down beside Anna and leaned in close. "Someone must have slipped her a happy pill."

Anna burst out laughing.

"In the spirit of cooperation," Morden said to Chang and the others, "I have some translations."

"Wonderful, wonderful. I can't believe you have something for us already." Chang sat opposite Morden, Churlstein quickly taking the seat beside him. Anna was also surprised that Morden could have translated anything yet. Even with computer analyses, it was a slow, painstaking job.

Morden opened a folder with a series of stills derived from the probe's image transmissions. "Using some image refinement techniques, I've been able to get readable inscriptions off of fifty different sources so far." He spread out the stills. "The majority are the hexagonal stone blocks, though also included are several pillars and the egg.

"This gave me a marginal sample to begin doing some preliminary translations. Keep in mind these are very rough. The language has thousands of different characters, though a smaller number seem more commonly used. I really shouldn't even begin without a sample at least twice this size, but I had some free time . . . . The language has some similarities to two little-known ancient languages, Kandarian and what's known as L5, and that gave me a starting point, though this language is much more refined and sophisticated. Those languages may have been influenced by this one. Anyway, let me review the characteristics of the language."

As Morden continued, Anna noticed how much more relaxed he seemed than when they'd first met. His hands were picking out various stills and sheets of notes, gesturing, expressive, broken free from the careful folded-hand position. His face was in motion, reflecting his thoughts rather than holding them back behind a frozen smile. These times still did not last; he would fall silent and the grief would pull him back into the quiet, careful world of desperate control, but she saw him escaping that world a few moments longer each day. As much as she would have enjoyed taking credit for it, his progress had very little to do with her and her attempts to draw him out. It was the expedition that had engaged him, body, mind, and soul, as it had engaged all of them.

"Certain phrases appear to be repeated numerous times. The most interesting case is the pillars. So far, the four pillars on which I've been able to get satisfactory resolution have carried the same inscription."

Chang brought the various stills of the pillars next

to each other, and Anna stood up to lean over the table.

Chang shook his head. "A ritual meaning?"

It was the most likely explanation, Anna thought. Repetitive structures most often had a ritualistic purpose or a practical one, and offhand it was hard to think of a practical purpose the pillars could serve, unless it was somehow related to their technology.

"The preliminary translation, very rough, is 'Every light casts a shadow.' "

"Part of some religious belief, perhaps," Chang said.

"The pillars could cast shadows at different times of the day—if there wasn't a storm. I'd say they were some sort of time-telling or distance-measuring tools, as used by Ptolemy, or at least carrying a similar ceremonial purpose, but the planet gets so little light. Shadows cast would be weak, if they existed at all."

Anna tilted her head, studying the pattern of the runes. "You're assuming atmospheric conditions have remained constant, and that they weren't worsened by the war fought here."

Chang nodded. "If the atmosphere was clearer at an earlier time, the pillars may have been tied to astronomical observation of some kind, as with Stonehenge."

Anna sat down. The inscription bothered her. It seemed innocuous, yet it made her think back to the mouse, to the image of the dark, towering machine. Who would this race be who would create technology of such sophistication and build pillars with such a simplistic message? What significance could it have for them?

"You have more?" Chang asked. Donne had returned, the box squirreled away. She stood behind Dr.

Chang. Petrovich and Standish had wandered in as well.

"One more," Morden said. "I really don't feel secure enough to share anything else." Morden pulled out a still with a close-up of some shaded lettering. "This was taken from the egg. It's by far the largest and simplest piece of writing on the object, and the only one that can be read in its entirety. The others lead into the various tunnels and hollows in the object. He brought his hands flat against each other, raised them to his mouth. "I'm not really sure on this. My tentative translation is 'what is desired,' though it may say 'all that is desired.'"

"That's the entire phrase?" Churlstein asked.

"Yes."

Churlstein's face wrinkled in frustration. "Is that a question? What is desired?"

"I don't know," Morden answered.

They were all silent.

"Could the device be a manufacturing center?" Chang suggested. "It may be requesting specifications of some kind."

"Perhaps it provided entertainment," Standish said, "and the inscription is more like an advertisement."

"It sounds more like a promise," Donne said. "Something you'd find on the side of an oil lamp with a genie inside."

And from the silence that prevailed after she said it, Anna realized it was what they had all been thinking.

"My shower's broken," she said, her shape a hazy silhouette behind the coated shower door. "Can I share yours?"

"It's not very big," John said.

The door opened and her head peaked in, brown hair in disarray, mischievous smile radiating heat. "I can squeeze in."

"Then by all means," he replied.

She stepped in with soap and shampoo, naked, all business. "Could I get under the water please?"

"Certainly."

They squeezed past each other in the small square stall, her body a brush of heaven, so familiar, so wanted. She stepped under the spray, and the water cascaded down her face, her shoulders, her breasts, her body like a blessing, she one of the ancient goddesses she studied, embodiment of life and vitality.

"You didn't wash your back," she said. "Turn around."

He did. She rubbed the soap over his back in a slow, serpentine pattern, and he felt his muscles relaxing, melting. Then she put the soap aside and it was her hands running in mysterious geometries across his skin, the rough sandpaper touch of her callused fingers bringing his skin to tingling awareness, revitalizing him, recharging him.

His link chimed.

"Don't go yet," she said.

He opened his eyes to the darkness of his quarters, the sensations persistent. He reached for the link, activated it. "Sheridan. Go." He found he was slightly out of breath.

"Coded message for you from General Lochschmanan, Captain."

Didn't the man ever sleep? John swung his legs over the side of the bed. "I'll take it in my office. Lights." He squinted as the lights came on, held out one hand to half feel his way into the office next door. He sat at his desk. His T-shirt and shorts would have to do, he supposed. "Computer. Accept and decode communication."

Lochschmanan appeared on the monitor, his tall thin frame looking as spit-and-polish as ever. "Captain, sorry to wake you."

John squinted up at the monitor, thinking of Anna and tact. "I was just getting up, sir."

"I've been authorized to share certain information with you that I've been unable to discuss before. It should not be shared with your officers until I give you the all clear. It is critical that you get your crew in shape very quickly now. We will need you and the *Agamemnon* for a mission in three to four weeks. We suspected this might be the case, which is why your ship was upgraded with the new stealth technology, and now we know for sure. We have been tracking the Homeguard faction responsible for the destruction of the Io jump gate. An agent of ours has infiltrated the group. He reports that they plan to attempt to blow up Babylon 5 at its dedication ceremonies next month. They are currently arranging a major buy of nuclear explosives from the Narns. We don't yet know where or when, but our agent will be privy to this information. The *Agamemnon* will intercept the Homeguard ship after the buy."

"Sir, you know some of the problems we've been having. To send out the ship this quickly, on this crucial a mission, seems . . . Why us, sir?"

"This decision comes from the top, Captain. Those at home are still very unsettled by the previous terrorist attack and the failure to apprehend those responsible. Now there is a threat to Babylon 5, after four previous failures. It weakens our reputation, not only among our own populace, but among alien governments. It weakens the authority of our stated desire for peace. That is why they want you, John, the hero of the Earth-Minbari War, making secure the peace. It will send a message to those who oppose peace, both at home and abroad.''

"But sir, with all due respect, is it worth endangering the mission, Babylon 5, and all those on-station in order to send a message?''

"No, it's not. And that's why I expect your crew to be in exemplary form before I have to send you out. So get to work, Captain.''

John let out a breath. "Yes, sir.''

The general terminated the communication.

It was time to show Earthforce that their faith in him wasn't misplaced. Hundreds of thousands of lives depended on it.

As John stumbled into the vibe shower, the memory of his dream returned. It was past midnight now; their anniversary was over. John felt horrible that he hadn't had the chance to see Anna, or even call her. She loved going on digs, but he'd gotten the impression from their talks over the last few months that she needed a break from IPX, and he feared she'd only gone on the expedition out of loneliness. Now another six months would slip away from them.

He'd let so many days of drilling, inspections, and battle simulations go by without making the time to contact her. Then when he'd finally sat down to do it, he'd realized he didn't even know where she was. He'd tried her apartment in Geneva, getting a prerecorded message explaining she was on a dig. Finally, last night, he'd looked through the expedition specs she'd sent him and discovered that she was shipping out from Station Prime, not Earth as he'd assumed. And she'd shipped out yesterday. She'd probably been staying at the Imperial Hotel all this time, waiting to hear back from him. He'd tried to contact her on the ship, only to be routed to IPX headquarters in Geneva, where they informed him all personal messages had to be prerecorded and cleared.

He'd be damned if he was going to let some IPX flunky listen to his private communication. So the anniversary had come and gone, Anna's ship slipping away from his, gliding out into the vacuum of space.

CHAPTER 8

Dr. Chang climbed out of the probe control module. "It's all yours," he said to Anna. "Just make sure you don't get a scratch on it."

Anna smiled. "Thanks, Dad."

She stooped to climb through the small hatchway, and Chang closed the door behind her. The control module was self-contained so that it could be moved from ship to ship or to various IPX office buildings. It was designed, she supposed, to take up the least amount of space on a ship. But that didn't stop her from believing that whoever had designed this thing had been a sadist. One small hatchway provided the only opening. Once inside, she could not straighten up. She had to squeeze into the control chair—how she could have done it if she were Churlstein's size she didn't know—then fit her legs into the two hollows nearly straight in front of her and bend her arms up at an awkward angle to reach the keypad and other controls. Once she was in contact with the probe, she had to put on a helmet to get the full holographic visual the probe was transmitting, and when she wanted to use any of the tester arms, she had to wriggle her hands into the thick moisture-retentive gloves whose movement controlled them. Once she was controlling the probe, caught up in its movements and perceptions, the claustrophobia faded away. But before and after, her skin crawled with the closeness of the module.

She noticed that Chang hadn't bothered to close down his session, so she could just operate the probe under his access code. She fitted on the snug helmet, found herself in the landscape she'd been observing down in the conference room with the rest of the team, jagged, harsh, the dust and the distance of the sun making the light appear dusky, even in the midday. The lights on the probe gave her a visibility of perhaps fifty to seventy feet.

She and the rest of the team had observed as Chang ran the probe through its paces, making sure all the manual systems were operational and getting a sense for the slight time delay remaining between the issuing of an order and the executing of it. He'd run a few new tests on the egg, then turned the probe over to her.

"Plot a course to cave 3A, sector 3," Anna ordered the probe. A visual of the projected course appeared below the landscape. The probe had discovered the first cave almost a week ago, and since then several others had turned up in the black igneous rock that made up the more mountainous areas of the landscape. The extent of the caves was still unclear. They seemed natural elements of the landscape; no evidence of artificial alterations or improvements had been discovered so far.

Cave 3A was the largest cave they'd found so far, in a rocky outcropping near the foothills of one of the smaller mountain ranges. Her instinct told her the caves were important. In general, caves provided less disturbed, better preserved artifacts—*if* they had been occupied, that was. With advanced civilizations like this one, it was unlikely this cave had been occupied for thousands and thousands of years, unless by animals. Yet Anna had noticed an odd lack of organic remains or personal possessions among the stone blocks that had made up some of the major structures of this civilization. If these buildings had been destroyed in a war, skeletons and possessions should have been among the ruins. Archaeologists loved catastrophic destruction, since it often left a perfect record of a moment frozen in time, the moment at which the civilization had been destroyed. Pompeii was the classic example. Admittedly, some artifacts would not have lasted as long as the stone, and some may have been buried in the deposits of sand and dust, but the dry atmosphere should have worked to desiccate and preserve remains. The probe had found nothing.

The lack of organic remains and personal possessions could be explained if the residents had outlived the buildings. But then where had they moved? Anna wondered if it might have been to the caves.

"Time to destination," she requested.

"Twenty-four minutes," the probe responded. The cave was only a little over a mile away, but the probe had to move slowly over the rocky terrain or risk serious damage.

"Execute," Anna said.

As the probe moved ahead, the holographic display showed the rocks moving behind her, new landscape coming into view. The illusion of movement always made her feel like a ghost floating over the landscape. It was a lonely, vulnerable feeing.

Anna's choice of destination sparked a lot of speculation from the team, who were watching the probe's readouts from the conference room and conversing with Anna though a com link into the module.

Donne's tight voice came through the link. "Why

aren't you investigating the egg?'' Anna could visualize her clenched jaw.

"The probe has done several preliminary tests on the egg. The purpose of the probe is not to do in-depth testing—that's what we're for. It's for advance scouting work. We haven't gotten any data from the caves yet."

"The egg is an incredible find," Donne persisted.

Anna didn't know what had gotten into Donne's shorts, but she found herself losing patience. Hadn't Chang gotten down to the conference room yet, and couldn't he get her away from the link? "Basic archaeological practice teaches that an initial, thorough examination of the site is the most effective way to prepare for an excavation."

"You're wasting valuable time and resources."

"Excuse me for saying so, Ms. Donne, but I think you've lost it."

There was silence from the link for several minutes after that, and Anna berated herself for losing her temper. Hardly professional behavior for the second in command. John would have loved to see this; she was always telling him to use more tact.

As time passed, the other team members got on and off the link, speculating about whether she would find anything in the caves. Within a few minutes Favorito had established odds and was taking bets. The team was excited about the results they might get now that they were close enough to manually control the probe, and there was a generally festive atmosphere. Anna supposed Donne must have left the room.

That morning they'd left the *De Soto* behind. After a series of jumps that had brought them as close to the rim as jump gates could, they'd rendezvoused a few days ago with the *De Soto*, an explorer ship that could form its own jump point. The *Icarus* had hitched a ride with the *De Soto*, which had dropped them out of hyperspace as close to their destination as was convenient. Although they had twenty days to go, with civilization behind them and nothing but open space between them and Alpha Omega 3, an atmosphere of expectation and excitement had begun to build.

Anna was glad that the probe seemed fully operational. Probes never lasted long. They were not going to be the artifacts to survive the Twenty-third Century to be dug up by future archaeologists. They were finicky devices, intricate and prone to accidents in the hazardous landscapes they roamed. While the body was a simple six-wheeled multiterrain vehicle, the technicians couldn't help adding bells and whistles until something was bound to break down. She and Chang had worried that the dust in the air might work its way into the probe's mechanisms, or that the rocky terrain might cause the vehicle to overturn. But so far all systems were in the green.

The transmissions being sent by the probe were coming through fairly clearly today, with only occasional surges of static, the dust storms granting a rare reprieve. The probe sent its transmissions up to the orbiter that had accompanied it, which then relayed the signals to the *Icarus*.

The orbiter was basically a jump engine with scanners and a series of probes attached to it. When it found a planet that conformed to its preprogrammed guidelines, it sent down a probe and acted as a relay station for communications between the probe and Earth. The orbiter often recorded useful information of its own about the planet below, though in this case the constant dust storms prevented the orbiter from gathering much significant data. The orbiter was programmed to abandon the probe and move on after one month if no findings that satisfied its guidelines were reported by the probe. In this case, the findings had been plentiful, and the orbiter had been ordered by IPX to remain until further notice.

Chang's voice interrupted her thoughts. "How are you doing in there?"

"Fine. I hate it, but I'm fine." Between the uncomfortable position and the claustrophobic surroundings, the module was suggested for use for only six hours at a time. Some people couldn't stand it for nearly that long.

"Tell Sheridan I bet ten credits against her," Razor called.

"Tell Razor I'm returning his Christmas present," Anna responded. You'd think they'd been in space ten years instead of ten days.

"Destination acquired," the probe said. In her helmet the image of the cave mouth waited, the probe's headlights sending the jagged edges of the rocks into high relief. The cave mouth opened like a dark scream.

Anna looked down, the probe's cameras mirroring the tilt of her head. She examined the talus, the sloping mass of rock fragments outside the mouth of the cave. Often the talus revealed signs of habitation within the cave. Items such as bones, stones, or pottery were often thrown out of the cave or eroded out onto the talus. But she saw nothing except jagged black fragments of rock.

The surface did seem smooth enough for the probe to proceed without difficulty. To cover uneven or mountainous terrain, a section of the probe with spider-like legs could detach, but Anna preferred not to use it. Just something else to go wrong.

"Ahead with caution," Anna ordered. As the probe moved forward, the darkness of the cave enveloped her.

"Lights on high," Anna said. The darkness around her lessened somewhat. She could see hints of cave walls, barely visible, to her sides. The lights of the probe seemed dulled, as if the rock absorbed rather than reflected them. The cave appeared perhaps twelve feet wide here.

"Safety lock engaged," the probe said, and its forward progress stopped. An alarm began sounding inside the module. "Communication endangered." Inside the confined space, the alarm was enough to give her an instant migraine.

"Cause of danger," Anna said.

"Increased depth of rock causing contact failure."

"Reverse to safe distance."

Her ghost drifted back several feet; it was hard to say how much in the darkness. The alarm stopped. "Maximum safe distance acquired."

"Shit," Anna said. Not only was the dust causing communications interference; now the rock was too. Which made sense, since the dust was made up of particles of worn rock. But that didn't mean she had to like it.

"No cave-trolling for you, Sheridan," Razor's voice said over the link.

"We'll see about that," Anna muttered to herself. If the probe went any deeper into the cave, it would lose touch with her and the orbiter. The safety lock had engaged to prevent that. Anna scanned the probe's position. It had stopped about ten yards into the cave. She decided to make full use of every inch of that ten yards. She'd run every scan in this tricked-up probe's menu. If there was something to find, she'd find it.

Sheeting joints and fractures ran through the walls of the cave. Cracks up to several inches wide painted a darker web against the darkness. When she got up close enough to see detail, she found the walls jagged and sharp with differential etching. The floor was covered with a mix of dark, sharp, ragged fragments and larger stones. Underneath, slabs of rock had been differentially lifted, creating a cracked, uneven surface almost like old rural roads broken by frost heaves back home. She was no geologist, but all indications were that the caves had been formed through dissolution, when water or some other liquid worked its way into the rock and selectively dissolved those sections of the rock made up of a certain chemical, such as in the limestone caves back on Earth. That dissolution—of both tiny veins of the chemical and larger deposits— would account for the jagged, etched look to the walls, the fractures, and the caves themselves.

What she wouldn't give for some sign of previous habitation right now. She ran through the menu of scanning options on her helmet viewer, thinking she'd tried every one likely to show something and even some that weren't.

"Run thermal scan," Anna directed.

"Time to pack it in, Sheridan," Razor said. "I have a bet to collect on."

"Was that the one where you said you could find the Centauri lost colony?"

"Ow—Sheridan, you're cruel."

"And you love it." The results of the thermal scan came up, and Anna jumped, banging her helmet against the top of the module. "There's a slight heat source . . ." They could see it on their screen. "A foot below the surface, beside the cave wall."

They were all quiet now, as she narrowed the scan

and clarified the dimensions of the heat source. It occupied about a cubic foot. Normally she would have hesitated to dig even a foot below the surface with the probe. No digging should have been done until complete measurements and records had been made. And then the digging should have been done in person, one thin layer at a time, with painstaking care and attention to any changes in the makeup of the deposits. But if she didn't find anything of significance within the cave, Anna knew Chang wouldn't choose it as one of their two initial excavation sites. And they might not have the chance to get back to the caves at all. Giving them four months to excavate an entire planetary culture was a joke, but then IPX wasn't interested in the whole culture. Only those pieces of it that might prove profitable. They had the mentality of treasure hunters—the enemies of every archaeologist. And Chang, though he would do his best to find out all he could about this culture, would run the dig according to IPX protocol.

Anna felt blindly in front of her, pulled on the thick gloves. She did the digging manually, a necessary precaution to preserve whatever was below. As she moved her arms, the probe's metal arms moved, the flat spatulate hand reaching down, scraping away a thin layer of rock fragments. The resistance of the rock against her hand registered as a dull pressure. It was an odd sensation, as if her body had been replaced by a machine body.

She took care to record what she found at different depths, though the jagged fragments appeared fairly uniform. Occasionally the shifting rocks surrounding the hole ran down inside, contaminating her data, making her wince at the poor procedure. As time wore on, the betting began again, with the most money predicting she would uncover the largest and ugliest bug on the planet.

When she had dug down to a depth of one foot, Anna realized the source was actually within the cave wall, rather than beside it. One of the larger rocks, when she moved it away, covered a cavity in the stone. The opening was barely six inches across, the size of the interior irregular and unclear. She extended her left arm—now a camera/light combination—into the cavity, and as she switched to the new feed let out a whoop as she saw the husk-like objects within.

Chang's voice came over the speaker. "I always said you left no stone unturned."

A chorus of groans accompanied hers.

She switched back to the main feed. Her right arm now a metallic claw, she reached into the hole. Even though it wasn't her hand, even though they were still twenty days away, she shivered as she reached out, feeling the darkness close around her.

She retrieved each of the two cocoons fairly easily, and they were narrow enough to fit through the hole. She set them down on the cave floor, her heart pounding. The husks appeared in good condition. Perhaps the closed confines and the dry conditions had put them into a suspended state. The husks were similar enough in configuration to the mouse that these either were mice or were very closely related devices. This confirmed that the mouse had indeed come from this culture. She ran a resonance scan. On the monitors, faint but steady, pulsed two heartbeats.

A variety of exclamations sounded through the link, and then money began to change hands.

Anna felt she'd been given a second chance. She could understand these devices, could learn how they were controlled, could learn who had created them and why. She'd go slower this time, be more careful.

"Sheridan, get down here," Chang said. "It looks like we're going to have a party."

She wanted to break open the husks now, to see the condition of the mice, to run a whole series of tests on them, but it was too dangerous a procedure to do with the probe. She could damage them. She should wait. She should wait.

"I'll just stay a little longer," Anna said.

"You've been in there eight hours," Chang said, surprising Anna. "Get out of there and come join the party."

She became aware of the aching in her legs and arms, the tightness at the back of her neck, the pounding in her head. Anna closed down the session, returning the probe to automatic, twisted her sweaty hands out of the gloves, and pulled off her helmet. She was exhausted. As she pulled herself out of the chair, her leg muscles spasming, she realized that she had totally lost track of her body. She had, in a sense, melded with the machine. For those eight hours, she had been the machine. And as she scanned the controls and panels and communications equipment surrounding her, it struck her: the machine had been the universe.

It was eighteen hundred by the time the general left him in his quarters. John was breathing hard, as if he'd been running rather than standing at attention while the general chewed him out. He leaned a hand against the bulkhead, lowering his head. He'd failed. He could feel his career slipping away from him, and the sensation was terrifying. Being an Earthforce officer was what he was meant to do. He couldn't imagine a life apart from the service.

He'd completely misjudged Ross, and that error in judgment might cost him his career. They'd been engaged in a battle simulation with the heavy cruiser *Hyperion*. During the mock battle, the *Hyperion*, in an ingenious maneuver, had managed a hit to the *Agamemnon*'s targeting system, knocking it out. John had ordered manual targeting, which required the four weapons officers to enter the hemispheric cages that projected a holographic image of the firing field of each laser cannon. There had been confusion in the weapons bay at that point; John wasn't sure what had happened. But at last, after an unacceptable delay during which the *Hyperion* scored two more hits off them, the manual targeting systems were operational and the officers began to fire at will. All, that is, except Ross.

John had brought the ship about in a way that exposed the *Hyperion*'s flank to the *Agamemnon*'s aft port cannon. And yet, despite John's direct orders, Ross had not fired. Before John could bring another cannon to bear, the *Hyperion* had scored a killing hit, the smaller cruiser triumphing over one of the most advanced destroyers in the fleet.

Afterward, in the privacy of John's office, Lochschmanan had chewed him up one side and down the other, condemning his performance as shameful and inadequate.

John straightened, his face drawn down, taut. He should have court-martialed Ross after the aborted punching incident. Well, he'd correct that error right now. He hadn't created this mess, but by God he was going to clean it up, if it was the last thing he did.

John jabbed his link. "Lieutenant Ross. Ross!"

There was no response.

He called security, told them to find and detain Ross. Then, unable to wait, he headed to Ross's quarters, breathing fire. Ross's failure during the battle simulation was much more serious than sloppy procedure or a bad attitude. It proved Ross incompetent: clear grounds for discharge from Earthforce.

He reached Ross's quarters just as two guards arrived. "He's in there, Captain," one said.

"Open it," John barked.

The guard punched his security code into the keypad. The door swung open.

Although it took the door less than a second to open, the wait seemed interminable to John. As the wedge-shaped opening grew, John saw a small worn brown rug, the corner of a bed with an Earthforce jacket thrown across it. Ross's quarters were identical to the other officers' quarters, except for the captain's and the commander's, which were larger. Ross shared a room with another officer, in their standard configuration the two sides of the room mirroring each other, desks on either side of the door, beds against the long walls, dressers against the far wall.

John ducked into the room before the door had fully opened. Ross was sitting on the bed, his huge bulk pushed up into the corner, his legs bent at awkward angles. John at first thought Ross was praying. His hands were clasped together beneath his chin, and his eyes were closed. *He ought to be praying,* John thought. Then he saw the half-empty bottle of bourbon leaning against Ross's hip. The two guards flanked John, and Ross's bloodshot eyes snapped open.

"Don't move," he boomed, his words slightly slurred.

As Ross spoke he lifted his head, and John saw

clenched in his hands a PPG, the barrel pushed into the skin beneath his chin. *Oh hell.*

John shook his head, astonishment crowding out his anger. "It's okay," he said to Ross. "We're not going to do anything." He raised his hands to the sides, holding the guards behind him. "Wait outside," he said to them. They backed slowly out of the room. "Give me the gun," he said to Ross, holding out a hand. Ross must have stolen the PPG from the ship's arsenal.

Ross blinked hard, his sharp mouth pressed into a line. "You're here to charge me, aren't you? Gross incompetence."

"You're drunk. Give me the gun." John took a step closer, and Ross whipped the PPG around at him.

"Stay back!"

The guards rushed back into the room, their PPGs drawn.

"It's okay," John said. "Wait outside. Close the door."

When they were alone, John backed away, sat on the opposite bed. Whatever problems had been eating at Ross had finally broken through to the surface today, with a vengeance. "I'll stay over here, all right? Until you're ready to give me the gun. I won't come any closer."

Ross tucked the gun back up under his chin, like a security blanket. His eyes met John's. "I'd like to apologize for my performance today, sir." His booming voice was cracking, fracturing. "I also wanted to apologize for—almost punching you, sir. You were absolutely right, about the promotions." Ross paused, swallowed. "I find myself unfit for duty, Captain."

After all the difficulties he'd had with Ross and the weapons section, the carelessness, the dereliction, the passive resistance to his command, this was the last thing he expected. John leaned forward, resting his forearms on his knees. "Tell me what happened today, Lieutenant."

Ross's voice had lost its power. It was uncertain, erratic now. "I delayed entering the manual targeting system, Captain. And once I did, when I had the *Hyperion* dead to rights, I failed to fire."

"But why did you fail to fire?"

"I couldn't fire, sir."

"Was there a failure in the manual system?"

"No, sir."

"Then why couldn't you fire?"

Ross shifted, the mountain of his body out of balance, insecure. "I remembered the last time I used the manual targeting system."

"And when was that?"

"During the Earth-Minbari War, Captain. At the Battle of the Line. Aboard the *Athena*."

That made sense. The targeting system was one of the most valued components of any warship, and so was protected as much as possible from damage and built with many redundancies. It was one of the most dependable components of the ship. Yet during the Earth-Minbari War, Earthforce had discovered that their targeting systems had been unable to lock on to any Minbari ships. The advanced Minbari technology eluded the targeting systems, and so required the entire war to be fought with manual targeting and manual firing.

He was finally getting to the heart of it, to what was bothering Ross. It was the breakthrough he'd hoped for. He clasped his hands. "What happened at the Battle of the Line?"

Ross's shoulders fell as he let out a breath. He

spoke slowly in the attempt to sound sober, but his voice quavered with emotion. "We'd been ordered to hold position, hold the line, no matter what. The Minbari were heading straight for Earth, and Earthforce sent up every ship they had in defense. Most of them didn't have a chance. The *Athena* was a destroyer, one of the linchpins of the line. They were counting on us."

John found himself remembering other accounts he'd heard of the horrific Battle of the Line, a battle he'd missed, a battle that had involved over twenty thousand Earth ships and had left only two hundred survivors.

"The battle happened so fast—twenty-five minutes total, someone said. Once the Minbari were on us, they destroyed our ships as fast as they could target and fire. I was doing manual targeting for the fore starboard cannon. When you're inside one of those systems, you feel like you're hanging out in space, all alone. The back of your seat feels like the hull of the ship against your back. You become very attached to it."

Ross removed one hand from the PPG, grabbed the bottle at his side, took a quick, hard slug. His hand returned to the gun, his eyes averted now. "I could see above and below the plane of the ship, which were clear. In front of the ship, to my left, a huge Minbari warship glided toward us. It look like a gigantic shark. And off our starboard bow, stretching off in front of me as far as I could see, a line of identical warships closed on ours.

"Both sides had launched fighters, but the enemy fighters didn't even try to evade us. Our starfuries didn't have enough power to damage them. They just glided ahead, destroying our fighters as they went.

And beyond them, down the line, the Minbari were destroying ship after ship after ship. The sparks of the explosions looked like fireflies.

"The *Curie* closed on our starboard side for protection, but it was too late. The Minbari warship had already made one direct hit, and it made another. The *Curie* exploded, taking out our two aft cannons, the cargo bay, and a whole section of our hull. We lost eighty-four of the crew."

Ross's torso began to rock slightly back and forth. "After it had destroyed the *Curie*, the warship targeted us. We started taking direct hits. I had fired into the belly of that beast, again and again. It had no effect. I started firing at the enemy fighters instead. Those I could destroy. I shot one after another after another. Their steady courses made them easy to target. Like shooting fish in a barrel. But there were too many. Our 'furies were destroyed within a minute, and after that the Minbari fighters swarmed over the *Athena*.

"We took hit after hit, the ship shuddering like it was caught in a feeding frenzy. Then the third laser cannon went out. Mine was the only one still operational. I just kept my finger on the firing button, cutting my line of fire through the mass of them. It wasn't enough.

"I had been linked to the command deck throughout the battle to receive orders, so I heard it when Captain Best gave the command. We all knew, when he gave the order, that it was treason. We'd been ordered to hold the line at all costs. Earth stood in the balance. But no one objected. We all knew that the ship was on the verge of destruction. The battle was lost. There was nothing we could do. So we retreated."

Ross raised his head, his eyes returning to John, and John nodded his encouragement. So the rumors about

Best had been true. Ross looked away again, and his sharp features seemed fragile now, as if they could break apart.

"The *Athena* began to swing back from the line, and Captain Best ordered the helmsman to open a jump point. We were all thinking it. Just one jump and we would be away. We would be safe. The next thing I knew a target had swung into my field of fire at point-blank range and was coming straight at me, as if it was going to ram. I fired. As my finger hit the button I realized it was one of our own 'furies. I saw the face of the pilot at the moment my laser hit him. Bjornson. I knew him.

"If we'd been using the computer targeting system, the friend-or-foe signal would have prevented us firing on one of our own ships. But on manual, there are no safeguards.

"I realized he'd been trying to make an emergency landing in the fighter bay before we abandoned him. The explosion, at point-blank range, took out my laser cannon and the jump engines, and another thirty-five of the crew were killed. Then we couldn't run."

A tear made a silent track down Ross's face. "The captain and those on the command deck must have seen what happened. But they didn't say anything about it. They were too busy trying to keep the ship together.

"The Minbari seemed to sense that we were helpless; they moved on to other targets, and I watched as their ships destroyed the remaining fragments of the line.

"After the battle, they started calling all of us who survived heroes, and Captain Best a hero for saving the largest surviving Earthforce ship. Those of the crew who didn't like Captain Best accused him of retreating. But others supported the captain. Most of them didn't know what had happened. No evidence survived to prove things one way or the other. Best and his cronies saw to that. Best claimed that a Minbari warship took out our jump engines. He said he'd feared the *Athena* might explode and damage some of our own ships, so he'd swung slightly out of position. I backed him up, along with many others. Best covered up for me, so I covered up for him.

"Of course, the rumors continued. They hurt the reputation of the captain and all of us who served with him. But Captain Best had strong enough allies in the service to survive it, and those of us loyal to him he rewarded. I owe my position as weapons chief to the killing of thirty-six crew members." Ross let out a hard breath, and his body settled further around the PPG, as if he had held this secret within the architecture of his bones.

John had never known anyone to be quite so honest with himself. No wonder Ross had kept this hidden inside so long. John couldn't imagine how he would feel if he killed one of his own crew by accident. Facing or discharging friendly fire was a fear of every soldier. "Best has kept your secret all this time, and you've kept his. Why tell me now?"

One of Ross's hands broke free from the gun, wiped impatiently at his cheek, returned. "Because it's poisoned me, sir. I didn't even know it until you came aboard. Captain Best never demanded much from us, and I realize now that after the Battle of the Line, I didn't believe I could do much. I made a lot of noise, but the crew under me knew they could do whatever they wanted. I was a hollow man. I didn't believe in myself. It was just like you said. I actually thought you'd found out about me.

"I didn't believe in Earthforce anymore either. How could I, and support Captain Best? My habits grew worse and worse, my duties neglected. The crew under me have been poisoned by my attitude. When you took command, I laughed at that welcome speech you gave. You seemed so naive and gung-ho. But then as time passed I started listening to you. And watching you. And I realized that you were what I had once wanted to be. And I realized that there was another path, and I had taken the wrong one." Ross curled the mountain of his body around the PPG with a shudder. "You're right that the past shapes us. I can't go back now. And I don't believe I can become the officer you want me to be, one worthy of this uniform. I don't believe I'm fit to be in Earthforce, Captain."

John stood, afraid to move forward, afraid that Ross would kill himself right then. "You say you've been promoted unfairly. Now you want to take the easy way out. Well, I'm not going to let you off so easily, mister. I want you to serve Earthforce in the place of those thirty-six men and women who can't anymore. I want you to earn that rank you carry. I want you to perform the duties you should have been performing. I will accept no excuses, and I will tolerate no less than excellence. I want your section to become an example to this entire ship. If you've been poisoned, then spit it out and be done with it. You have a debt to pay, and I'm going to see that you pay it, in duty and honor."

Ross's head was inclined.

"Hand over the gun, Lieutenant." John extended his hand.

Ross raised his head, his sharp, fragile features like a lost child's. He straightened, handed the PPG to John. "Yes, sir," he said uncertainly.

"Come to attention, Lieutenant Ross."

Ross pushed himself to the edge of the bed, setting the bottle of bourbon carefully on the floor. He stood.

"I have processed Watley's request for a transfer, and I expect she'll be off the *Agamemnon* within a month. But that still leaves you with Spano and some of the more difficult gunners to handle. Will you be able to deal with them?"

After a few moments Ross's lost look began to fade. His body straightened, his shoulders squaring, the mountain rebuilding itself on firmer ground. His sharp mouth hardened again into a line, though it seemed now not resistant, but determined. When he boomed out his reply, the uncertainty was gone from his voice. "Yes I will, sir."

CHAPTER 9

Anna typed in her access code again. No answering response came from the probe. She cursed, her voice dampened in the cramped confines of the probe control module. Claustrophobia was building.

She checked the instrument settings, typed in the access code again: HOME-RUN ANNIE. Her nickname in college. The probe made no response.

SEND TEST SIGNAL TO PROBE, she typed. The test signal should simply be bounced back by the probe, whether her access code was working or not.

TEST SIGNAL NOT RETURNED, the computer reported.

SEND TEST SIGNAL TO ORBITER, she typed.

TEST SIGNAL RETURNED. ORBITER IN POSITION.

So it wasn't a problem with the orbiter. The problem was definitely with the probe. Perhaps the weather was disrupting communications. The probe's transmissions had suffered almost constant distortion from the dust, though they'd never been completely blocked. In the twenty hours they'd been manually operating the probe, the communications had been fairly clear.

ACCESS ORBITER. CODE HOME-RUN ANNIE.

ORBITER ON LINE, came the response.

WHAT IS STATUS OF WEATHER IN PROBE
SECTOR? Anna typed. COULD WEATHER PRE-
VENT COMMUNICATION WITH PROBE?

PROBE   SECTOR   UNKNOWN.   CONTACT
WITH PROBE LOST AT 05:00 12/14/56.

That was three hours ago. WHY WAS CONTACT
WITH PROBE LOST?

CAUSE UNKNOWN.

WHAT WAS STATUS OF WEATHER IN PROBE
SECTOR AT 05:00 12/14/56?

WEATHER IN STATUS GREEN.

Status green meant above average weather conditions. So the loss of contact wasn't due to the weather.
It looked like either a breakdown or an accident, as she
had feared. The probe must have been on automatic
control at that time, since if it had been under manual
control, Chang would have told her the probe was out
of commission.

WAS PROBE UNDER AUTOMATIC OR MAN-
UAL CONTROL AT 05:00 12/14/56?

MANUAL CONTROL.

Anna tapped her fist against her mouth. Chang had
only authorized himself and Anna to access the probe.
In the hours when neither of them were available, the
probe functioned automatically. Perhaps Chang had
given someone else access, and that person had failed
to notify Anna about the loss of contact. *Probably
afraid to admit they screwed the pooch,* Anna thought.

WHOSE CONTROL? Anna asked.

MISSION COMMANDER CHANG.

Anna's fist went still against her lips. Perhaps
Chang had just forgotten to inform her of the breakdown. But she would have thought he'd have been
very upset about it. They were still nineteen days away

from the planet, and with the probe out, that would mean nineteen days of exploration and preparation lost. And it would mean nineteen days she'd have to wait before she could study the two mice she'd discovered. Compared to the egg, maybe they weren't spectacular, but Anna felt she'd already made so much progress toward understanding them that they might offer the key to this race's technology.

Perhaps Chang had turned over the probe to someone else without closing down his session, as he'd done with her yesterday. In any case, the records of the probe's activity could tell her how the breakdown had occurred and how serious it was. She closed her session with the orbiter and accessed the control module itself. The module received the transmissions from the orbiter, recorded them, and relayed them to other parts of the *Icarus*.

PLAYBACK PROBE RECORD 04:59 12/14/56.

NO PROBE RECORD 04:59 12/14/56, the module responded.

Perhaps she was cutting it too close to the loss in contact. PLAYBACK PROBE RECORD 04:50 12/14/56.

NO PROBE RECORD 04:50 12/14/56.

PLAYBACK PROBE RECORD 04:00 12/14/56.

NO PROBE RECORD 04:00 12/14/56.

How could there be no record at four o'clock if contact wasn't lost until five? It was impossible. Anna began to get a horrible feeling that somehow the entire record had been lost. PLAYBACK PROBE RECORD 19:00 12/13/56. That was around the time she'd found the mice.

NO PROBE RECORD 19:00 12/13/56.

Shit. The little data she had on them was gone.

PLAYBACK PROBE RECORD 10:00 12/13/56.

Chang had first taken manual control of the probe a
little after ten.

LOADING.

Anna squeezed her head into the helmet. The visual
was there, and at her command the data and readouts
came up. She watched as the probe went about its business for a few minutes, then, at the point Chang must
have called for manual control, the interior of the helmet went black. She pulled the helmet off.

PLAYBACK PROBE RECORD 10:05 12/13/56.

NO PROBE RECORD.

It looked as if the module had somehow stopped
recording when the probe was put under manual control. This seemed like a possible mechanical glitch,
except that Anna knew it was impossible. Last night in
her quarters, excited by her discovery, she had played
back sections of the probe record from that day. It had
existed.

She had to talk to Chang.

"I haven't had the probe on manual since that first
session yesterday morning," Chang said. "I meant to
get up this morning and get on, but I guess you beat
me to it." The drained, slack look that had seemed
vanquished since he'd boarded the *Icarus* had returned; he looked older sitting in the narrow chair in
his pajamas, his rounded stomach and knobby knees
poking at the fabric. His weathered cheeks were covered with a white stubble. The news of the loss of the
probe had hit him hard.

"Did you give anyone else access?" Anna asked.
"Or did anyone else know your access code?"

"No. Only you and I had access, and only you
know my access code." He rubbed his eyes with one
callused hand. She'd woken him up when she'd rung at

his quarters. He'd asked the same questions, and come to the same conclusion, that Anna had: someone had put the probe out of commission and covered the evidence by erasing the probe record. His hand came down with a slap against his leg. "How are we supposed to do a decent job with all this damn intrigue going on?"

"Even if someone had your access code," Anna said, "only a few members of the team are checked out on the probe. And I don't know how any of them would have the expertise to delete the probe record. I couldn't do it."

"I've never tried," Chang said.

Anna leaned forward, her knees nearly touching Chang's in the cramped quarters. "Could Donne have gotten your access code telepathically?"

"I suppose so. Though that would violate one of the basic tenets of Psi Corps. But even if she did, she wouldn't know how to operate the probe."

"I know, but she's the person I least trust."

"You're way too trusting." Chang waved a tired hand. "You should widen your horizons. There are one hundred thirty-nine people on this ship to mistrust."

Chang seemed a bit paranoid to her. But even if he was right, only a handful of people could operate the probe. Petrovich and Standish. Favorito, Razor, and Scott. Chang himself. And Anna. She didn't know if Morden was checked out on it or not. "But what's the motivation? What does anyone gain by knocking the probe out? It hampers our advance planning, but we will still get there, we will still find whatever we're going to find."

Chang picked at his callus. "I don't know."

"We have to find who did this. Keep them away from the dig so they can't cause any more harm."

"Sheridan, we're not set up to mount an investigation."

"I could do it. I could question the crew, check the ship's logs. What else are we going to do now until we get to the site?"

"We have no evidence. You'd never be able to prove anything."

"How do you know until we look?"

Chang's eyes met hers. "It's not what IPX wants."

That stopped her. She didn't know how to react. "What does IPX want?"

Chang's voice had taken on its neutral tone. "They want us to do our jobs, and come back with the goods. They knew they were sending us out with a nest of vipers. And they expect us to deal with it. I want no hints to the others that the probe's malfunctioning was anything but accidental."

"We may never find out who's responsible."

"Worse things have happened." With a sigh he turned to the side, leaned toward the bed. "By the way," he said, reaching under the pillow, "did John ever teach you how to shoot?" He brought out a small PPG. "I've begun carrying this with me. You take it. I'll sign out another one." He handed her the pistol, a weight in her hand.

Anna shook her head. "We're sitting on the find of the century. Don't they see that we need to be able to do our jobs—"

"That's just it, Sheridan." He sank back in his chair, a slump in his chest. "It *is* the find of the century. And the find of the century is not found with the calmness of the find of the year, or the find of the month. This technology is going to change everything. And whoever controls it is going to control everything. We're way out of our depth here. That's what being a part of history means.''

January 2257

"One thing is necessary: to journey to wells."
—JOHANNES EDFELT

CHAPTER 10

"I know you're out of touch, and you probably won't get this for months, but I just wanted to say happy New Year. There's a godawful party going on here, with an ancient goddess and prancing professors wearing ceremonial dewlaps and stuff that would send you into a cold sweat, but all it reminds me of is that New Year's when we were in Lucerne, on the lake, and the fireworks, how they seemed to cover the sky, and how we both shivered under that coat you borrowed, and the way you looked at me . . ."

"I don't know what evil spirit possessed me to cancel our vacation. I should have gone AWOL. I miss you so much tonight. I even miss those sandpaper hands of yours. I tried to reach you on our anniversary, but I was notified that all communications had to go through IPX. Is that some new policy? It seems a bit extreme. Anyway, I gave up. I didn't want your bosses watching some mushy anniversary message from your lonely husband. And then tonight I realized, who cares if they see it? So long as you see it. I know where you are this message won't reach you for days, but I just wanted to say I love you to my wife on New Year's Eve. I still love saying 'my wife. . . .' "

*   *   *

"I know you felt guilty about canceling, and you shouldn't. I'm so proud of you. I've been worried that we've been letting obstacles get between us—borders. But I realized tonight that I feel as close to you as I ever have. It's fifteen minutes to midnight, and I can feel you near me, thinking of me, loving me."

"I'm so sorry that I snapped at you the last time we talked. I can't wait to see you and make it up to you. I love you, Anna."

"I love you, John." Though she hadn't heard from John in over a month and had no idea when she would hear from him, she could feel him, his love, his concern, the sheer integrity of his presence, as if he were in the next room. Anna hesitated, then ordered, "End message. Send. Access code Idol Worshipper." Chang's code.

"Message sent," the com station said, and Anna stood, preparing to leave the lab and, God help her, reenter the party. She could hear the beginnings of a Gigmosian chant coming from the conference room next door. "Message error," the com station said. "Communications off-line."

Anna went to the com station, not sure what had happened. She hadn't used the com station in the main lab before, but the conference room was occupied, and only Chang's quarters came equipped with a full com station. "Captain Hidalgo."

After a few moments, he appeared on the screen. "Hidalgo here."

"The com system says communications are off line."

"Yes, communications went down a few minutes ago. We're looking into it."

"What happened?"

He shot her an irritated look. "We'll know that after we look into it."

"Right. Thank you." She ended the communication. She wondered if her message to John had gotten through. The system had said "Message sent" first. She wasn't sure if there was some way to find out whether the message was stuck in the system or not. She certainly didn't want the mushy message floating around in Dr. Chang's mailbox.

"Com system check unsent mail, access code Idol Worshipper."

"Two messages."

Two? Perhaps Chang had sent a message as well that didn't get through. "Play message one."

She recognized herself instantly, hated hearing the sound of her own voice. "Stop. Transfer message one to mailbox access code 120349." Her wedding date. Once the communications were back on line, she could use Chang's access to send it. At least this way it wouldn't be floating around for him to find until then. She wondered what the second message was. Of course, it was private, but she should make sure that it wasn't some duplicate of her own message, created through the malfunction in the system.

"Com system who is sender of message two?"

"Mission Commander Chang."

As she'd suspected. But for the sake of completeness . . . "Who is recipient of message two?"

"Mission Supervisor Galovich."

Chang's boss at IPX. The fact that it hadn't been sent was curious. Either the message had been caught by the same malfunction as hers, which meant the attempt to send it had been in the last few minutes, during the New Year's Eve party, or he'd purposely left it unsent.

"Time of message creation."

"Zero hundred hours thirty-two minutes, 1/1/57."

A few minutes ago. She knew Chang had been at the party at midnight; they all had, except Donne. A few minutes later, when the head-bobbing ritual show of dominance began, she'd seen Chang leave and thought it would be a good idea to take a break herself and send a message to John. Odd that he would leave the party to send a message to his boss. Even IPX execs had to take New Year's Eve off. It must have been urgent.

The message must have been caught in the same communications malfunction she'd experienced. She wondered if Chang knew it hadn't been sent.

What would he have to tell Galovich that was so important? Since the probe had stopped working two and a half weeks ago, they'd spent their time sifting through old data, mapping out the most promising excavation sites, planning strategies, and playing poker. Only she had found herself in a state of paranoia, as if she'd caught it from Chang, thinking constantly about the probe and who might have been able to access and operate it. She wanted to discuss it with someone, but the only other person who knew was Chang. And since she'd gone to him with the news about the probe, she'd felt a growing distance from him. The whole expedition was in jeopardy, and he was more concerned with keeping the home office happy than with running an effective, accurate, scientifically valid mission.

She forced herself to thoroughly consider the ethics of the situation for three seconds before telling the com system to play the message.

Dr. Chang appeared on screen, wearing a suit, sitting in the narrow chair in his quarters. Despite his obvious attempt to present a polished exterior, his thumbnail was picking at the callus on his index finger, and his chest was heaving, as if he couldn't catch his breath. She'd never seen him this upset. "This is an unscheduled report." His tone was carefully neutral. "It's twenty-five minutes after midnight on New Year's Day. The team was holding a New Year's Eve party. I left a few minutes after midnight to go to bed. I decided to stop at the observation deck for a few minutes. On the way there, I happened to catch a glimpse of Ms. Donne down a side corridor. I followed her. She met with Captain Hidalgo. I didn't hear everything they said, but I heard enough to know that they have made an arrangement of some kind, I'm not sure of the scope of it. . . ." The word caught in his throat, and he paused, swallowing. "He has agreed to smuggle artifacts for her that will be turned over to Psi Corps once we reach Earth. I don't know whether she plans to get the artifacts past us into the ship, or whether she simply plans to take them out of our inventory somehow.

"I've cooperated with Ms. Donne on a limited basis, per your instructions, but this puts our whole expedition into jeopardy. By herself I don't think there's much she can do. But I don't believe I can run an effective expedition with the captain cooperating with Psi Corps. We depend on the captain. I know I don't have the authority to remove him. I need you to give me the authority to remove him, or to order him to step down yourself. I'm not sure how much of the crew is part of his plan. He must have some of them involved in order to do what he's promising." Chang paused again, and Anna could see him attempting to calm himself. "Please get back to me on this A-S-A-P. The ship is our lifeline back to you."

He stared blankly ahead for a few moments, then, as if coming back to life, with a deep breath he straightened. "Oh, as per your request, I ran a scan of the sector. There are no other ships, biomechanical or otherwise, within our scanning range. This and the failure of the orbiter to detect any ships or other activity supports Dr. Morden's hypothesis that the ships you tracked here from Mars were on automatic and have perhaps gone into a dormant state, like Dr. Sheridan's mouse. But that's still quite speculative at this point. . . . I'll be waiting to hear from you. I know tomorrow—today—is a holiday, but please do whatever it takes to get the authorization. We'll be making planetfall in thirty-one hours, and I don't want to do it with Captain Hidalgo in command." The message ended.

Anna had glanced nervously toward the empty corridor throughout the entire message. Now she spoke quickly. "Copy message two. Send copy to mailbox access code 120349. End."

She brought a hand to her mouth. The first part of the message was frightening enough: the captain couldn't be trusted. But the second part implied something much worse: Chang couldn't be trusted. He had lied to her. She couldn't believe it, even as the words of his message ran through her mind. If ships had flown here, ships with technology similar to the mouse, biomechanical ships that had been on Mars and had been tracked by IPX, then they knew a lot more about this planet, and about biomechanical technology, than they had admitted. And if the probe hadn't detected any ships, then the ships had arrived before the probe. IPX had become interested in Alpha Omega 3 because they'd tracked the ships here, not because a probe had happened upon it. She remembered Chang's call to her on Station Prime, how he had related the "exciting news" of the probe's discovery. But the probe had been sent to follow up, to observe. The higher-ups seemed to think the ships had been functioning automatically, but to Anna, active ships implied an active culture, or at least the possibility of one. Which brought into question the whole concept of sending out an archaeological expedition.

The promise of biomechanical ships, lying empty and dormant, waiting for pilots and mass production, must be sending IPX into raptures.

Dr. Morden's hypothesis . . . He and Earthforce must have been involved in whatever happened on Mars. Which explained his presence here. Someone else she couldn't trust. Someone else with secrets. And John's precious Earthforce had kept those secrets, had allowed IPX to send them out with incomplete information, as long as Earthforce's representative was on board.

But it was Chang's deceit that hurt her the most. He had withheld facts from her about the site, the culture, and the technology. Her lack of accurate information would most likely render her research redundant or invalid or irrelevant. He had betrayed her, in the worst way one archaeologist could betray another. She felt as if this whole expedition was a giant hoax, like the Cardiff Giant. And she'd fallen for it hook, line, and sinker.

She wanted to shake Chang, to scream in his face and land a few good, solid punches with her fists, but at this point she wasn't even sure how he would react to the news that she'd watched his message. Perhaps he'd decide she needed to be removed from the expedition.

Besides, it was her turn to keep secrets now.

There was only one thing she needed to tell him. She activated the com system. "Dr. Chang."

After a few moments, Chang appeared on the monitor in his quarters. He was back in his casual clothes, now. "Yes?"

"I wanted to let you know that the communications system is down. It went down about twenty minutes ago. I tried to send a message out."

Chang was rocking back and forth on his feet, something she'd never seen him do. "Yes, I know. Captain Hidalgo informed me."

She saw it in the slackness of Chang's mouth. Hidalgo had made sure that message didn't go through. She felt so stupid. Of course communications had gone out. Hidalgo must have been monitoring Chang's transmissions, seen the message she just saw, and arranged for a convenient breakdown. Chang knew he had done it, and knew why he had done it, and could do nothing. "All right then," she said.

Chang nodded his head absentmindedly. "Good night."

"Good night."

Anna wandered out of the lab, unsure what to do. The whole expedition was falling apart around her, and they hadn't even reached the site. In the passage, the music of the party enveloped her. She followed it into the conference room. The Gigmosian aspect to the party seemed to have finally ended. Churlstein, Favorito, Razor, Scott, Morden, Petrovich, and Standish were seated around the table, all drunk out of their minds, playing a heated game of poker.

"That *is* a three!" Standish yelled, waving a card in front of Churlstein.

Churlstein squinted, his head swaying along with the card.

Morden, seated at the head of the table, saw her first. He was pounding his finger into the table, making a point to someone.

"Now you wish we'd raised the stakes," Scott said. "Hey, Sheridan!" She waved at Anna, a goofy grin on her face. Her short white hair was standing up every which way. "Come help me beat the pants off these boys."

Several of them turned toward her, called encouragement.

"No thanks. I'm beat."

Morden stood, took a long gulp from his mug, and wiped all of his chips onto an empty plate. "Deal me out," he said over the protests of the others. He approached Anna. "What's wrong?" A mild look of concern moderated his smile.

"Nothing." Anna shook her head. "I just tried to send a message to my husband and found out the communications are down."

"Oh. Well, I'm sure they'll be back on line soon. It can't be serious, can it?" His dark eyes studied her.

"I don't know." She looked back over at the table, her hand tapping nervously at her leg. She couldn't trust him. She couldn't trust anyone. "It's just, you know how it is, it's the holidays, and you want to talk to someone . . ."

His smile rose, and she realized what she had said. "I understand," he said.

"Oh. Listen. I almost forgot. I have something for you." The box was in her sweater pocket. It seemed odd now, her giving him a present, but she'd done it and she might as well give it to him. She should keep acting normally.

"Sounds mysterious."

"It's just a little New Year's present. Let's go next door."

They went into the main lab, and Anna turned on one of the workstation lights, which illuminated a table and various hanging pieces of equipment. They sat on two stools on the same side of the table. The rest of the lab hung around them in shadow.

Morden laid his plate of chips on the table, the harsh overhead light creating pools of shadow in his eyes, below his nose, his lips. "That was the weirdest New Year's Eve party I've ever attended."

"Same here. But it looks like you made out pretty well," she said, indicating his pile of chips. She realized then that Morden's pile had been the biggest of anyone's at the table.

His voice was smooth. "I'm a pretty good poker player."

"You're not drunk at all, are you?"

"I'm afraid I'm a maudlin drunk. I wouldn't have been any fun at all."

"You like misleading people, don't you?" The words came out before she could stop them.

He folded his hands, careful, noticing the change in Anna. "Not misleading, no. I don't enjoy that. Except in poker. But I don't wear my heart on my sleeve. I don't enjoy broadcasting my private life to the world. I suppose I did that right after the explosion. I was out of control. And I regret it." His body settled with a breath. "But I don't go about my job the same way as Ms. Donne, if that's what you mean. I find I'm much more effective if I go about my job quietly."

"And what is your job?"

"To represent Earthforce interests in any new technology and to cooperate with IPX in as much as it furthers our mutual understanding of the technology. I've never hidden that." His head tilted as he studied her. "Is this an interrogation?"

Anna smiled. "I'm sorry. I guess I'm a little jumpy now that we're so close to planetfall. And I guess I'm a bit depressed, being unable to get my message out to John." She dug the small box out of her pocket. "But I feel blessed to have found such a love. And I know you were blessed too." She handed it to him. "This is to remembering, healing, and living. I hope you won't be mad."

"Why would I be mad about getting a present?" With his smile securely fastened, he ripped away the plain paper wrapping and opened the box. He took out the love stone she had removed from his quarters yesterday. One end of the stone was now pierced by a silver loop that was attached to a silver chain. His expression remained fixed as he held it up, as if he didn't recognize it.

Anna was afraid to speak, felt the growing, inexorable realization that she had unintentionally inflicted a horrible wound.

"I didn't even notice this was missing," he finally said, a musical tone to his voice.

"I just took it late yesterday," she said.

"I used to look at it every night, every day, every hour, sometimes several times in an hour. I used to go to sleep with it in my hand, and I used to wake up with it in my hand."

"Just because—"

"I didn't notice it was gone. How long did you have it? Twenty-four hours?"

Anna nodded. It was actually longer.

"I didn't notice. I didn't look." His face spasmed. In the harsh light it seemed almost something alive ripping through his features. Another spasm wrenched his face, and another. She'd never seen anyone in this much pain. It was horrible to watch, more horrible because she had caused it.

"I'm sorry. I'm sorry." She had ripped open the wound of the past, destroyed the callus that had begun to form. She took his hand—the one not clenched around the stone. It shook with the violence of a seizure. She wondered if she would be in this much pain if John died.

"You think it doesn't matter, forgetting about those you once loved? I promised to love my wife forever. And here it is, six months later, and I'm already forgetting. Twenty-four hours I didn't think of her!" A quick spasm across his face, a glimpse into his inner world. "Do you know that I can't hear the voice of my daughter? I can't hear it. I can watch her on our home movies and I hear her laugh and talk, but she's like a stranger. That's not what my daughter was to me—the brush of her as she went past, her smell, freshly scrubbed, the rhythm of her footsteps on the stairs, her cry of delight when I would come home from work. She's leaving me. They both are. And all I feel is relief."

They sat in silence, and after a time Anna felt his shaking begin to subside. "I'm sorry," he said. His face began, again, to reassemble itself.

"It's okay. I'm sorry for upsetting you." She realized that this hurt would never go away for him. It would always be there, under the surface, no matter how deeply buried. She'd never been hurt that deeply.

"I give you this big speech about how I don't wear

my heart on my sleeve, and then I break down." He
withdrew his hand from hers.

"It's okay. I understand."

Shadows pooled in his eyes. "No, you don't. And I
hope you never do." He opened his fist, revealing the
stone. "This was very thoughtful of you."

"Not thoughtful enough, I'm afraid."

"I really do appreciate it. Thank you. Would you
help me put it on?" She took the necklace and went
around behind him, opening the clasp. "This way,"
he said, "I'll never be able to forget."

"I hope you'll remember that they loved you, and
that they'd want you to be happy. This way you can
carry their good wishes with you." She draped the
necklace around him so that the name of the god inscribed into the stone faced his chest, and fastened the
clasp.

She sat down beside him again. The shadows on his
face were off. His features had failed to align into their
old familiar facade and seemed unsettled, uncertain.
She had ripped the wound open, and it would take
some time for it to heal over. Perhaps, right now,
there was a chance. A chance to make a real human
connection untempered by politics or secrets. She
leaned closer.

"Tell me about Mars," she said.

And he did.

CHAPTER 11

GENERAL Lochschmanan turned away from the weapons control system, his aide following without making a notation on her comp-pad. John held in his smile and gave a tight nod in Ross's direction. Ross stood stiffly at attention, but there was a certain set to his shoulders that told John he was proud. John felt the same thing in his own stance. Beside Ross, Spano stood with hands clenched. He remained a problem, but John wanted to give Ross a chance to handle him.

The general and his aide preceded John and Corchoran out of the weapons bay, the inspection completed, and they returned to John's office.

"You have my congratulations, Captain. The inspection was outstanding."

The smile broke over John's face. "Thank you, sir."

Lochschmanan reached into his jacket. "I have some more information on your mission to share with you at this time. You may fill in Commander Corchoran after I leave. This data crystal contains the scheduled time and place and the few other pieces of information we have regarding the explosives buy. It will occur in approximately thirty hours. You will make way to that location as soon as I leave. The plan of this Homeguard faction is to load the explosives onto their ship, travel to Babylon 5, and then, during the dedication ceremonies, to make a suicide run at the station, exploding on impact. Those dedication ceremonies will take place in three days.

"You are to observe the transfer of explosives, using the new stealth technology we have installed to remain undetected. Wait until the Narns selling the explosives have left the area. We don't want to provoke them and create an incident. Immediately after they have left, you must disable or destroy the Homeguard ship. It must not reach Babylon 5."

"Yes, sir."

The general made a regulation turn toward the door, hesitated. "Captain," he said, his back to John, "I need not remind you of the power and influence of the Homeguard."

"I understand, sir."

"Very well." The general continued out, his aide following.

Corchoran turned his glum expression on John. His frown made his dark brows even more pronounced. "He's sending us out on a critical mission when we've barely learned how to pass inspection?"

John laid a hand on his shoulder. "That's what I said. But I think we're ready now. We can do this."

"Tell me about this Homeguard group. What's the general's source of information?"

John waved him away. "I'll explain later. Right now we need to get underway. And as soon as we do I want you to initiate radio silence. I don't want any specifics about this getting out to the crew. But just in case word of this does get out, and any of them happens to be a Homeguard sympathizer, I don't want to

take the smallest chance that information might somehow get back to them.''

"I understand, sir.''

John clapped Corchoran on the shoulders. "Cheer
up, Commander. The days of drilling are over!''

The ship sang of beauty and order, the harmony of the
spheres. The peace of its silent passage through space,
the symmetry of its form, the unity of its functioning
wove through its melody. It served willingly, faith-
fully. Within the song, Kosh Naranek altered its
course, and the ship with joy slipped the surly bonds of
gravity and turned onto its new heading.

Kosh reviewed the data that had been sent to him.
The perceptions of the Vorlon buoys were clear. The
danger was imminent. He had known this day would
come for three years. He had waited.

He entered his encounter suit, sent out the communication that was his only recourse.

"Ambassador Kosh," said the one called Nerid,
with a bow. "We are honored by your call. Ambassador Delenn is just preparing to return to Babylon 5.
We hear that you will be joining her there for the dedication ceremony.''

Delenn approached, dismissing Nerid. She bowed,
her expression anxious. "This is most unexpected.''

The voice generated by the encounter suit echoed.
"The humans have gone to Z'ha'dum.''

For long moments she was silent, and he was reminded again how strongly the younger races instinctively avoided the truth. "What possible interest could
they have there? By what means could they have even
found it?''

"They must be recalled.''

"What will they find there?''

"The past. And the future. Stop them." He ended the communication, having conveyed all the necessary information. Delenn liked to question, and he did not like to answer.

He removed himself from the encounter suit, immersing himself again in the music, the music that would bring him to Z'ha'dum. He could do nothing there, but he must know what would happen. He would arrive just before the Earth vessel, if Delenn was unable to have it recalled. The humans themselves were of little consequence; it was the events they would trigger that would shift the currents of time and space. And he must follow.

"Meet you back at the *Icarus* at seventeen hundred," Chang said through the link in Anna's EVA suit. "Good luck."

"I read you," Anna said, keeping her tone distant, impersonal. From the small observation portal beside her seat near the front of the crawler, Anna could barely see the two crawlers carrying Chang's party turn off to the south, toward the egg and the major pillar. They had decided to start the dig with a focus on two sites: the area of the egg and the major pillar, and the area of the major cave Anna had explored with the probe. Since Anna's discovery of the mice, exploring the cave had become a top priority. Chang headed the pillar group with Churlstein, Scott, Petrovich, and Donne, while Anna headed the cave group with Morden, Favorito, Razor, and Standish.

Most of the team was salivating to explore the egg. Between the uniqueness of the find and Donne's constant discussion of it, as if she were its PR agent, excitement was high. She'd questioned them all constantly about what they'd discovered about it, and particularly on their opinions regarding the inscription Morden had translated. Anna had thought it odd that Chang had been willing to give up a space in his party to Donne. His assignment of Donne to his party was even more peculiar given the message Anna had discovered. If Chang knew Donne was planning to smuggle artifacts, why take her to see the most prized find so far? But Chang had assigned Donne to his party. He probably wanted to keep an eye on her. Anna was grateful. Let them deal with all their plots and counterplots. Maybe she could get some actual archaeology done.

Each group had two crawlers and, in addition to the members of the archaeological team, forty techs from the science support crew. Anna had briefed the techs herself, all the while wondering which of them were part of Donne and Hidalgo's plan, which of them would try to steal artifacts. Out of them all she could put names to only a handful.

As her crawler stopped in front of the cave site, Anna pulled herself out of her chair in the bulky EVA suit. She wished they didn't have to wear them; the atmospheric analysis had revealed oxygen with some harmless miscellaneous components, but it had also showed low levels of carbon monoxide. The ship's doctor had explained that over perhaps twenty to twenty-five hours, this carbon monoxide would build up in the blood, preventing oxygen from binding to the hemoglobin as it should. The result would be death. Even so, breathers and jumpsuits were all the protection necessary. No hazards had been detected that would require a full EVA suit, and the temperature, with a daytime average of fifty degrees, was well within habitable limits. Unfortunately, this was standard first-contact protocol. They had to wear the suits for the first twenty-four hours.

The claustrophobia from the EVA suit wasn't quite as bad as that from the probe control module, but it was still there, a constant dis-ease, as well as a serious handicap to her work. She might as well try to work with her hands tied behind her back. And with the gravity one point three times that of Earth, the extra weight would exhaust them quickly. She felt like an elephant lumbering around in the thing, an accident waiting to happen.

She touched her thigh pocket, feeling the cushioned outline of the PPG Chang had given to her. After keeping it in the back of a drawer in her quarters since he'd given it to her, she'd decided this morning to bring it with her, although it was making her more nervous, not more secure. She doubted she could even get it out of her pocket in under thirty seconds, and once she did, she wasn't even sure she could make the thing work. She'd never fired a gun before.

Anna headed into the rear section of the crawler, followed by the other archaeologists. Along each side of the crawler ran a row of seats for the techs, while in the center was stored their crawler's share of the heavy equipment: a dozer, several drills, a heavy-duty resonance imager, the sonic probe, and a disassembled mobile elevator platform. She gave the tech the signal to open the door, and the door broke open along the ceiling, unfolding out to create a ramp. The techs and archaeologists began heading out. Anna's steps came more slowly.

The landscape of Alpha Omega 3 was more desolate and more majestic than any world she had visited. The craggy rocks and sharp, upthrust fingers of stone stretched to the limits of vision, where the misshapen forms of massive mountains distorted the horizon. It was easy to feel lost, insignificant here among the huge blocks of stone, the towering pillars, and the vast scale, like a bug in the land of the gods. She remembered feeling this as a child, in Rome standing beside Trajan's column. These pillars stretched over twice as high, higher than the EVA suit would allow her to tilt her head back to see.

The sky was a turbulent reddish brown, the dust constant, and heavier since they'd landed than when the probe had recorded it. Its color added an air of distance and unreality to the landscape, almost as if she was observing something removed in time, or in some other dimension. As Anna stepped off the ramp, she realized that the unreal feeling of the landscape was more than a creation of the dust; it was the light. It came from the distant sun, frail, refracted by the dust and other elements in the atmosphere. That explained the darkness of the planet, as if it existed in twilight, but it didn't explain an odd, fine, threadlike quality to the light that had not come through in the probe's transmissions, as if the light had been filtered through a polarizing lens, or strained into a shifting, fibrous curtain in the dusk.

As Anna rounded the side of the crawler, she saw the low, trailing fragments of the smaller mountain range up close. The black rock of these dust-weathered remnants erupted from the reddish-brown stone of the landscape in a series of rocky outcroppings. Dunes of sand and dust had formed along their base. Near the end of these mountains, beside an outcropping of black stone approximately fifty feet high, the crawler had stopped. Anna moved away from the crawler toward the outcropping, climbing the slight dune. Gradually the sand gave way to the dark shards of rock that formed the talus. There, before her, lay the cave mouth, its shadow a darker black than the blackness surrounding it, an opening seventeen feet across and fourteen feet high.

Anna turned on her flashlight and aimed it at the edges of the opening. The flashlight illuminated a beam of blowing dust and, faintly, the ragged edges of the rock. The presence of the mice in the cave suggested it had once been inhabited, or at least visited. They didn't have enough data yet to know during what period that had been true, but she hoped to find out soon. In general caves were used for shelter, for storage, for mining, for strategic location, as holy sites, or as tombs. Most often cave activity was focused around the mouth, where access to the outside and food was easy, though there were a few cultures where habitation was far below the surface. The extensive ruins on the surface were indicative of surface dwellers, but she'd been troubled before by the complete absence of bones and personal possessions on the surface. Perhaps, during or after the war, they had taken shelter in caves. Perhaps they had died out there. Or perhaps, considering what she now knew about Mars, they hadn't.

Anna turned back to the crawler and to the pillar that rose up behind it. Morden had refined his previous work on the identical pillar inscriptions. Previously he'd translated them to read, "Every light casts a shadow." He'd now corrected that to read, "Every light carries a shadow." This, unfortunately, hadn't led to any insights. Anna felt no closer to understanding this race than she had been back on Earth.

Morden had revealed last night that the only reason he'd been able to make the progress he had in the translations was because he'd obtained a few textual

samples from the ship on Mars. Though those had
been insufficient for translation, he had, in the three
intervening years, discovered their similarity to two
very obscure ancient tongues, which he had then studied. When the probe had begun transmitting new samples, Morden had been ready for them. Unfortunately,
the work was still very difficult, and without the probe
transmitting new source material, he'd been unable to
make any further translations. Both teams had been
instructed to record any writings they discovered.

Anna headed down the dune toward the others. She
had given Razor the job of overseeing the assembly of
the mobile elevator platform, a complex and critical
piece of equipment for cave excavation. With the platform they could move heavy equipment into the cave,
raise or lower it through vertical shafts, into pits and
crevasses, and maneuver it through tight spaces. The
assembly would take most of the day and over half of
her support crew. Standish supervised the rest, running a survey of the area surrounding the cave, taking
various readings to fill in gaps in the probe's data, and
establishing a datum point, from which all site measurements would be made. She consulted with both of
them and made sure things were progressing smoothly
before she asked Morden and Favorito to accompany
her on a preliminary exploration of the major cave.

Morden was the one she felt she could trust the most
now. He'd told her about Mars, about IPX's discovery, three years ago, of a ship buried at Syria Planum.
The ship had utilized biomechanical—or as he called
it, organic—technology, unlike anything they'd ever
seen before. As soon as the ship had been exposed to
sunlight, it had sent out an automatic coded message.
IPX, in a bit of a panic, contacted their friends at
Earthforce New Technologies Division, and Morden

was sent over as a consultant along with a team of others.

Morden advised that the signal was most likely an automatic distress call, and if the owners of the ship were still around, they would send someone to retrieve it. After taking samples from the ship and planting a homing device, IPX pulled back quickly. Three days later, an identical ship arrived, finished excavating the buried ship, repaired or activated it somehow, and they both flew off. IPX had tracked the ship to Alpha Omega 3.

After much debate and political wrangling, a probe had been sent to follow up. IPX had cut Earthforce out of the testing of the samples from the ship, which were IPX property, but had agreed to provide reports on their progress, which turned out to be nonexistent. When IPX reported that the probe detected no signs of sentient life on Alpha Omega 3, Morden theorized that the activity of the ships might have been automatic, that it was possible the culture was long dead. Endless arguments ensued over the theory and what course of action should be taken. Until Anna. And the mouse. Earthforce learned from IPX that the mouse had many of the same characteristics as the ship found on Mars. Suddenly the prospect of using and mastering this technology seemed much more immediate, and the appropriate course of action was clear: send an archaeological team, including Anna Sheridan.

Anna remembered Chang telling her he "needed" her for the expedition. Anna had thought he'd meant he needed her because he knew she would do a good job. Now she understood that he needed her because others wanted her on the team—others at IPX, and others in Earthforce. While this thought had angered her before—Chang may not even have wanted her on the expedition, in fact he'd seemed disappointed at her acceptance—now as she thought about it she wondered if he'd been disappointed because he'd known the potential dangers of the trip and had wanted to protect her from them.

Morden had told her that Chang and IPX had been under strict orders from Earthforce to keep the discovery of the ship on Mars a secret. Although Morden hadn't said it, and she thought he would disagree with her if she did, Anna was left with the sense that Earthforce was using them all as pawns—IPX, Anna, and the rest of the team, even Morden himself—in the attempt to secure this new technology.

After Morden had told her about Mars, Anna had told him about the probe, and about the smuggling arrangement between Donne and Hidalgo. He seemed unsurprised—he said when communications broke down that he assumed Donne must be responsible, and that Donne must have help among the crew—but he was hungry for details, details which, unfortunately, Anna couldn't provide. But at least she felt she had an ally.

Even at her most paranoid, she found it hard to believe Churlstein, Favorito, Razor, or Scott would do anything to hamper the expedition, but neither did she think it would do her any good to confide in them and try to enlist their help. They would probably go straight to Chang in disbelief, or if they didn't, they might become victims of the power struggle that was sure to erupt. As second in command, she had to keep their safety in mind.

She, Morden, and Favorito gathered their equipment. Anna had to readjust her old tool belt to get it around the EVA suit. She and Favorito each had preferred hand tools they carried with them all the time, from hi-tech sonic scrapers to the old dependable trowels and brushes to Anna's favorite antique dental picks. Then there was the larger equipment: scanners, lights, and a camera. Anna directed them to travel as light as possible, since this was just a scouting trip. Of course Favorito brought his ever-present comp-pad. It bothered Anna a bit that Morden's tools were all new, standard issue. They went along with his smooth palms. He must do most of his work behind a computer, not in the field.

They reprogrammed the links in their suits to treat the three of them as a subgroup. That way they could communicate among each other automatically, and link out of the subgroup to the main group when they wanted to talk to the rest of their party. Favorito activated the camera, a saucer the size of a dinner plate that floated along behind him like a trusty dog, automatically recording everything he took an interest in. He checked the manual controls, in case the camera needed to be taken off automatic for special, detailed work.

Then they headed up the dune that led to the mouth of the cave, Anna feeling the familiar rhythmic tapping of the hand tools against her body. She had told herself again and again that they had four months on site, but she had a sense of insecurity about the entire expedition that made her feel rushed. Besides, she wanted to retrieve the mouselike objects she had found before Donne or anyone else got to them, and if she could locate the probe as well, it might provide the evidence about who had destroyed it and why.

They paused at the cave entrance as Favorito made sure the camera was recording, Anna and Morden searching with their lights for signs of any artificial component to the cave or any signs of habitation. It appeared to be a natural formation of the landscape, despite some odd, jagged outcroppings along the floor that looked almost like teeth.

Anna led the way into the cave. It sloped steeply downward, and she had to keep her light trained on the ground to watch for differentially lifted slabs of stone and fallen rocks. As they moved away from the entrance, they became enveloped in darkness, their three lights shining damped and ineffective in the space surrounding them. The cave walls seemed to swallow their light. Anna had spent a good deal of her life in caves, cathedrals of mystery and beauty and truth. She'd never seen darkness like this.

"We'll have to start with the floodlights," Anna said to Morden. He was carrying a supply.

He nodded. "They're not going to go far in here." His smooth voice, through the EVA suit links, was reproduced with an almost uncanny quality. It seemed as if he were standing right beside her.

Morden took a floodlight out of his pack, held it against the cave wall, and activated it. It sealed itself against the wall and flickered on. The light would last for approximately six months, longer than they'd need.

Anna followed the cone of bluish illumination out along the cave floor. "It doesn't seem as bright as it should be. Are we getting full output?"

Morden checked the side of the device. "It's at one hundred percent. These walls seem to absorb the light."

Anna checked her coordinates with the hand-held scanner, moved toward the cave wall, a few yards down from the light. She found the small hole that she had dug with the probe. "Can you bring your lights over here?"

Morden and Favorito came closer, following her lead and pointing their lights at the jagged stone fragments and larger stones that made up the cave floor.

"This is where I left the two mice." She couldn't believe it. They were gone. "Do you see them?" Anna crouched, a difficult maneuver in the bulky suit.

Morden was shining his light down the hole. "This has filled partway in. Do you think they slid back down?"

"I didn't leave them that close to the hole."

They searched the surrounding area. Anna ran a focused thermal scan using the weak, hand-held scanner. The three of them were the only heat sources in the immediate area. The mice were not there.

The probe wasn't there either, of course. It had been taken somewhere to be destroyed. Knowing what she now knew about Mars, Anna supposed it was possible that a surviving member of this race had destroyed the probe, but that wouldn't explain the erasure of the probe record. Someone from the *Icarus* had destroyed the probe and had taken the mice as well, and either hidden or destroyed them.

The idea of someone destroying the mice infuriated Anna. They might be the only such devices remaining in existence. One of the first lessons archaeologists learned was that they had only one chance to discover the secret history buried by time. If the data taken during an excavation were incomplete, or an artifact was damaged, there was no way to put everything back the way it had been. The mice were precious. Anna hoped that if Donne was somehow responsible, she had hidden them in hopes of smuggling them back to Psi Corps with the help of Captain Hidalgo. Anything would be better than their destruction.

"All right," she said, "they're not here. Let's move on."

"But where could they have gone?" Favorito asked. "It's not like somebody could have come by and taken them."

Anna exchanged a glance with Morden. Then she pressed a control on the arm of her suit to link to her party outside. "Razor."

"Razor here," came the response, again as if he were standing right beside her.

"I'm about thirty feet into the cave. How's my transmission?"

"Clear as a bell."

"Okay." This had been where the probe's safety lock had engaged as it had begun to lose contact with the orbiter. "Keep talking for a minute." She walked further into the cave.

"I don't know what to say."

"That's got to be a first."

"What was that?" His voice was breaking up.

She stopped. "Can you still hear me?"

No response. She checked her position, backed up a step. "Razor." Backed up another. "Razor."

The reply was faint and crackly. "Sheridan."

She checked her position, took another step back. "Razor."

"Sheridan. I read you."

"It looks like our communications are only good up to thirty-six feet inside the major cave. After that, we're going to have to communicate by runners."

"Too bad Churlstein's not on our team. It would be a perfect job for him."

"Don't be cruel, Razor, you know that's my job. How's the platform coming?"

"We're progressing on schedule, meaning we're

about fifty minutes farther along than when you left fifty minutes ago."

"I've bet Favorito a ten-spot that you won't finish on schedule." Favorito pointed a finger at her to show he accepted the bet.

"You want to double that action?" Razor asked.

"You're on. We're going out of communications range now. Expect to be out for two hours. If you need us, follow the blue lights."

"Find any bugs in there?"

"Just the one that's going under your pillow tonight."

They continued into the cave, which sloped downward at a steep angle, their boots sliding on the loose rock fragments. Morden crisscrossed from side to side to set up the floodlights. Favorito supervised the camera and made constant notations on his comp-pad. Anna ran the several scans available to her on the hand-held scanner, searching for any signs of artifacts or habitation. The results showed nothing, but then these hand-held scanners were crude devices, without the capacity to convey the detailed information that she needed. Usually her eyes were the best tool on a preliminary survey like this anyway. Often the surface contours of the cave floor could indicate habitation. But she saw no such signs.

The cave gradually widened, the darkness around them growing vaster, and as Anna scanned it, she found that the cave was branching apart. "The cave is separating into three branches," she said.

"Door number one, door number two, or door number three," Favorito said.

As she widened the scan to determine the size, direction and route of each branch, the scanner showed a vast network of caverns overlaying caverns, multiple, contradictory patterns stretching to the limit of the scanner's range. "Hey, look at this."

The other two came close.

"It must be some sort of reflective effect," she said.

Morden looked off into the darkness. "The cave rock must interfere with scanning as well as communications."

"I've got the title for my expedition report," Favorito said. "Archaeology in the house of mirrors. This will be a challenge."

"The scan seems accurate up to about thirty yards," Morden said.

"Let me get the sonic probe in here," Favorito said. "That will tell us what's down there."

Favorito was right. But unfortunately, the sonic probe couldn't be brought in without the mobile elevator platform. For today, they were winging it. "Let's go with door number three."

They turned down and to the right, Morden lighting the entrance to their branch. Without accurate scanner readings past thirty yards, those lights were their only way out. Anna thought of Hansel and Gretel, marking their path with bread crumbs.

The new branch was narrower—about ten feet across—and steeper, the fragments on the ground making the going slippery. The cave ceiling descended to a level about six feet high, forcing Favorito to stoop and Anna and Morden to keep a sharp eye out for headache stones. Only a short distance in, Favorito called out. "Eureka!" He knelt down as Anna and Morden approached. "Look at this. It's almost perfectly preserved."

They shone their flashlights down with his. A small

desiccated corpse lay near the cave wall, partially buried in the rocky surface.

"Incredible," Morden said.

Favorito carefully brushed some of the rock fragments away from the area of the corpse, the camera hovering over his shoulder. "What is that?"

It appeared nearly intact, strings of dried muscle and tendon holding it together. The dry environment had helped to partially preserve it. It wasn't a mouse; the shape and structure were different. It was roughly circular, about a foot in diameter, but only about two inches thick. The bones and connective tissues were a rust color, the bones extremely delicate, narrowing to needlelike thinness for much of their length and widening to about one-quarter inch at the joints. The configuration of the bones seemed more geometric than organic, on the top bones radiating out from the center of the circle to its edge, joined to short bones that went halfway down its side. The bottom was a mirror image of the top, the overall shape reminiscent of a spoked wheel. The inside of this structure was mainly empty, except for its center, where an odd dried-out twist of connective tissue fastened a smaller formation of bones to the top and bottom of the outer skeleton.

In her mind the division was made automatically and instinctively: the outer skeleton and the inner skeleton. The inner bones poked through the remnants of a layer of tissue. They were cruder, more of a uniform thickness, and whiter, and they also appeared more familiar and more functional. She could see what appeared to be limbs, and a skull. But what would limbs and a skull be doing at the center of this creature? Structurally and evolutionarily, it made no sense. She would have liked to believe that the larger creature had swallowed the smaller one, but that would not explain the connective tissue. This was either a single organism of a totally new, unfamiliar type, or two organisms tied together in some symbiotic or parasitic fashion.

Except that the outer organism did not appear natural. The bones had the same look as the mouse bones, crafted, elegant, artificial. The mouse had also had an odd interior skeletal structure, but it had been much more subtle than this, much more complex.

This appeared quite obviously to be two separate organisms. It looked almost like a small flying saucer with a tiny pilot inside. That made her think of their saucer-shaped camera, and as she imagined a tiny pilot inside, her mind flashed to the probe control module, to the feeling that for a few moments she and the machine had been one. It was crude, and this was sophisticated, but she felt sure, as she studied the small skeleton caught in the suffocating grip of tissue, that she knew the key to biomechanical technology. The realization sang through her with a rush. "That small skeleton inside was a living creature," she said. "They took something living and hooked it into their machines. That's how they worked."

She straightened as Morden did, and his mouth opened, awe breaking over his face. "That's what you sensed with Donne's mouse fragment."

"Yes." She felt the same excitement she saw on his face, the adrenaline high of the breakthrough better than any stim junkie's fix. "That may be why the devices seem to work telepathically—one living being communicating with another."

"And I thought humans won the award for sickest culture." Favorito rose into his stooped standing posture. "How did they do it? How could they plug a living creature into something else like some interchangeable component?''

''I don't know. But the artificial section, remember, also has a biological element. Somehow they work together, in some sort of symbiotic or parasitic relationship.''

''Parasitic, I'd say.'' Favorito made some notations on his comp-pad. ''This doesn't look like a mutual thing to me.''

Morden had turned away, thoughtful. Now he marked the location of the artifact with a light. ''I only have two lights left.''

''We need to be heading back soon anyway,'' Anna said, but her mind was racing, eager. ''Let's just go a little farther.''

They went as far as the two lights would take them without finding anything else, then continued beyond the last light until it was a weak glimmer in the darkness. The cave ceiling descended further, until it was about five feet high. They had to move very slowly then, crouched over, the blackness hiding obstacles. That's when her light caught on it, about twenty feet away, a smooth, oily blackness that reflected her light back at her, totally unlike the jagged, absorbing black of the cave walls. They all saw it, and as they approached it they closed ranks, instinctively moving closer together in the darkness. They stopped about six feet from it. The surface, in their lights, appeared shifting and oily, almost iridescent.

''It looks alive,'' Favorito said, sending the camera around the side of it.

Anna scanned it. ''I'm not getting any reading on this at all.''

''You sure that scanner's working?'' Favorito asked.

"It reads all of us. I'll check it when we get back."

They moved their lights across its surface, remaining side by side.

"It looks like a perfect sphere," Morden said. "Maybe eight-foot diameter."

"It's blocking the passage," Favorito said. "There's no way around it."

For some reason that made Anna nervous. The space containing them seemed to contract around her. She thought of the long way back up to the surface.

And yet she didn't want to leave the sphere with such little information. Without the scanner, all they had was a visual recording of a round black ball. The sense of life, of movement in its surface, seemed almost to pulsate, the shifting reflections moving in surges, as if tied to the act of breathing. The nodule had an odd sense of flatness to it that came and went, as if she were looking at a two-dimensional representation of a three-dimensional object, or, perhaps, at a projection or shadow of something that existed in a fuller form elsewhere in the darkness.

"We should leave," Favorito said, and Anna realized she had no idea how long they'd been crouched there. The camera was hovering beside Favorito's shoulder.

"I want to take a sample," Anna said and, feeling this statement required further explanation, added, "since we can't get any scanner readings." The black membranous surface disturbed her and drew her. They had to find out what this was, whether it really was alive.

Morden opened a small specimen case. "How are you going to get the sample?"

"I don't know. I guess I'll have to test the surface first." She forced herself to take a step forward, then

another. She was right in front of it now, the oily
blackness subtly shifting, realigning itself. She raised
her hand. She was glad, now, she was wearing the
EVA suit. She brought her fingers to the membrane, as
if to tap the surface of a pond. Her hand passed
through it as if there were nothing there. She could
still see her hand, and she could still see the blackness
beyond her hand, as if she had misjudged its distance.
But then the blackness moved, and this movement was
totally unlike the liquid shifting she'd been studying;
this was the structural movement of a body, and she
realized it was no longer the surface of the nodule she
was seeing but something equally black inside it,
something that in the shadows gave the impression of
rising. With it rose an odd, symmetrical pattern of dim
lights, like a tiny constellation separated by aeons of
cold space, and as she looked longingly toward that
tiny, distant constellation of light rising through the
darkness and it stopped even with her at eye level, her
depth perception shifted, and the lights were no longer
at a vast distance but inches from her face, and they
were no longer stars but eyes, that were watching and
had been watching, tiny suns of knowledge, malice,
and desire, an ancient intelligence, a furnace of hunger
that engulfed star systems and galaxies, that unfolded
inside her a black well, as if all her life she'd been
hollow, waiting only for this moment to open, need
burning through her like a scream.

She stumbled back, her oxygen tank jamming into
her spine as she hit the ground.

Morden was beside her. "Are you all right?"

She grabbed on to him, pulled herself to her feet.
She was gasping, couldn't catch her breath. She took
his hand, grabbed for Favorito and got his arm, began
pulling them, crouching, away from the nodule.

''What is it?'' Morden was looking back over his shoulder.

As she pulled on them they began to run uphill, toward the tiny glimmer of blue light enveloped in darkness.

CHAPTER 12

LEAVING her robe of office behind, Delenn hurried from the Great Hall and out into the sunlit, crystalline passages of the city, which glittered with the brilliance of spring. She had no time to appreciate them. She was anxious to take action now that the Grey Council had authorized it, for she had lost a day already since Kosh had contacted her, and she sensed that every moment was precious. Kosh would not have called on her if the situation were not critical. The ship might even now be arriving at Z'ha'dum.

Her office was a medium-sized, functional room, yet with its few carefully placed crystals, she thought it fostered an environment of peace. Today, however, that peace seemed to elude her. She ordered her assistant, Nerid, from the room, composed herself as best she could, and put through the call. She was soon connected to Commander Sinclair, who appeared to be in his quarters on Babylon 5.

"Ambassador Delenn. I hope you'll be rejoining us in time for the dedication ceremony." Delenn had not had much personal contact with him yet, but the commander projected a warmth, intelligence, and honesty that made him seem superior to other humans.

"I have been delayed, Commander, but I plan to

leave for Babylon 5 shortly. Unfortunately, an urgent matter requires your attention. I hope you may be of some help.''

His eyebrows—a most expressive feature on humans—rose. ''I'll do what I can, Ambassador.''

''An Earth vessel has been sent to a planet near the rim of known space. You call this planet by the name of''—she checked her notes—''Alpha Omega 3. This ship must be recalled immediately. It is a matter of the gravest importance.''

''Minbari territory is nowhere near the rim. What is your interest in this matter?''

She chose her words carefully. ''The vessel poses a potential danger to us all, Commander.''

His eyebrows now contracted. ''What kind of danger?''

''I am not at liberty to say more. But many lives, far more than those aboard that ship, lie in the balance. You must have that ship recalled, Commander Sinclair. Please do everything in your power.''

''What is on Alpha Omega 3, Ambassador?''

She took a step forward. ''I hope, in the new spirit of cooperation among our races, and as the first diplomatic challenge faced by Babylon 5, that you will be able to grant our request.'' There. Humans loved to be challenged. Perhaps that would work.

The commander smiled. ''I'll do everything I can, Ambassador.''

''Thank you so much.'' Delenn bowed and ended the communication. He did not know how much was at stake. But she had told him all she could.

She directed Nerid to have her belongings loaded on board the ship at once.

* * *

They ran up the ramp into the crawler, Anna still gripping them, unable to let go. She shot a nervous glance over her shoulder. Behind them, dust blasted in through the opening, shifting its angle like a living thing as the ramp rose, closing. The camera slipped inside, settling over Favorito's shoulder.

"Are you all right?" Razor said. The rest of the party was already in the crawler, some seated, some standing, all watching them.

"Yes," Morden answered for her. All three of them were hunched over, gasping for air, breathless and exhausted after the long run in the EVA suits in heavy gravity. "I think so. What happened to the weather?"

"About an hour ago it suddenly got worse. I don't understand it. None of our projections predicted anything like this. We had to take shelter in here." With a vibration Anna felt beneath her feet, the ramp sealed shut against the side of the crawler, and the pressure of the wind died into stillness.

"What did you find?" Standish asked, the light reflecting off his EVA helmet.

Anna found her voice. "Have you heard from Chang's party?"

"No," Razor said. "We tried to reach them to share information about the storm track, but no response. It's probably just interference from the storm. I was able to reach Captain Hidalgo, but the transmission was distorted. I couldn't read him."

Anna saw the tech who drove their crawler standing behind Razor. "Get us over to Chang's site, now. Tell our other crawler to follow."

"Yes, Doctor." The tech headed toward the front of the crawler.

"I really don't think the storm is anything to worry

about," Razor said. "The crawlers can handle it. Chang is probably already back at the *Icarus*."

"Let's just make sure," Anna said. "Keep trying to reach Chang."

Razor nodded and headed for the front of the crawler. Standish remained, watchful, curious.

"Standish, could you get me the latest readings on the storm?"

Standish reluctantly retreated.

As the crawler started to move, the techs all found seats in one of the two rows that lined the crawler's sides, facing center. The large open center section was still filled with the sonic probe and other heavy equipment they had meant to leave at the site.

Instead of going up front with the rest of the archaeological team, Anna pulled Morden and Favorito, still attached to her, to three empty seats. The camera followed. Right now Anna didn't know what to think. She was ashamed of her performance in the caves, running away like a schoolgirl in a spook house. Chang was probably fine, was probably back at the *Icarus*. But she was no longer sure. What she had seen changed everything. She tried not to think of it.

"What happened in there?" Favorito asked.

She forced her fingers to open, releasing Favorito's arm, and linked down to their subgroup. Her hand shook slightly. "Deactivate that camera."

Favorito took hold of the camera and deactivated it, setting it on the floor beside him.

"I don't want you to tell anyone about that nodule we found," Anna said. "Not until I give the okay." She waited until they both nodded.

"What was it?" Morden asked.

"It was alive," Anna said, "and it was watching us. This race is not dead."

They sat in silence until Standish found them. He grabbed the hand bar above them to keep his balance. Anna's link chimed as he linked into her subgroup. "I thought you were coming up front." He handed her a comp-pad with the latest information on the storm. "It's concentrated over this whole region. Winds are gusting up to seventy miles per hour. It looks like it's going to be with us for the next few days at least."

She handed back the comp-pad. "When we looked at the data from the orbiter this morning, it didn't predict a storm."

"I know. For some reason the computer hasn't been able to come up with a terribly accurate model. There must be factors influencing the weather that it's not taking into account." He took a few steps to maintain his balance as the crawler slowed to a stop.

As she went to stand, Anna realized she was still holding Morden's hand. Although they were separated by two layers of bulky gloves, she could feel the substance of his hand, its return pressure against her. The simple human contact was reassuring. With an embarrassed smile she released his hand, pulled her arm out from his. She didn't say anything since it would have automatically gone out over the link.

Anna linked back to the main group and went up to the front of the crawler, followed by Morden, Favorito, and Standish. Out the front windows, through the sheets of blowing dust and sand, the major pillar was intermittently visible. To its left, perhaps thirty yards off, were Chang's two crawlers. He was not back at the *Icarus*.

"The egg is gone," Razor said. He was staring out the window. "I wasn't sure at first. The scanners are giving us some trouble with the storm. But you can see. It's not there."

"That's impossible." Favorito elbowed his way to the front. "Why don't you turn on the lights?" As Favorito flipped on the crawler's floodlights, the answer became apparent. They reflected back off the curtains of dust, reducing visibility to almost nothing.

Razor turned the lights off, and they all stared into the shifting curtains of dust outside.

As the dust lessened for a few moments, the area around the base of the pillar became clear, a jagged plain of cracked, reddish-brown stone. The egg was gone.

"Could they have moved it?" Standish asked.

Favorito snorted with contempt. "They'd know a lot better than to move something that valuable before it could be studied and mapped and its soundness checked."

"Maybe they thought the storm would damage it and moved it into the crawler," Standish persisted.

Favorito turned to face Standish and cross his arms. "It's been there for *a thousand years*. Maybe that's how you do things on your team. We do things a little differently. We use our intelligence."

"It's too big to put into the crawler," Morden said quietly. "And they didn't have any other equipment with them that would have been able to move something so large and heavy. Not all in one piece."

"Have you tried to reach Chang?" Anna asked Razor.

"I've been trying." Razor's voice was subdued, not like his normal, teasing tone at all. "No response from the links, no response from the crawlers."

The possibility that something had happened to Chang and his party suddenly seemed very real. Anna kept her own voice calm as well. "Have you scanned for life signs?"

"I'm not picking up any life signs. But it could be the scanners."

"Have you scanned for their links?" Anna asked. Each link had a built-in locator beacon.

Razor looked like a lost dog. "I got a reading on one, near the pillar."

Anna's heart was pounding. "We'll split into two groups. Razor and Standish, take group one and check out the crawlers. I'll take group two with Morden and Favorito to the area around the pillar."

Razor looked back down at the scanners, as if their readouts might have changed.

"Go," Anna said.

Outside, the dust and sand seemed to have intensified. Visibility averaged around thirty-five feet. Occasionally Anna could see farther than that, though occasionally the dust came so fast and furious that she couldn't see the ground. Since it was uneven, that could be treacherous. "Stay together," she said to Razor and Standish as they headed off with their group of twenty techs. Anna had her group stand in a line an arm's width apart and then sweep down toward the area of the pillar. If anything was here, she wanted to find it. She prayed that, whatever had happened to the egg, Chang and his party were in the crawlers safe and sound, waiting out the storm. But what could have happened to the egg? She thought of those eyes on her, watching her as if they had *been* watching her. If there was still a living race on this planet—underground perhaps, or somehow shielded—had they detected the probe and expected the *Icarus*? Were they watching, now? She told herself she was jumping to conclusions, focused on keeping her footing on the uneven stony ground.

"I see someone!" Favorito yelled. He was pointing ahead.

There, about ten feet to the right of the pillar, was the white of an EVA suit. It lay against the ground, partially covered by sand and dust. Favorito broke ranks and ran ahead, and Anna followed. The white swam in and out of vision like a ghost, and then she was there.

"Oh, God!" Favorito cried.

She knelt down beside him and peered down at the white shape. Anna felt her mind functioning very clearly. Chang's helmet had been removed and tossed aside. His body, lying on its side, had created a small drift of sand, and his cheek appeared to be pillowed on it. Chang looked as if he were asleep, mouth hanging askew, eyes closed, weather-beaten face slack. Sand clung to his eyelashes and collected in the pocket of his lips. His fine grayish-white hair blew raggedly around his face. His life-signs detector was flashing red. Favorito had cleared the sand away from his chest. A hole had been burned through his suit and through the top several inches of his chest cavity. She was no expert, but from what she'd seen on the news feeds, it looked like a PPG blast. Suddenly her fear of aliens jumping out of dark caves seemed ridiculous, and she thought of Donne, who had been in Chang's party.

Favorito began to sob, the sound coming through the link.

"Chang has been shot," she told the others, who were beginning to gather around. "Look for a PPG." The ship had been equipped with arms, though they were only in case of emergency. Chang had access, and perhaps Captain Hidalgo did—she didn't know. She remembered Chang, in his quarters, handing her the PPG. He'd been worried, and he'd warned her.

She felt the pockets of his suit, searching for the PPG he'd said he was going to get for himself. It was in the thigh pocket, just as hers was. She worked it clumsily out. The gun told her nothing. It seemed unlikely that anyone would have shot Chang with it and then returned it to his pocket.

Morden knelt on one knee on the far side of Chang and linked to the subgroup. "If he'd known what was coming, he would have taken that out."

"He could never have shot anyone."

Morden's face had the careful smile on it, and Anna realized how uncomfortable he was with the reminder of death. Anna sandwiched the PPG in her gloves, extended it toward Morden. "Here. You take this. No one else knew he had it."

"You should keep it. You might need it."

"I already have one. Here."

Morden took the gun, slipped it into his pocket. "He looks very peaceful, doesn't he? There's something reassuring about seeing him like this."

Favorito stumbled to his feet beside Anna. "You're sick!" he yelled at Morden, and then he walked away into the dust.

Anna couldn't understand why Chang's helmet had been removed. If someone wanted to kill him, suffocation from the carbon monoxide would take way too long. She remembered catching him asleep once, in his office at the University of Chicago, slumped back in his chair, head tilted to the side. He looked like that now, as if he could open his eyes at any moment.

She linked out to Razor's group. "Razor. This is Sheridan. We found Dr. Chang. He's dead. He's been shot by a PPG."

There was no response.

Anna's calmness was wearing away. She could feel

the wind scraping it away, the panic beneath it beginning to rise. "Razor."

"I heard. I can't believe it." There was some static on the transmission, but she had no trouble reading him. "What happened?"

"That's all we know so far. What have you found?"

"We've done a thorough search of both crawlers," Razor said. "No one is here."

Anna felt a strange tightness around her throat. "Split your group between Chang's two crawlers and take them back to the *Icarus* immediately. We'll follow. Keep scanning for locator beacons from the missing EVA suits." As if only suits were missing, not people. "I want you to check back in with me every five minutes until you get back to the *Icarus*."

"Okay."

Anna stood, directed two nearby techs to take Chang's body back to the crawler. As they picked him up, and his arms flopped loosely back and forth, she brought her fist up to her mouth, the action kept from completion by her helmet. She'd barely spoken to Chang since she'd listened to his message, furious at him for withholding information that could have helped her research. Over the years he'd helped her again and again. He'd listened to her, guided her. So what if he played the corporate game, kept their secrets, told their lies? He'd been good to her, and she'd failed him. As second in command of the mission, she should have been looking out for his safety. He'd warned her about the danger, and she hadn't taken him seriously. What if he'd known that Donne posed a serious threat? Perhaps he'd taken her in his party to keep Anna out of danger. And Anna had gladly let him. Even watching his EVA suit disappear into the dust, she couldn't believe he was gone.

Her body was trembling all over. She forced calm into her voice. "Morden, can you show me exactly where the egg was?"

He walked up to the pillar, stepped back a few paces, then took a few steps left. "The center of it was just about here. Then it extended about twenty feet to each side, and fifteen feet to the front and back."

Anna stood beside him and did a slow circle, staring into the dust.

"They couldn't have moved it," Morden repeated.

"Then either someone else moved it," Anna said, "or it moved itself."

"Watch your step," Morden said.

To her right, a crevasse in the stone widened from a few inches to about two feet across, remaining at that width for about ten feet before narrowing back down again. "I don't remember seeing that in the probe's transmissions. Was the egg on top of it?"

Morden approached the crevasse. "It must have been."

The dust tended to brown out everything behind it. Yet the crevasse stood out like a stream of blackness, as if the blackness saturated the very air, persistent, leaving a negative afterimage as a bright light left a positive one. Anna knelt. The reddish-brown rock of the surface continued to a depth of less than a foot here. Below was the black, light-absorbing rock of the caves. The sides of the crevasse were jagged, vertical. "I can't see how deep it runs. But they couldn't have climbed down here. They'd have needed to set up a platform."

"They could have fallen in," Morden said. Above her, obscured by sand, his expression was unclear.

"The stone is jagged." Anna leaned down into the crevasse. "I don't see any pieces of clothing or equipment." She didn't want to admit that she couldn't see much in the darkness, and that the wind might have blown away any scraps.

"That still wouldn't explain what happened to the egg. The dimensions of the crevasse are too narrow for it."

Anna stood. She was exhausted, and she had run out of ideas. Could they all be dead—Chang, Churlstein, Scott, Petrovich, Donne, and forty technicians?

"Do you really think the egg might have moved under its own power?" Morden asked.

"Why not? It's basically a tool or machine of some kind. Its purpose might involve locomotion. I admit the shape doesn't suggest it, but this technology is so different from ours, we really don't know what its purpose is."

"All that is desired." His tone was wistful.

"If that's what it's promising, then it's failing miserably." Anna linked up to the rest of her group and ordered them to return to the crawlers.

Her leg muscles ached as she trudged back through the wind. Morden fell in beside her. "You're going to have to watch your back," he said. "You're in charge now."

CHAPTER 13

JEFFREY Sinclair rested his head in his hands. "Tell me it's all resolved, Michael."

"It's *almost* resolved?" Garibaldi replied.

"Try again. Harder." He was dealing with a thousand crises, and he'd like to have a simple resolution to one of them.

"It *will be* resolved, as soon as I track down Marco."

Jeff's head came up. "You haven't found Marco yet?"

Garibaldi raised his hands. "We've tracked him to Brown 3. We're almost there. Just give us another hour."

"Fine. Just don't show your face around here until you've got him. Less than forty-eight hours to our dedication ceremony and the whole place falls apart."

Garibaldi slid his hands into his pockets. "Ready to start looking for another job?"

"I'm ready to ask for a raise. Now get out of here." Garibaldi left the office, and Jeff leaned back in his chair, contemplating all the other crises demanding his attention. His top priority was still to follow up on Ambassador Delenn's request. He'd talked to Senator Hidoshi, who had referred him to President Santiago's science advisor, Dr. LeBlanc. Then chaos had taken over. He put through a call to the doctor, and after a minute it went through, and she appeared on the Stellarcom monitor.

"Doctor, I'm Jeffrey Sinclair, commander of Babylon 5."

"I've been hoping to have the opportunity to meet you. Congratulations on your appointment." She was an elegant woman in her fifties, her platinum-blond hair swept back, a scarf fastened with a gold pin at her shoulder.

"Thank you. I'm afraid I have a rather serious situation on my hands, and I need to ask your help."

"I'm intrigued. Ask away."

"The Minbari ambassador contacted me earlier today. She said that we have a vessel en route to a planet near the rim, Alpha Omega 3, and that it must be recalled. Senator Hidoshi referred me to you in the belief that this must be a science vessel of some kind. Ambassador Delenn called this a matter of gravest importance, and said the ship poses a potential danger to all of us."

LeBlanc straightened. "A ship near the rim? I'm not aware of any such mission. It must be from the private sector. Did she give the name of the ship or any other information?"

"Unfortunately, no."

"Do you know the source of her information?"

"No. She—"

"Did she explain why the Minbari had taken an interest in this expedition?"

"She said that many lives were at stake. She wouldn't say any more than that."

LeBlanc tapped a polished, pointed fingernail

against her desktop. "What's your take on this ambassador, Commander Sinclair?"

"I've only known Ambassador Delenn a short time, but I've found her honest, and she is not prone to exaggeration. If she says there is a serious danger, I believe her." He surprised himself with his words. He *had* only known Delenn a short time, and here he was going out on a limb for her. But he did believe the danger was real, and if it was, he had to do everything he could to help.

LeBlanc ran her index finger along her jaw. "Surely you can't believe the Minbari ambassador is being totally forthright?"

"I didn't say she wasn't keeping secrets. But that doesn't mean that what she has told us isn't true."

"You have an interesting outlook, Commander. In any case, I don't know of any mission to the rim. I'll have to check on this and get back to you."

"Please hurry, Doctor. I believe this danger is very real. And even if you don't, as a matter of interplanetary relations it may be in our best interests to cooperate with the Minbari. The peaceful resolution of diplomatic issues such as this is the main reason President Santiago began the Babylon Project."

LeBlanc gave him a tight smile. "I'm well aware of the diplomatic implications, Commander. I'll be in touch."

The Stellarcom logo returned to the monitor.

Jeff heaved a sigh and leaned back in his chair, rubbing the knot in his neck. He could do nothing more until he heard back from her. Nothing more, except deal with the nine hundred ninety-nine other crises that had to be resolved within the next forty-eight hours.

* * *

"Go to battle-alert status," John ordered.

In this empty place between stars, the two ships ahead of them were not even visible on the large observation screen. John kept his distance. That was how he wanted it. If he couldn't see them, they couldn't see him. John had directed the *Agamemnon* to stand by during the transfer of explosives at the limit of their scanner range. The *Agamemnon*'s scanners could monitor the enemy ships, but with this new stealth technology, Lochschmanan had assured him neither Narn nor human vessels could scan the *Agamemnon*.

"The shuttle is returning to the Narn ship, Captain," Corchoran said. "I believe the transfer has been made." John had thought that perhaps Corchoran would liven up when they saw some action, but his mood still seemed gloomy, somber. Maybe it was just a misleading impression his features gave.

Corchoran checked the scanner readout. "Narn ship is pulling away and opening a jump point."

"Good. What's the cruiser doing?"

"The cruiser has set course for the Carutic jump gate, a Narn jump gate approximately ten hours away. From there they can jump to Babylon 5." So far everything was developing by the numbers. The thing that bothered John the most was that on the scanners, the Homeguard cruiser had the signature of an Earthforce vessel. The friend-or-foe signal definitely marked this ship as friend, which meant either that the signature had been faked, which was supposed to be impossible and would carry very troubling implications if it were possible, or that the cruiser had been stolen from Earthforce, or that an entire faction of Earthforce was in collusion with the Homeguard.

"Is the Narn ship away?" John asked.

"Narns away," Corchoran said.

John turned to the other officers on the command deck. They had all shaped up nicely. They were a good crew. And they all looked a bit nervous knowing that this battle alert was not just another drill. "All right, this is what they pay us for. Helm, bring us within weapons range. Weapons, stand by. Communications, it's time to let them know we're here. Open a—" John's link chimed. He brought it to his mouth. "Sheridan. Go."

"This is Ross, sir. The laser cannons are nonoperational. Repeat, nonoperational."

"How serious is it, Ross?" John asked. Corchoran approached, his worry for once seeming totally justified.

"I think you should come down here, sir."

"Stand by." John clenched his jaw, thinking. "Helm, are we within visual range yet?"

"Almost, sir."

"Come around. Bring us back out to the limit of scanner range. Set a parallel course to the cruiser. Communications, maintain radio silence." At this distance, radio silence was critical, since any external communications would be detected by the cruiser.

John got up from the command chair. "Commander, let me know if there's any change."

"Yes, sir."

John hurried down to the weapons bay. He'd thought Ross had made a real change. His performance had been outstanding since their talk in Ross's quarters. What could have gone wrong? And now, of all times.

John entered the weapons bay, expecting it to be filled with gunners and officers responding to the battle alert he'd called five minutes before. Ross sat alone before the weapons diagnostic system. "Ross, what's going on?"

Ross came to attention. His voice boomed. "I'm sorry, sir. I ordered the weapons crew into the mess. I came on duty thirty minutes ago, and when I did I conducted a routine inspection of the weapons bay. I found this." He raised his hand, and in the center of his palm was a tiny electronic component, about an eighth of an inch across. John took it, held it up close. "It was on the floor just down here." Ross indicated the space below the weapons diagnostic system.

"What is this?" John asked.

"It's from the weapons diagnostic system. It's a bridge. Nothing fancy, it just conveys information from one spot to another. But without it, the information won't get where it's supposed to go." John returned the component to him. "I thought there might have been some repair work done while I was off duty, so I checked the logs, but they showed nothing. So I opened up the diagnostic system and ran some checks to see if everything was in order. It turns out the information pathway regarding the optics was interrupted. A bridge had been removed. The optics were reading green on the diagnostic system because no other information was reaching it. So when I put in a new bridge, I got the actual status of the optics, which is, as you can see, in the red."

"How serious is the damage?"

Ross shrugged. "It seems to be limited to the primary mirror, but I can't really tell without getting in an EVA suit and going up to the tube."

The optics were in the red, and the one system that would have warned them of the failure was missing a key component. If Ross hadn't found it, John would have issued a warning to the Homeguard cruiser, revealing the *Agamemnon*'s presence. They were both thinking the same thing, John knew. That was why Ross had sent the weapons crew out of the room. "In your opinion, Lieutenant, how did this happen?"

Ross slid the bridge nervously across his huge hand as he spoke. "These components don't just fall out, though I would have said it happened as a fluke if I'd replaced the bridge and everything had stayed in the green. But the fact that this specific bridge prevented information about a critical failure from reaching us suggests"—he looked up at John—"it was taken out on purpose. And that perhaps the optics were also damaged on purpose."

John nodded. "You were right to order the others out of the weapons bay. Tell me, who would have the knowledge to carry out this type of sabotage?"

"The gunners service the optics, so most of them would be able to do some kind of damage there. But the diagnostic system . . . the weapons officers are really the only ones fully trained. I suppose it would have to be one of us."

"Or more than one," John said. "When was the last time you were on duty?"

"I got off last night at zero hundred."

"And do you think that you would have spotted this bridge if it were on the floor last night?"

Ross squared his shoulders. "I'm positive, sir. I ran the same inspection last night that I did today."

"So if we assume that this was done sometime between zero hundred last night and sixteen hundred this afternoon when you came on duty, who had the opportunity? Who was on those other shifts?"

"Watley had the first watch, sir, and Spano the second."

John let out a breath. "All right. I'm going to put a

guard on this door with instructions to admit no other weapons crew but you. And I'm going to have your fellow weapons officers questioned. Good work so far, Ross. Now I need you to get into an EVA suit and get out to the tube. I need your repair estimate ten minutes ago. We have to be able to fire before that cruiser reaches the jump gate.''

"They're obviously all dead.'' Favorito's voice was quavering. "We've got no life signs, no locator beacons. If they were alive, they would be here or they would have contacted us.''

"Not necessarily,'' Razor said, fiddling nervously with his comp-pad. "With the dust from the storm interfering with communications, they could be unable to reach us. And our scanners could be unable to pick them up.''

Favorito pounded with the flat of his hand on the conference room table. "That doesn't explain what happened to them.''

"I'm afraid we're out of our depth here,'' Standish said, chewing on a fingernail. He'd been white as a ghost since they'd gotten back. "If we could only repair the com system, we could consult with—''

"Good news,'' Captain Hidalgo proclaimed from the doorway of the conference room. "The com system is repaired.'' He was filled with false good cheer. He didn't have to worry about Chang sending his message to IPX anymore, but Anna knew, from all the questions he'd asked her, that he was worried about losing Donne and his fat payoff.

"With this storm, the signal probably can't even penetrate the atmosphere,'' Favorito said.

"Then we can just leave the atmosphere and send a message,'' Standish said, "on our way home.''

This touched off another round of arguing.

"We're not leaving," Anna said, quieting the others. She sat at the head of the table, feeling very out of place in Chang's seat. "We don't have time. Those EVA suits our missing crew are wearing only have enough oxygen for ten more hours. We're going to spend every minute of that ten hours searching for them. After that, we'll have all the time in the world for going home. Before that, every minute is precious, and I want every member of the crew involved."

"But some of my crew aren't trained for EVA activity," Hidalgo protested.

"I want them all out there," Anna said. She wouldn't put it past Hidalgo to take the ship up while they were out searching. "Those who aren't trained can use breathers. The atmosphere's safe for them and we don't have enough EVA suits anyway."

"That violates protocol."

"Losing forty-five people violates protocol too. Look, I'm going to use a breather myself. They're perfectly safe." To avoid further argument, she changed the subject. "Razor, have you been able to get any additional information from the ship's scanners?"

"There are still no life signs and no beacons showing, but I am reading an energy source of some kind from the cave site where you were today."

"I'm not going back into those caves," Favorito yelled. "This planet—"

"Dr. Favorito," Anna said. "If you're suffering from claustrophobia, I'll put you in another group."

Favorito went to rub his forehead and knocked the reading glasses from his head. He was ready to crack, and Anna couldn't let that happen. If the others knew there were living natives on the planet, it would very likely push them over the edge. As archaeologists, they weren't used to dealing with unknown dangers. They were used to dealing with the unknown, as long as it hadn't moved in a couple of centuries, and they were used to dealing with dangers, as long as they were familiar—cave-ins, falls, mechanical accidents. A situation like this was totally unprecedented. Anna had no idea how to handle it either. She was just taking one step at a time.

"We will search an area centered on the major pillar, extending for a radius of five miles." She called up a map on the monitor. "Razor, you take Captain Hidalgo and search sector one, the area of the pillar. You may need to investigate the crevasse Dr. Morden and I described to you. Favorito and Standish, take sector two, which includes some low mountains and many stone blocks. Morden and I will take sector three, which includes the cave site, and we'll investigate the energy source you're reading."

The search already seemed destined for failure. Razor seemed steady, but Hidalgo couldn't be trusted. But he couldn't be left on the ship either. Favorito and Standish—God knew how effective they would be, left to their own devices. She would have put Morden into one of the other groups, except that the secret of what they had found in the caves had to be preserved, as long as possible. She wondered if she was turning into Chang now, keeping a secret from her own team, a secret that might endanger their lives. "Each group will include thirty techs. Standish, I want you to set up a group of techs as runners, with multi-terrain vehicles, in case our communications are cut off."

Standish seemed to snap out of a paralyzing meditation at the mention of his name. "Can we at least try to send a message home?"

"It will take us a half hour to prep the EVA suits and organize our teams. If it can be done in that time, we'll do it. Standish, I want you on the runners. Razor, can you work with Captain Hidalgo on sending out a message?"

Razor nodded. "If we can just get our message to the orbiter, we can order the orbiter to retransmit from there. I'll need your code to access the orbiter, unless you want to do it."

"Shouldn't we be armed," Favorito asked, tapping his glasses against the table, "against—whoever killed Dr. Chang?"

Anna could see Favorito with a PPG, shooting at anything that moved. "I don't want to give arms to a group of people who aren't trained to use them. We'd end up with a lot more shootings that way. If you feel you want a weapon, bring a tool or a piece of equipment that you know how to use." Anna took a deep breath, let it out. She wished for John, wished it with a depth she'd never felt before. She wasn't trained for this sort of situation. She didn't want anyone else to die. They were all depending on her. "I want your teams briefed and ready to go in a half hour. No later. Our team members are counting on us to find them. We have to come through for them. Go."

As they filed out, she realized Morden had not spoken through the entire meeting. His features were relaxed, an unfamiliar peace in them. She wished she could feel so calm. She approached him. He was wearing the necklace, had been since she'd given it to him. "Can you brief our team and meet me in my quarters in twenty minutes?"

"Do you need me for anything else?"

"Just keep an eye on . . . everyone."

He nodded, left.

Razor remained, waiting for her access code. He had refastened his comp-pad to his belt and stood as if at a loss.

She told him the code. "I'll record the message right now and send it up to you on the command deck. Let me know if you're able to get through to the orbiter."

Razor nodded and started to squeeze past her.

"Wait," Anna said quietly, lowering her head. "I'm sorry to be sending you with Captain Hidalgo. If there was another way I could break the team up, I would."

Razor had been struck silent by her tone.

"He can't be trusted," Anna said. "He made an agreement with Donne to smuggle artifacts for Psi Corps. Chang found out about it, and Hidalgo took the com system off line so Chang couldn't report him." She reached into the pocket of her baggy sweater. "I want you to have this." She laid the PPG in his callused hand, closed his fingers around it. "Chang gave it to me."

"And look what happened to him," Razor said with a weak exhalation of a laugh. His lost-dog eyes looked up at her. "Shouldn't you keep this?"

"I'll be with Morden. I won't need it."

"You sure?"

"Take it. I feel guilty enough sending you off with Captain Cutthroat as it is."

He pocketed the gun. "A razor beats a cutthroat in any poker hand."

And then she was alone. She made the message brief. "Mr. Galovich, Dr. Chang is dead. He was shot by a PPG. We don't know who shot him, though it appears to be a member of his party. The remaining members of his party—Doctors Churlstein, Scott, and

Petrovich, Ms. Donne, and forty techs—are missing. The egg artifact that Dr. Chang was investigating is also missing. Conditions on the planet are interfering with communications and scanners. We can read no life signs and are picking up no locator beacons from their links. We are going out to search for our missing crew in twenty-five minutes.

"Given that IPX, as well as other organizations, has a high interest in Alpha Omega 3, and given that you have much more information about this planet and its technology than you have shared with us, perhaps you would send us the information we need to do our jobs, or send people whom you would entrust with that information.

"I have encountered life on this planet, and I have reason to believe it may be hostile, that it may be responsible for our missing crew. But that may not surprise you." Her voice was beginning to shake, and this message had gone on far longer than she had intended. "You sent us in with no warning, knowing that this race, thousands of years more advanced than us, might still be alive. You didn't want to confront them, so you sent us in as pawns."

She forced herself to stop. There was no point to this, and no time. She let out a breath. "I'm attaching Dr. Chang's last message to you. End."

She sent the message up to Razor, then headed for Donne's quarters. She had to know if Donne had killed Chang, and why.

Donne's quarters were identical to Anna's: bed and narrow closet on the left, dresser/desk combination on the right, narrow passage in between leading to the tiny bathroom at the back. Donne's possessions were minimal, and organized with military precision: several black suits, shoes, identicard, a credit chit, toiletries, a pair of pajamas, several pairs of gloves, socks, underwear, the small lead box with the mouse fragment inside. The only personal touch appeared to be a photograph in a simple frame on her dresser. It showed a man and a woman standing outside the door of a house.

They were both in their thirties, both blond, the man's harsh face carrying a strong resemblance to Donne's. From the style of the clothes—the man's shirt had a wide collar, the woman's skirt was short and neon-pink—she guessed the picture had been taken about twenty years before. She turned the frame over and opened it in the hope that someone had labeled the back of the picture. But it was blank. Anna refastened the frame and turned it back over.

The woman's smile seemed about as natural as Morden's, and she had raised a hand as if waving—hello or good-bye?—to someone. With her bright clothes and teased hair, she looked as if she were trying very hard to present a cheery exterior. The man had grabbed the woman's other hand and held it up against his stomach as if preventing her from moving. His whole body seemed stiff. He had the same wide shoulders as Donne, the same hard jawline. The man's expression was closed, clenched. They must be her parents, Anna thought. It seemed odd that Donne would bring their picture with her, perhaps because Anna had never thought of Donne as actually having parents. It seemed especially odd that Donne would choose this picture, which didn't seem to show her parents in the best light.

Anna returned the picture to the dresser and continued to search the room. It was a small room, with few potential hiding places. The bed was made tightly, precisely—the military mind-set again. That was why she was so surprised when under the pillow she discovered a satin lingerie roll.

Anna couldn't imagine Donne ever wearing lingerie. It seemed so totally opposed to what she was, and to everything else in the room. The roll was a soft, glossy turquoise, about eighteen inches long and five inches thick. In disbelief, she untied the delicate turquoise string, let the roll unroll. It formed a rectangle approximately eighteen inches by thirty, the rectangle broken up into smaller rectangular pockets of varying sizes, their covers transparent silk so their contents could be seen. At first Anna didn't recognize what she was seeing. Inside was an odd assortment of items, not lingerie. A lock of hair, a signet ring on an odd ring post. Anna dropped the roll and jumped back. The satin slipped into an iridescent pool on the floor.

It was a finger. A finger, in the lingerie roll. In the next pocket over was a dark, shriveled item that looked almost like a leaf. She took a step closer, bent tentatively toward the roll. Curving lines of contours ran in a semicircular shape. Her fist went to her mouth. It was an ear. As if her mind had clicked into a new mode of sight, she quickly recognized the rest of the items: a toe, a dark lock of hair, a nose, an eye from a Narn, a piece of tendon, the shapes repeated, the sizes varying. Several pockets remained empty. Along the bottom row were nestled a series of cutting tools, and in the last, corner pocket, a small insignia, about one inch across. Anna took it for a Psi Corps insignia, but when she leaned closer, she saw that it was similar, but that in its center was a black square. She'd never seen one like it before, and she was sure that the insignia Donne wore did not have the black square.

She sat on the bed, looking down at the satin rectangle, her mind simultaneously racing and blank. This wasn't what she'd expected to find. At last she remembered to check her watch, found that only a few minutes had passed. She still had five minutes before she had to meet Morden. She stood up, determined to pull some information from this room. This was her job. Study the artifacts left behind, deduce the culture of those who had left them, reconstitute their behavior, recapture their thoughts.

The precision of the creased, identical suits in the tiny closet, the mirror-polished shoes below, the socks rolled and lined in neat ranks—it all spoke of a military training. Anna had thought Donne looked more like a soldier than a telepath when they'd first met. The insignia must belong to a special unit of Psi Corps, perhaps a unit with military training of some kind, like the Psi Cops, but not dedicated to tracking down rogue telepaths, instead dedicated to . . . eliminating threats to telepaths? Donne appeared to be an expert killer. Was that what she had been trained to do? Anna began to pace in the tiny space, carefully avoiding the satin roll. Donne's killings could be her own—hobby— unrelated to her position in Psi Corps, but the inclusion of the insignia in the pouch suggested a connection. Why would Psi Corps have sent an assassin on the expedition?

Donne had made some kind of arrangement with Hidalgo. He was going to smuggle artifacts for her. But what artifacts? As Chang had wondered, had she expected to pocket them under the science team's noses and sneak them back to the *Icarus*? Or had she planned to sneak catalogued items out of the hold and expected no one would notice? It seemed unlikely she could get them by the entire science team's notice. Theft had been a constant danger throughout the history of archaeology, and they took automatic precautions to prevent it. Killing Chang wouldn't be enough. They were all meticulous when it came to mapping and cataloguing. Those were an archaeologist's life. She would have had to kill the entire science team. And perhaps with Hidalgo's help, it could all have been passed off as an accident, a terrible accident that had destroyed all the artifacts.

Anna was exhausted, and the theory smacked of paranoia. Why would Psi Corps be so desperate to keep this technology away from anyone else? Terrence had been hurt, yes, but was the threat really serious enough to justify this? Yet Donne may have already completed half of her task.

She thought of Chang, and she remembered now as they had removed the body from the crawler, she had gone to smooth his wispy, wind-whipped hair. There had been an odd patch on the side of his head, stubbly and short. Donne had cut away some of his hair to keep. That was why Chang's helmet had been removed. The thought that Donne would treat Chang like some sort of trophy made Anna sick with fury.

She searched the room again frantically, now late for her meeting with Morden. But she found nothing else. Her lips pulled back from her teeth, she crouched down and began to roll the satin rectangle back up. As she reached the top, she saw the finger again, and the ring, and something made her look up at the photograph displayed on the dresser. The father's hand, holding the mother's tight against him. He was wearing a ring, gold and wide, like the one on the finger. It was too small in the photograph to see details, but it looked like it could have been the same ring. She looked back down at the signet ring in the pouch, found it was embossed with the letter D, in a simple,

sans serif typeface that made the letter look almost like
a half-circle. *Donne*. She had killed her own father.

Then Anna remembered the small scar on Donne's
cheek, in the shape of a D. The size of the scar
matched the size of the letter on the ring. She felt
Donne's life laid out before her, the way she sometimes felt on a dig about someone long dead. There
had been an initial hurt, a scar on her face, the buildup
of scar tissue, calluses, the acceptance into a group,
Psi Corps, the new feeling of power, the desire to
exercise that power, to celebrate it, to memorialize it.
Out of the past had been created a monster. If Donne
were long dead, Anna would have felt sorry for her.
But since she wasn't long dead, and might not be dead
at all, Anna felt only fear. This woman loved to kill; it
was her life. Anna took a deep breath and resumed her
work. She tied the delicate turquoise bow, returned the
roll to its place under the pillow. Just in case Donne
was still alive. Just in case she came back.

She left the room unseen, found Morden waiting
outside her quarters. "Sorry I'm late. We better head
down there."

"What's wrong?" Morden asked.

Anna began to walk, and he followed in the narrow
passage. "What do you think happened to Chang?"
she asked.

"Donne killed him."

"Why?"

"I'm not sure," Morden said. "It may have something to do with the egg. He may have confronted her
about her arrangement with Captain Hidalgo. He may
have caught her taking something."

"But what was her plan?"

"If you're asking me, then you must have a pretty
good idea."

She stopped. "I expect better from you."

He nodded. "I don't know. I only have a theory. And it's probably the same one as yours. The only way for her to smuggle artifacts back undetected would be if she eliminated at least the entire science team, possibly some of the crew as well."

"But why would Psi Corps go to such lengths over this?"

Morden tilted his head. "You were there."

"I know. Terrence Hilliard. Donne said he would never recover."

Morden hesitated, as if he expected her to say more, then let out an odd laugh. "I thought you knew. It wasn't just Terrence Hilliard who was caught in that feedback loop. Every telepath with Terrence's rating—P5—or below within a three-mile radius of your lab became a gibbering vegetable. They did a good job of covering it up, but within thirty-six hours we figured out what had happened." His hands clasped in front of him. "You don't even know what you've discovered. You've discovered a bomb that takes out only telepaths. God knows what would have happened if a P12 had set it off."

Anna continued down the corridor, numb. More deaths, or virtual deaths, on her hands. But now Donne's presence made sense. Psi Corps wanted that technology at all costs. It didn't matter whether destroying telepaths was the mouse's real function or an accidental by-product. It could be used for that purpose.

And maybe that *was* its real purpose, Anna thought. This technology seemed to work through some sort of telepathic contact. Telepaths would wield a great deal of power and could, potentially, pose a serious threat. On Theta Omega 2, the planet where they had found the mouse, the J/Lai had revered those among them they called Thoughtseers, who could, according to their writings, make the thoughts of others visible. Perhaps the mouse had been brought there as a weapon.

Razor met them in the hallway and fell in behind. Anna could see from his face that he had bad news, and she didn't want to hear it. "I tried to send your message to the orbiter," he said. "It seems to have gone the way of the egg. It's gone."

Anna continued walking.

"I tried sending the message straight through to Earth, but I doubt it had the strength to make it much past the atmosphere. No way of knowing for sure. Without the orbiter, we're limited to ground information on the weather. Which, by the way, shows the wind intensifying."

"What is it," Anna said, "my birthday?"

The teasing tone returned to Razor's voice. "Well, I was planning to strip for you."

"That would really send me over the edge," Anna said.

They entered the locker room at the end of the crawler bay, and as Anna stripped down to her underwear and pulled on an orange jumpsuit, she realized that she was wasting her time with distractions, with the probe, Donne, Hidalgo. Donne was not responsible for the missing egg. Donne was not responsible for the missing orbiter. Those were beyond her power. The creatures of blackness and stars had been watching, and had been acting, quietly, carefully. As Morden had pointed out, it was often easier to go about one's business quietly. She had to forget the distractions and do her job, study the artifacts left behind, deduce the culture of those who had left them, reconstitute their behavior, recapture their thoughts. Their lives depended on it.

Across from her, Morden zipped up his jumpsuit, tucking his necklace within it.

CHAPTER 14

"**W**E've got Marco," Garibaldi said.

Jeff smiled. "You've got him? You just made my day."

On the Babcom monitor in Jeff's office, Garibaldi's lips twisted to the side. A bad sign, Jeff had learned. "There's just one thing."

"Yes?"

"He was selling stims to the Brakiri high holy priestess at the time—"

"The Ribkiri," a Brakiri standing behind Garibaldi interrupted.

"Right, this Ribkiri, and the whole thing is threatening to turn into a big diplomatic incident."

Jeff smiled again, refusing to let go of the good feelings. "So you caught Marco." If he let every little thing get to him, he wouldn't even make it to the dedication ceremony.

"Did you hear what I said, Jeff?"

"Thank you, Michael. I have every confidence in your abilities to resolve the situation. If you need any help, just let me know. Out."

No sooner had Garibaldi's puzzled face disappeared from the monitor than the Stellarcom terminal informed him he had an incoming communication. It was Dr. LeBlanc. Her smile was a little hard for Jeff's taste.

"Commander Sinclair. I appreciate your coming to me with this situation. I've discovered that there is indeed a mission to the rim. I've spoken to everyone concerned, including the president. We're quite concerned about the source of Ambassador Delenn's information. It's rather discomfiting to know that the Minbari are monitoring our scientific expeditions. Are you sure she didn't give any indication of where she got this information?"

"Positive." He leaned forward. "Doctor, what is the purpose of the expedition?"

"And she gave no indication what this alleged danger was?"

Jeff's good feelings were rapidly dissipating. "Only that it was a threat to all of us. Doctor, can I assume from this that you are going to refuse Ambassador Delenn's request?"

"We cannot set a precedent of letting other races limit our explorations and progress. What kind of position would that put us in? She hasn't even given us any concrete reason to grant her request."

"You don't believe any danger exists, do you?"

LeBlanc ran her index finger out along her jaw. "Frankly, I think there is a danger. To the Minbari. I think we must be on the verge of discovering something so powerful they don't want us to have it. Which is all the more reason to continue with this mission."

Paranoia, self-interest, a hunger for power—and he was supposed to be running a station devoted to peace. "Have you been in touch with the ship? Have they reported any trouble?"

LeBlanc brought her hand back down to the desk. "The ship is temporarily out of contact. But they've

reported nothing out of the ordinary. Please inform
Ambassador Delenn we regret we cannot grant her
request. If she'd like to provide us further information, we'll reconsider. In the meantime, I hope your
plans for the dedication ceremony are progressing
smoothly." With a perfunctory nod she broke contact.

Jeff forced himself to take a deep, calming breath.
It didn't work. He'd known the chances of them granting the request with such little information had been
slim, but it still frustrated him. What if the ambassador
was right and there was a serious danger?

He put through his call to her, dreading the conversation. Though he barely knew her, and he generally
felt uncomfortable around Minbari, for some reason he
hated to disappoint her. He also worried about how she
and the Minbari government would react. This had
seemed very important to them.

The call was routed to her ship, where she sat in an
office similar in its austerity to her office on Minbar,
but much smaller. The harsh planes of her face were
exaggerated in the bright light.

"Ambassador Delenn. I regret to inform you that
the Earth Alliance cannot grant your request. There is
an Earth science vessel investigating the world you
specified, but without hard information clarifying the
threat, we feel it is premature to abort the mission."

She shook her head. "This is very bad news, Commander."

"Is there any further information you can give us
about the danger?"

Her red lips, the only spot of color on her face,
tightened. "I have told you all I can. Has your government contacted the ship? Have they—landed on the
planet?"

There was something in the way she said it—as if

the very idea was abhorrent to her. "I was informed that the ship is temporarily out of contact."

The red lips fell open in a crooked shape. "It is too late then."

"Too late for what? Ambassador, what is on Alpha Omega 3?"

Her mouth closed, and her head tilted back, restoring the sense of aloofness he so often got from her. "The Minbari government is displeased with your government's lack of action, Commander. We serve you fair warning. If any additional Earth ships are sent to Alpha Omega 3, we will consider it an act of war and make immediate retaliation." She terminated the communication.

Jeff began to knead the back of his neck. *Great,* he thought. *Babylon 5 hasn't even been dedicated yet, and we might already have another war on our hands.*

"We found Spano," Corchoran reported over the link.

John's eyes narrowed. "Good. Bring him to me in the weapons bay." After Ross had left for the laser tube, John had ordered Corchoran to question the other weapons officers, who were assembled in the mess. But when Corchoran had arrived there, he'd reported that only Timmons and Watley were present. Spano was missing.

John had suspected that Spano was responsible for the sabotage ever since Ross had confirmed that one of the weapons officers must be involved. Spano's disappearance had reinforced those suspicions. John regretted not bringing him up on charges earlier, not getting him off the ship before they were deployed. Now the mission was in jeopardy.

John was sitting at the weapons diagnostic system,

waiting to hear from Ross. He pressed his link.
"Ross."

"Ross here."

"Have you reached the optics yet? I need that estimate."

"I'm opening the tube hatch now, Captain. Stand by."

John tapped his hand on the console. The laser tube ran down the center of the ship, where there was no gravity and no oxygen. Any activity was time-consuming. Ross was moving quickly, John knew, though every minute that passed brought the cruiser and its load of explosives closer to the jump gate and Babylon 5.

Corchoran came in, Spano behind him held by two guards.

John stood. "Where did you find him?"

"I was in the gym," Spano yelled, pulling against the guards. "This is ridiculous. Ross orders us out during a battle alert and tells us to wait in the mess. I got sick of waiting. Don't you think this is a little extreme?" The tense muscles in his neck stood out.

John pulled a chair out into the center of the room. "Sit down, Spano. And wait until I ask you a question."

John stepped aside with Corchoran. "We found him near the gym," Corchoran said. "He claimed he'd left the mess after a few minutes and that he'd been working out since then. He resisted coming with us."

John nodded. "What about Timmons and Watley?" Watley's transfer hadn't come through yet. She was another wild card.

Corchoran's face was grim. "I've questioned them both, Captain. They both have periods of time when they were alone in the last sixteen hours, but the times they claim to have been with others have checked out.

They both claim to have no involvement in the sabotage. I believe them.''

"We need to gather more information. I want all the gunners questioned, particularly the ones who were on duty for the last sixteen hours. Check the ship's logs and see if they provide any evidence. I want to know who's used an EVA suit recently. Have the quarters of all four weapons officers searched. And check the crew records for anyone else with a weapons background.''

"Yes, sir. Captain''—Corchoran hesitated—"do you think we should try to call in reinforcements?''

John had been considering this already. They were isolated in this sector, which is why the Homeguard had chosen it. There were Earthforce ships at Babylon 5, but the trip through hyperspace took twelve hours. The cruiser would already be in hyperspace by the time the reinforcements came out of the Carutic jump gate. And destroying the cruiser with its nuclear explosives at the other end of the jump, when it would be so close to Babylon 5, would probably destroy the station. "I think it's unlikely in the extreme that another Earthforce ship is in range. But let's ascertain the extent of the damage first, before we make any decisions. I don't want to break radio silence unless we absolutely have to.''

"Yes, sir.''

As John approached Spano, Ross's voice came through the link. "Captain, we have a problem.''

John turned away. "Go ahead.''

"Not only has the primary mirror been destroyed, but it's been fused to the tube itself. I'm going to have to cut it out and then replace the mirror and a section of the tube.''

John shook his head. He'd never heard of a section

of the tube needing to be replaced. The entire interior surface of the tube was also mirrored. Replacing any section of it and restoring its reflective integrity would be a lengthy, demanding job. "How long is that going to take?"

"I've never done this exact thing before, Captain. I know I can do it, but I'm not sure what snags I might run into along the way. I'll need two gunners to assist me. And it would really help if I could have another weapons officer."

"How about Timmons?"

"I would feel comfortable with that, Captain."

"How long, Ross?"

"My estimate would be about seven hours, sir. Give or take one or two hours."

"That give or take puts us right into the red zone, Lieutenant."

"I'm sorry, sir. I'll do my best."

"Get on it. And let me know if there's anything else you need." John made the decision at that moment not to call for reinforcements. Chances were that no other ship was within range, and if they broke radio silence and revealed their presence, the cruiser would accelerate to maximum speed, giving them even less time to make repairs.

John linked out and faced Spano. He sat slouched in the chair, clenched fists on his thighs, flat eyes carrying a hint of fear.

"Did you sabotage the weapons system?"

"What?"

"Did you sabotage the weapons system?"

"I have no idea what you're talking about. I was called down here for the battle alert. I was ordered away. I went to the gym."

"You were on watch before Ross today. I want you

to tell me exactly what happened. Were you alone at any time in the weapons bay?"

"I'm alone a lot of the time in the weapons bay. You know that. I sent the gunners out to do a maintenance check on the aft port cannon. That's what was scheduled by your new best friend, Lieutenant Ross. He's been scheduling lots of activities to keep us busy. You know you've ruined a perfectly good officer."

John narrowed his eyes. "Did you do any maintenance on the weapons diagnostic system?"

"No, that wasn't on my schedule."

"Did you do a general inspection when you came on shift?"

Spano shrugged. "I looked things over like I always do."

John thrust the bridge at him. "Do you know what this is?"

Spano looked at it, and his face grew curious. He held out his hand, and John gave the bridge to him. "It's an electronic component, probably from the diagnostic system. It looks like a bridge. Where did this come from?"

"From just where you said. Ross found it on the floor when he came on duty. Any idea how it got there?"

Spano handed it back and regarded him with his opaque, flat eyes. "No."

"A few weeks ago, you seemed pretty eager for a war. You wanted to be a war hero. How much do you want it, Spano? Enough to kill a quarter of a million people?"

"What are you talking about? How can I kill anyone if the laser is inoperative?"

John clenched his jaw. Spano had a short fuse. The way to get him to confess was to light it. He began to pace in a circle around Spano's chair. "This is not a drill, Spano. We are tracking a terrorist Homeguard ship filled with nuclear explosives. If we don't stop it in the next eight hours, it will proceed to Babylon 5, where it will make a suicide run on the station and kill hundreds of thousands of humans and aliens. Some weapons expert aboard this ship has sabotaged our laser system, leaving us unarmed. I think about why someone would want to do that. Maybe they hate aliens. Maybe they don't like the idea of us living in peace with them. Maybe they wish we'd go back to war. And on all counts, Spano, you come up first on my list."

Spano was sitting up straight now, his head turning to follow John's course.

"But then I think of what a cowardly act this is. Sneaking around the ship, damaging systems. And in the aid of an even more cowardly act, the peacetime bombing of innocent civilians. And I remember that you thought mines were cowardly, and I think, how could Spano possibly be involved in something so low?"

"Captain, I'm not! I swear I didn't do anything." Spano was nervous now.

"And then to deny it."

"But I didn't do anything."

John turned on him and began to yell. "You want to convince me you're not responsible? Then give me information to help figure out who is. Because right now you're looking like the only game in town. And that means you better enjoy being spaced."

Spano held out his hands. "I don't know anything. I worked my shift, I went to bed, and I woke up when the battle alert sounded."

"You're not helping, Lieutenant. The sabotage

probably occurred during your watch. If you didn't do it, then who did?''

Spano's nostrils were flaring, but this time in fear rather than anger. ''I—I did leave for a few minutes during my shift. I know I'm not supposed to, but while the gunners were on their way back from the maintenance on the cannon, I went down to the mess and had a drink.''

''How long were you there?''

''Maybe ten or fifteen minutes.''

''Did anyone see you?''

''No. No one was there. I just helped myself.''

''A lovely story.''

''It's true, sir. That must have been when it happened.''

''Are these trips to the mess a regular habit of yours, Lieutenant?''

''I go about once a shift.''

''You didn't happen to see anyone go in or out of the weapons bay while you were on your travels?''

''No. Sir, you can't blame me for this. I didn't even know about these terrorists.''

John felt his face go red, and he stabbed a finger at Spano. ''Yes, I can blame you, and I will blame you. Even if you didn't sabotage the laser, your failure to run an inspection when coming on duty and going off duty prevented the problem from being discovered for hours, and makes it harder now for us to pin down when it happened. Your abandonment of your post may have allowed the sabotage to occur. And your disobedience of Ross's orders to stay in the mess has caused us to waste valuable time looking for you. You *are* responsible. You think your bad attitude and disregard of procedure has no consequences? Well how about these consequences—you kill two hundred fifty

thousand people.'' The thought of those people dying
terrified John. The thought that he would be responsible if they did. ''You want to know what a hero is? A
hero is someone who does what's right, even if he
doesn't think it will make a difference. Because it's the
right thing to do.''

He had run out of words. He couldn't tell if Spano
was responsible or not. The truth was, he sensed that
Spano was telling the truth. And if he was, then the
saboteur was still walking freely on the ship. John
crossed his arms, feeling more alone than he had since
the war. ''You're being charged with insubordination,
desertion of post, and dereliction of duty. Other
charges may follow.'' John turned to the two guards.
''Take him to the brig.''

The scanners, once again, were of little use inside the
cave. They identified the energy source that had been
detected as some sort of plasma energy, but it seemed
to be coming from all directions. The reflective effect,
again. Anna led her team down into the darkness of the
cave, to the spot where it separated into three
branches. Even with the thirty techs, each with their
own light, and the string of floodlights from their first
trip, the darkness of the cave seemed to envelop them,
a watchful presence that could absorb any amount of
light.

Anna scratched uneasily at the back of her neck.
Dust and sand had gotten under the collar of her jumpsuit on the walk from the crawler to the cave. In her
jumpsuit and boots and the breather, a clear oxygen
mask that fit down over the front of her face, she usually felt quite comfortable, much more so than in the
confines of an EVA suit. But now they left her feeling
exposed to the darkness. The cool stillness prickled

along the backs of her hands, the back of her neck, her
scalp. The jumpsuit felt a flimsy, inadequate protection
against the sharp-etched stone of the cave and the creatures who lived within it. The great, vaulted darkness
conjured up awe, but it was no longer the awe of rev-
erence; it was the awe of fear. She'd never felt an
unease like this before. She wished she'd worn an
EVA suit.

She'd determined in the trip over in the crawler to
confront the creature in the nodule. Try to communicate with it, threaten it, kill it if necessary. Morden
had the PPG, and she had her favorite digging tools. It
had all seemed very logical in the crawler. Now the
thought of facing its malice and hunger again made her
want to run back into the open air.

She ordered her team to split, fifteen techs down the
left passage, fifteen down the center, her and Morden
alone to the right, down the passage where they'd
found the nodule. The techs found this division a little
strange, she could tell as she gave the orders, but they
obeyed, each group starting a new series of lights into
the darkness. She felt bad sending the techs off with
such little knowledge of what they might face. But then
what did she know about what they would face?

She and Morden started down the narrower passage, following the trail of dim blue lights. Morden
was carrying a full bag of floodlights and a scanner
that he checked periodically. He'd left his shiny digging tools behind. After all, they were here to search
for missing crewmen, not excavate. Anna turned off
her link, using the remote control adhered to the back
of her hand. The listening and speaking mechanisms of
the link were built into the breathers. But with the link
off, she and Morden could both communicate merely
by speaking, their voices transmitted through the

screens of the breathers. If the others needed her, they would link in.

"You seem to have a plan." His voice, through the screen of the breather, was smooth.

"Not really. I'm going to try to communicate with that creature. It knows where the others are. We could search these caverns for days without finding them. If it won't cooperate willingly, maybe we can threaten it. And if that doesn't work, we'll try to kill it."

"You don't believe in the indirect approach, do you?"

"We don't have time. And unless we can locate that energy source, I have no other ideas. You don't have a better idea, do you?"

"Calling in a squad of GROPOS would be nice."

They approached the desiccated corpse they'd found before, and as Morden ran a scan of the area, Anna paused beside it, thinking of the living creature trapped within the biomechanical shell. For this race, inferior creatures were simply biological components to be inserted into their biomechanical tools. Anna wondered what purpose the living creatures served. Did their brains serve as some sort of processing center? Or were they somehow utilized as an energy source? A circulatory center?

Whatever their purpose, it seemed that bigger or more complex tools would require bigger or more complex biological components. She'd seen only small tools so far, nothing like the spaceship Morden had described.

They continued farther down into the cave, forced once again to crouch as the walls closed around them. As they reached the end of the lights, they slowed as Morden installed new ones at regular intervals. The darkness felt close and thick around them, as if they were the only ones in this place, and this place was the only place in the world. Her sense of uneasiness grew as they approached the location of the nodule. She hit her link. "Group one report." She waited, the link silent. Of course they'd drifted too far away from each other. As she'd discovered before, their links couldn't work through more than thirty-six feet of rock. "Group two report." No answer. She and Morden were totally isolated from the others. If anything happened to the techs, she wouldn't know. And if anything happened to her and Morden, the techs wouldn't know. The techs could send a runner, of course, but only if they were able.

Anna swept her light ahead. She couldn't see the nodule. They continued farther, the floor sloping down, down. Then the cave started to widen again, the ceiling rising to the point where they could straighten up. They had passed the location of the nodule. It had been at the narrowest point in the cave. And now it was gone. Her breath hitched in relief.

"I've got a clear reading on the energy source." Morden came over to show her on the scanner. "It's just ahead."

They moved forward, their flashlights sweeping the ground before them. Anna's flashed over something, and she slowed, bringing the beam back onto it. Morden's beam joined it. It was a piece of machinery, human in origin, a metal box about two feet by two feet that was emitting a low hum. They crouched down over it, the darkness closing around them.

"This looks like a plaser generator," Morden said. "I think it might be from the probe." His tone had an odd quality she couldn't name.

"The probe couldn't have gotten this far. The

safety lock wouldn't permit it. Besides, where's the rest of it?'' She cast her light across the cave floor.

''I don't know,'' Morden said, standing.

Anna remained crouched beside the generator. She realized that the cave floor here was smoother. There were no large rocks in the way and most of the fragments were gone as well, leaving large slabs of stone visible. As she ran her light across the ceiling, she saw that it was smoother than it had been up to that point and more of a uniform height. No headache stones here. Someone had cleared them away. ''That nodule was here before to block our way,'' she said. ''They didn't want us to get any farther. On this side I see definite evidence of improvement to the cave.''

''If there is a living society on this planet, it's most likely underground,'' Morden said, ''where our scanners haven't been able to read.''

Perhaps it was the stillness, the darkness that focused her thoughts. Or perhaps it was her decision to block out the human distractions and focus on the culture they had encountered. But connections were becoming obvious to her. Either they had moved underground during the war, or they had always lived underground and the structures on the surface had been a diversion. The cave entries were kept natural to disguise their presence. This was a secretive race, a race who worked through diversion, misdirection. ''I think they knew we were coming. Could they have found the beacon on board their ship?''

''Why do you think they knew?''

''It's all too neat. They live underground, where our scanners can't detect them and our probe can't go. Above ground, all we find is ruins . . . and one astonishing, living artifact. An artifact that promises 'all that is desired.' And everyone who goes to investigate that artifact disappears.''

"Given my choice I would have gone there, instead of the caves."

"Maybe they thought they would catch us all that way. With that bait. They didn't expect us in the caves. When we came in, they blocked our way."

"And now the nodule is gone. Does that mean they're ready for us?"

"Yes, it does." She stood. "They provide an intriguing energy source to draw us in. And here we are. But what I can't figure out is why they would want to hide from us and then attack us. They don't even know us. You were there on Mars. Did something happen that you didn't tell me? What was one of their ships doing on Mars anyway? It suggests they've had some connection with humans in the past."

As she talked, a strange change came over Morden's face. The muscles went slack, his carefully composed expression melting away. He reached into the pocket of his jumpsuit, and as she realized he was going to pull out the PPG, she remembered his encounter with this race on Mars, his shiny tools, his smooth palms, Chang's warning to her, and Donne's, and his statement, almost a warning in itself: *I find I'm much more effective if I go about my job quietly.*

As the PPG came clear of the pocket and began to rise, she shoved him, hard. The gun went off with a reverberating blast. She lost her balance, heard rocks falling, and then a flash and she hit the cave floor. She covered her head with her arms and tucked her body into a ball. She'd been in rockfalls several times before, all minor, so she'd always thought Chang had been joking when he'd described the cave-in at Almover: *it was like being an ant in the center of the*

bowling pins when God hits a strike. But that was exactly what it felt like. The world collapsed around her,
huge rocks clashing and crashing in a great cascade
like thunder. One rock slammed into her legs, another
into her back, the heavy gravity increasing the impact.
The ground shook as if she were in the middle of an
earthquake. Her arms squeezed desperately around her
head. From the thunder, the rockfall seemed to be concentrated a few yards up the passage, where Morden's
PPG must have hit. Two great slabs of rock shattered
against the cave floor, and then the rumbling trailed off
into silence.

She forced herself to remain in a ball for the count
of thirty, while unstable rocks dropped haphazardly
from their unlikely resting places. Then she straightened, her body throbbing. She was in total blackness.
The floodlight farther up the passage had either been
knocked out or blocked by the cave-in. She groped for
her light, forcing herself to ignore the sound of the
rocks settling. Her hand closed around the familiar
shape. She turned it on, and a dim light illuminated the
cave floor. She shone it toward where Morden had
been standing.

He looked as if he had been picked up and thrown at
the cave wall. He was twisted up against it on his side,
the orange jumpsuit over his chest fluttering with
quick, shallow breaths. On the right arm of his suit
was an odd, dark shadow. She thought at first that a
rock was somehow balanced on it, but as she looked
at its edges she realized that it was a burn. His right
hand still gripped the PPG. Another cascade of rocks
sounded behind her, and with his left hand Morden
pulled the PPG out of his clenched fingers.

A light shone off the mask of his breather, and
Anna followed the beam back behind her, farther

down the passage than they had gone. Her link chimed as someone linked in.

"He destroyed the probe." Donne's voice ran like poison into her ear. "Did your good friend tell you that?"

CHAPTER 15

JOHN was in his office, reviewing all the ship's logs for the sixteen hours during which the sabotage had occurred, as well as interrogation transcripts and investigation reports. So far he hadn't found anything helpful, and he was about ready to throw these down, climb into an EVA suit and try to help Ross. Time was running out. It was almost twenty-three hundred. They had only three hours until the cruiser reached the jump gate. Ross's estimate had him finishing an hour before then, if all went well, but what if he didn't finish in time? The starfuries didn't have enough power to take out a cruiser, not one that was fighting back, anyway. Without backup from the *Agamemnon*, it would be a slaughter.

John's link chimed, and a surge of nervous adrenaline shot through him. "Sheridan. Go."

"Captain." It was Ross. "I'm afraid we've run into a major snag. The damage to the laser tube is much more extensive than I thought. It's very subtle. I didn't spot it until we removed the section around the primary mirror. We're going to have to remove a much larger section. Then the whole thing is going to need to be realigned."

"How long?"

"I need more help, Captain. This is delicate work. The gunners aren't qualified for it."

He hated to put either Watley or Spano out there. If either of them was involved in the sabotage, the laser system would never get fixed in time, and they might pose a danger to Ross and the other crewmen. "How long if you don't get more help?"

"Nine more hours, sir. I'm sorry."

"How long if I send you just Watley?"

"Maybe six hours."

John's jaw clenched. "And how long if I send you Watley and Spano?"

"Maybe three hours."

So there it was. The only chance of repairing the ship in time was to trust the two people who had most likely sabotaged it. "I'll get back to you, Ross. Keep on it."

"Yes, sir."

John tapped the desktop. His instinct told him that neither Watley nor Spano was responsible for the sabotage. Yet logic insisted otherwise. No evidence implicated any of the four weapons officers, but if they were the only ones qualified . . . John searched through the reports for the information he'd requested, of any other crew on board with weapons training.

His link chimed. "Sheridan. Go."

"Captain, Lieutenant Spano is asking to speak to you."

If it wasn't one thing, it was two things. John spread the reports out over his desk. "Did he say what he wanted?"

"He said he had some information, sir."

"Put him on." He couldn't find the report. He started going through the entire pile again.

"Captain, I've been thinking about what you said,

and about some things Lieutenant Ross has said to me.'' The voice didn't sound like Spano's. The word *Captain* had even been spoken with respect. A stay in the brig with the threat of a court-martial did wonders. Or else he was putting on a good act. ''You're right. My negligence has endangered this ship and this mission. I'd like to help, Captain. You asked me for information, and I think I've come up with something.''

John got to the bottom of the pile and still hadn't found the report. ''Cut to the chase, Lieutenant. We don't have much time.''

''I wondered if you had considered officers who had previously served in the weapons section.''

John put the pile of reports down, the information he was looking for missing. His mind began to make connections. ''Was there someone specific you had in mind, Lieutenant?''

There was silence from the other end of the link.

''Commander Corchoran was a weapons officer very early in his career, Captain.''

John had a vague recollection of reading that in Corchoran's file, though the service had been so far back in Corchoran's career that John had forgotten it. The information he had requested from Corchoran about crew members with weapons training was missing—information that would have implicated Corchoran. ''Thank you, Lieutenant.''

He broke the link and activated it once again. ''Commander Corchoran.''

Corchoran's voice replied almost instantly. ''Corchoran here.''

''Commander, I'm missing that report on other crew members who have had weapons training in their past,'' John said.

''It was in with those other reports I gave you, sir.''

"Well it's not here now. Can you get another copy down to me in my office immediately?"

"Yes, sir."

John linked out, checked the time. He went through the pile of reports again, checked the floor under his desk. Spano might just be trying to divert suspicion from himself. He might still be the saboteur. John could send Corchoran out to help Ross instead. Corchoran's performance had been quite competent since John had taken command.

But now instinct and logic were telling him the same thing. Corchoran had been constantly available, attentive, cooperative. But he had been little actual help with the discipline problems on the ship. John had been forced to take on duties that should have fallen to Corchoran. And then there was Corchoran's uncharacteristic violation of procedure, routing Anna's call to him during a battle alert, in front of the general. It was a small thing, but it suddenly seemed significant. Perhaps, for some reason, Corchoran wanted him to fail. And the destruction of Babylon 5 would be a spectacular failure.

John had been thinking that the saboteur was motivated by sympathies to the Homeguard. But perhaps the motivation was more personal, more direct. Corchoran had not been promoted in four years. As a commander under Captain Best, he'd been trapped in a dead-end job. Perhaps, when Best had been "promoted," Corchoran had expected to receive command of the *Agamemnon* himself. And instead he'd been given a new captain.

John's mind returned to Best's "promotion" and what little he knew about it. Best had made a serious error. Procedure dictated that all ports be confirmed closed before opening a jump point. Best had failed to do that, and through his negligence had endangered his ship and crew. But checking ports was a precautionary measure, as many procedures were. No port should have been left open in the first place. John had assumed, with good reason, that the engine port had been left open through incompetence or carelessness on the part of Best's crew. But what if it had been left open on purpose, by someone who knew that Best would not check before opening a jump point? The gamble would have been risky, but perhaps not unacceptable for someone desperate enough to take chances. John had heard of a handful of other such jump point misfires, and while they could generate dangerous displacement effects and do serious damage to a ship, none had ever destroyed one. The error would be showy enough that it couldn't be ignored, but most likely not fatal.

He gave Corchoran five minutes, ten. The report did not come.

John linked down to the brig. "I want you to release Lieutenant Spano immediately. Tell him to get into an EVA suit and get out to the laser tube with Lieutenant Watley on the double. Then I want you to find and detain Commander Corchoran. Make that your top priority."

"Yes, sir."

John rested his forearms on his knees and tapped his hands together. He felt like he'd made the right decision. But if he was wrong, they would be unable to stop the Homeguard cruiser and Babylon 5 would be destroyed, and all those on-station would be killed.

Anna stood and caught Donne in her light, the EVA suit a brilliant white against the darkness. Donne's movements seemed shaky as she climbed over the irregularly shaped rocks scattered across the cave floor. In her right hand, the metal reflecting the light, was a PPG, aimed at Morden. Anna looked back down at him, still caught in Donne's light, his gun wavering now, but clearly aimed at Donne. On his right arm was a PPG burn. Skin and blood, muscle and tendon had all been fused into a black mass. Morden hadn't been aiming at her. He'd been trying to defend them from Donne.

"He hid the two artifacts you found, the mice," Donne said. "Luckily I found them." Her tone was low, tight. Anna could hear the tension in her jaw.

Morden's careful smile was slipping as he looked up at Anna. "I knew that if Donne had her way, Earthforce wouldn't see a single artifact from this dig. I had to try to protect our interests." Donne's activation of the link gave his voice an odd doubled quality. Anna heard it not only over the link but through the screen of his breather.

"You mundanes would love to have a weapon against us telepaths," Donne said.

"It's more than that. A lot more than that." Morden was resting the butt of the PPG against the cave floor now. He shook his head, as if to stay conscious.

"What happened to Dr. Chang and his party?" Anna moved in front of Morden's chest, careful not to block his aim.

"I know where they are. Tell Morden to put his gun down first. He's making me nervous."

"Why don't you both put your guns away," Anna said.

Donne stopped about four feet away, her face obscured behind the reflection off her faceplate. "Let Morden put his gun down first."

Anna wondered if Donne had already decided what
body parts to keep after she had killed them. She
crouched down in front of Morden, his hand with the
PPG extending to her left. She kept her eyes on
Donne, on the clenched face, the narrowed eyes. She
almost looked afraid, though the thought was ridiculous. How could two archaeologists possibly scare a
trained assassin? Unless something else had scared
her.

Anna reached down with her left hand, found
Morden's hand beneath hers. She squeezed it. He had
to trust her. She'd distrusted him in a critical moment,
and he'd been shot. If only she'd trusted him, Donne
would probably be dead now.

His hand opened, and she reached into his smooth
palm and scooped out the gun. She brought it up in
front of her, keeping it aimed at Donne. "Okay, now
put your gun away."

"This isn't what I had in mind."

"You don't think I'm going to shoot you."

"You seem to have your loyalties reversed. He's
the one who destroyed your probe. Do you want to see
its pitiful remains? It's on the other side of the outcropping."

Anna felt time slipping away. Morden was injured.
They only had a few short hours to find the rest of
Chang's party. She couldn't even tell in the dark
whether they were trapped or not. And in the darkness
the watchers were watching. "This is what we're going to do. At the count of three we're both going to put
these PPGs into our pockets. Then we're going to
search for a way out; Morden needs help. And while
we look, you're going to tell me what happened to Dr.
Chang and his party."

Donne nodded.

"One." Anna brought the PPG next to her jumpsuit pocket, and Donne did the same. "Two." Anna tucked the tip of it into the cloth. "Three." Anna slid the gun into her pocket as Donne did the same. They both brought their hands away. "Good. Now let's go up the passage and see if we can find a way out of here."

Donne picked her way farther up the passage, toward the center of the rockfall, and Anna knelt beside Morden. "How are you?"

"I'm sorry about the probe." Behind the glare of the breather, his face was pale and shiny. "I didn't have a choice."

"I'm sorry I distrusted you. If I hadn't shoved you, you wouldn't have gotten shot."

He smiled as he braced himself against her arm, pushing himself up. "If you hadn't shoved me, I think she would have killed me."

She helped him to sit, his body settling into a lop-sided position.

"I'll be okay," he said. "This isn't a fatal wound, as much as it feels like it. Just let me catch my breath."

Anna nodded. "Stay here."

She took Morden's scanner, located Donne with her light, and worked her way over. Her legs ached, from the rock that had hit them and from exhaustion. "The scanner shows about a five-foot barrier of rock between us and daylight. Do you see any openings?"

Donne had climbed to the cave ceiling and was shining her light along the rocks. "It's hard to tell, since it's dark on the other side. But I don't see anything."

Anna narrowed the focus of the scanner and examined the barrier of rock blocking them in, wishing

she could trust the readout more. Donne was right. It
would be difficult to visually spot an opening. And so
far the scanner wasn't offering any hope. Anna
climbed along the barrier, scanning, shining her light
into crevices. The rocks were huge, sharp, irregular.
Too heavy to move. And even if they were able to
move a few of them, it could cause another rockfall.
The whole area was unstable. "Do you know another
way out?"

"I came in through an opening on the other side of
the outcropping, near where I found the probe. I'd
been heading for your site, but I got lost in the storm.
The passage eventually led me here, where I saw the
floodlights you'd set up. No one was here, and I
couldn't reach anyone by link. I set up the plaser generator, hoping the signal was strong enough to get
through."

It was a good story, except that it didn't explain
why she'd brought the generator into the caves in the
first place, or why she'd set it up far inside the caves,
beyond the line of floodlights. That seemed more like
an ambush than an SOS. "This way looks totally
blocked. Can you find your way back?"

"Yes. That's the way the others are. It will lead us
out on the other side of the outcropping, though. It's a
long walk. Maybe you want to leave Morden here. We
can come back on the other side with some heavy
equipment and dig him out."

Donne definitely didn't trust Morden. Perhaps that
had been the whole reason for the ambush: to kill
him—or to kill all of them. Perhaps the others were
already dead. Anna couldn't figure out why Donne
hadn't killed her yet. She had no illusions that Donne
was afraid of her quick draw. Donne must need her for
something. Perhaps to help her with the thing she was

really afraid of, the thing Anna was afraid of too. "We're not leaving Morden."

As they climbed over toward him, Morden pushed himself to his feet, using the cave wall for support. "I'm feeling better."

Anna searched for his light, found it and the bag of floodlights crushed flat under a slab of rock.

Anna linked off for a moment, turning her face away from Donne. Morden did the same.

"Can you walk?" Anna asked.

"For now."

"I can help you."

"Watch Donne. She wants you for something, but eventually she will try to kill you." Morden's voice was smooth, his features, though pale and sheened with sweat, relaxed. It was as though the worse things got, the more hopeless they seemed, the more he felt at peace.

"We'll get out of this," she said.

He turned back to Donne.

Anna linked back in. "Lead the way, Ms. Donne."

Morden needed her help at first, to get over the rocks from the cave-in, then, as the way became clearer, he slid his hand from hers, moving with a cautious, controlled gait to the other side of the passage. He was creating two separate targets for Donne.

Ahead of them, Donne paused to pick up something. It was an isocase; it looked like one taken from the probe. She continued down the passage.

"Are those the mice?" Anna asked.

"Yes. I found this hidden on the side of the outcropping." Donne seemed to have recovered from her earlier shakiness. Her stride was confident, strong as she led them deeper and deeper underground. The cave floor here had been artificially polished, and the ceiling was a smooth, uniform eight feet high. If the caves were still inhabited, they were getting closer to the site.

"You shot Dr. Chang, didn't you?"

"Yes." Donne didn't even bother to turn to face them. She was sure Anna wouldn't shoot her. Anna and Morden needed her to guide them out. "When I first saw the images of the egg, I felt drawn toward it. At first I thought I was just interested in it because it was the most promising find. But when you took the probe to the cave and I objected, and you told me I'd lost it, I realized the egg had some sort of attractive power. As a telepath, I was the most sensitive to the attraction. I don't know how it worked, over all that distance, through a recording. I thought there might be a subliminal message or signal, and I examined the recording for one, but there was nothing I could find. I've never heard of anything like it. But once I was aware of it, I was able to block it out.

"When we landed on the planet, I think the rest of you started feeling the attraction as well, though it was subtle. Close up, though, the attraction was much stronger. As soon as we got to the site, everyone went to the egg, even though they'd been assigned different duties."

"Wait a second," Anna said, and Donne turned back with impatience. "You said you discovered the attraction that day I took the probe into the cave, and that you were able to block it. That was almost three weeks ago. You've done nothing but question us about that damned egg and talk about how important and fascinating it is for the last three weeks."

"I needed to know what kind of power it had that could draw me to it from so far away. Once Morden translated the writing on it, I realized it was a trap of some kind, designed to draw us in. I had to find out how it worked.''

"So you encouraged Chang's party to study it.''

Donne shrugged and resumed walking. "They really didn't need any encouragement. The attraction was so strong at that point, even I couldn't look away from it.'' Her voice slowed. "It was a translucent milky white. The letters on its surface formed a grayish pattern that shifted when you weren't looking. It was riddled with hollows, curves, holes, tunnels. They seemed to invite habitation, and I remember thinking of a Venus flytrap. The sense of malice was clear, to me at least, at the same time as the attraction.

"Churlstein climbed onto it first. Churlstein, who looked like a snowman in his EVA suit and could barely scrape one thigh past the other. He'd somehow managed to climb up onto the thing, using the indentations and twists as footholds. He acted like he was king of the mountain. When Chang asked him what he was doing up there, he said he was going to record some of the inscriptions for Morden. Everyone seemed to like that excuse, and they all got close to it, some climbing into the holes and indentations, following the inscriptions with their scanners into the interior.''

Anna walked faster to catch up to Donne. Within the EVA suit, Donne's face was a shadowed profile.

"I'm not sure when it started happening, but I realized that the internal shape of the egg had changed, that a large opening that had been on its front had closed over, and that Scott, who had been in that opening, was gone. One of the tech's voices, over the link, trailed off in a sigh. It took me a few minutes before I could actually catch the egg changing, and then I saw it. It was like a trick of the light, like catching a reflection off of something you hadn't known was there, like a pane of glass, and the reflection shines the light back at you, turning something from clear to white. Except that instead of turning clear again, the white stays, as if it has always been that way. Petrovich was gone. Chang must have seen it too, because he stumbled a few steps back and started yelling at everyone to get away from the egg. And then the whole thing seemed to—ripple, like the hot air makes things in the dessert ripple, and the egg was solid. It was like the Trojan Horse, but in reverse. They were all gone except for Chang, who had taken a few steps away. He seemed . . . stunned. He turned toward me, and then the reflection thing happened again, and the egg was around Chang's foot. His whole body seemed to relax, and I heard him sigh, like the tech had sighed. When he started to turn back to the egg I shot him. I'm not sure when I drew my gun but it was in my hand. . . . I wanted to see what would happen. When he fell, the egg released him. Apparently it has no interest in the dead.''

Anna swallowed the tightness in her throat, running her hand over the pocket with the PPG. Why couldn't Donne have tried to save Chang? Perhaps, with her telepathic abilities, she could have stopped the egg somehow. "You shot Dr. Chang out of curiosity.''

Donne glanced toward her. "Would you rather I said I shot him out of love?'' Her eyes narrowed. "The egg was quiet for a few minutes, still radiating attraction, and I didn't move. I think in blocking the attraction I had blocked its perception of me. Anyway, it didn't come after me. It started to ripple again, and after a few minutes it seemed to be getting smaller. I didn't realize what was happening until it was almost gone. It had changed shape again and it was oozing down into a crack in the ground.

"I didn't move for a few minutes after that. I could still sense the attraction of that thing as it moved underground." Donne stopped, looking from Anna to Morden, and her voice lowered. "There's something else I haven't told you. Since we landed, I've sensed something. Some things. Below the surface. Moving. Watching. I didn't know what they were, except that telepathically, they registered almost as negative presences, almost like holes opening up in my mind. And cold. The sensation has caused me considerable discomfort, though I've been able to partially block it. Down here, though, it's much stronger."

"You've known this the entire time and didn't tell us?" Anna said. "Would it have killed you to share information? You were planning to kill us all anyway. What difference would it have made?"

Donne's face clenched. "I needed to see what they were going to do. I needed to see what their plans were. This technology, and this race, pose the single largest threat that telepaths have ever had to face."

"And if we all get killed in the meantime, that just makes your job easier."

"I'd prefer that you destroy them, frankly."

Anna ran her hands up under her hair, dug her fingers into her scalp. "We're archaeologists, for God's sake!" She paced off, caught Morden's exhausted gaze, paced back. "You sensed the egg underground. Then what?"

"I wasn't thinking too clearly, but I realized it might be necessary to leave the planet sooner than planned. I wanted those mice, at least, for Psi Corps to study. I knew Morden had hidden them and figured he'd sent the probe off a cliff. From studying the terrain earlier, I had a good idea of where he'd done it. I was right. By then, the storm was so bad I didn't think

I could make it around the outcropping to find you. I decided to go through the caves. That's how I found the others. And the rest you know.''

Anna began to walk again. "When you say you found the others," Anna said, "you mean you found the egg?''

"No. They're not in the egg anymore. Quiet. Turn out your light.''

Anna turned off her flashlight and noticed that there was a low level of light in the cave now. Morden was cradling his arm, his boots occasionally scuffing against the polished floor. As they continued around a curve the light increased. Donne motioned them over to the side of the passage and had them crouch. As Anna did, she realized she'd lost her tool belt. It must have come off in the cave-in, and she'd been so shaken up she hadn't noticed. She felt naked without it.

Donne led them a few feet forward. A large, lighted opening was ahead. It was not the outdoors; the light was too diffused, the air too still for that. Besides, she could hear a sound echoing in the large space. It took her a moment to identify, because the sound seemed so out of place here, on a planet on the rim, in the depths of the caves of an alien race with a technology thousands of years ahead of theirs. It was the whirring of a drill.

CHAPTER 16

"TIME until cruiser reaches jump gate," John requested from his command chair.

"Twenty minutes," Lieutenant Commander Ving replied.

Twenty minutes. The weapons were still off-line, and Corchoran continued to elude security. He did know the ship well. John had considered bluffing the cruiser, saying he would destroy them if they didn't stop, but he didn't think that would deter them. They were ready to make a suicide run on Babylon 5. If they knew the *Agamemnon* was there, they would probably just make a run for the jump gate. The only other plan John had been able to come up with was to place the *Agamemnon* directly in front of the jump gate. Again, it most likely wouldn't stop the cruiser. They were already suicidal. They might even think they could win the game of chicken. This strategy would stop the cruiser and save Babylon 5, but at the price of his ship and crew.

The only thing that seemed to be going right was the weapons crew. Ross had reported that Spano was working harder than Ross had ever seen him, and that even Watley had been inspired to put in some effort. It seemed he'd finally solved his problems with them, though probably too late.

Ross had been on standby on his link, and now his voice came through. "Laser cannons back on line, Captain."

John licked his lips. "Good work, Ross. Now get someone into that manual targeting system and we'll finish this."

"Manual targeting, sir?" The uncertainty had returned beneath Ross's booming voice.

"Yes. You know the Homeguard ship has an Earthforce signature. Our targeting computer won't let us fire on it."

"With everything going on, Captain, I forgot."

John was acutely aware of time passing. "Why don't you let Spano make the shot? You told me his work on the tube has been incredible."

"I'm the only officer here, sir. The others aren't back from the tube yet."

John's jaw clenched. "Then get in there, Lieutenant. We don't have a minute to waste."

"Yes, sir," Ross said. "Stand by."

John narrowed his eyes. "Helm, I want you to bring us down right in front of that jump gate ahead of the cruiser. Best possible speed. Position the ship broadside, with its starboard side facing the cruiser, so that it will form the most effective blockade to the jump gate." If Ross couldn't make the shot, they'd stop the cruiser. One way or another. Of course positioning the ship side-on not only created the most effective barrier, it also put the occupied section of the ship in the most vulnerable position, right in the path of the cruiser. But if that was the only way they could stop the cruiser, so be it.

He thought briefly of Anna, longing for the warmth

and vitality of her presence, the sandpaper caress of her hands. He wondered if she'd gotten his New Year's message yet.

"I'm in, Captain," Ross said. "Fore starboard cannon. I'm okay."

"Stand by for my order," John said. "Communications, open a channel." The cruiser was within visual range now, its image filling only a small space at the center of the observation screen as they decelerated into position in front of the jump gate. The familiar dark gray gun-barrel shape of the Earthforce heavy cruiser was silhouetted in the starlight of nearby Carutic. It was a smaller ship than the *Agamemnon*, without a rotating gravity section, but it still carried significant firepower, as well as a fighter squadron of its own. "Unknown Earthforce cruiser, this is the *Agamemnon*, Captain John Sheridan commanding. You're carrying illegal explosives. Surrender immediately and prepare to be boarded, or we will open fire."

The communications officer, who looked like she should still be in school to John, turned to him, her eyes huge. "No response, Captain."

"The cruiser is increasing speed," Lieutenant Commander Ving said. The ship's image covered about five percent of the screen's surface now.

John spoke into his link. "Ross, target engines and fire."

There was no response.

"Ross." John activated his link. "Lieutenant Ross."

No response.

Then he heard a voice, distant and hollow, through the link. "That's it. You just sit there. Just like you did during the battle simulation." It was Corchoran. "When the terrorists blow up Babylon 5, John-Sheri-

dan-war-hero's record won't get him a commission on
a paper airplane. Then I'll finally get the command I
deserve.''

John pointed to the security officer, then to his link.
The security officer nodded, rushed off the command
deck.

"They're coming straight at us," Ross said. "The
captain isn't going to let them pass."

The cruiser's image was growing faster now, as it
accelerated. It filled about ten percent of the screen.
The fore fighter bay and guns were etched clearly in
the starlight, though he could see no identifying mark-
ings on the hull.

"Sheridan's not going to commit suicide. When he
can't reach you, he'll pull out of the way."

John was communicating with Lieutenant Commander Ving through hand signals. He tapped his
wrist, then made his two hands into fists and brought
them together.

Ving checked the scanners, then raised two fingers.

The passage led onto a stone parapet overlooking a
huge chamber beyond. Holding the carrying case with
the mice up off the floor, Donne crawled out to the
three-foot-high parapet, and behind her Anna followed. Her heart was pounding, her hard breath creating a recurring circle of fog on her breather. Behind
her Morden followed in a crouch, his arm tucked
against his body. The whirring noise echoed into silence.

The chamber stretched far above them, with rows
and rows of parapets above and ramps linking the various levels. The ones she could see appeared unoccu-
pied. The stone of the walls was carved into ornate,
spiky patterns and covered with runes. The great

vaulted space and dark, carved surfaces reminded Anna of a cathedral, but this was a cathedral devoted to darkness, not light. Far, far above, she found the sole source of the light: a long, narrow crack in the rock, similar to the one they had seen by the egg. Anna considered the distance they had walked, and the direction, as well as she'd been able to estimate it. The crack could be the one that had been below the egg.

Donne was pressed up against the side of the parapet. "Look over," she whispered, "and tell me what you see." Here, Anna sensed, was the source of Donne's fear.

Anna raised her head slowly, Morden beside her doing the same. The light in the chamber had a muddy coloration, and the threadlike, filtered quality she had noticed earlier seemed more pronounced here, as if the lines of reality were fraying apart. The far side of the chamber was shrouded in shadow. Anna estimated it was one hundred feet across. She could make out only one specific feature on the far wall, and it was a column, embedded in the cave wall, yet distinct from it. It was made from the reddish-brown rock of the planet's surface, which meant either that the rock had been brought underground for this purpose, or that a vein of the rock had existed here. The column had the same type of inscription as the pillars above ground, and in fact was similar to those in diameter, yet in better condition in the shelter of the chamber. Anna estimated the distance from the crack to the column. The column actually could be positioned directly below the major pillar. They could be part of a single, massive structure. Anna followed the column down to its base in the floor of the chamber, perhaps forty feet below. It was embedded in the black rock of the chamber. The column could continue even farther underground.

Arranged in orderly rows on the chamber floor
were clear tubes, approximately seven feet long, three
feet across. Some of the tubes were empty; some had
people in them. With a start she recognized Petrovich.
The tubes reminded Anna of the cryogenic chambers
that used to be necessary for extended space voyages.
She looked farther, thinking to identify others from
Chang's party, but instead she found Captain Hidalgo.
From her mouth escaped a small sob of air. She'd sent
him with Razor's group to explore the crack. Farther
on, in the row closest to her, was Scott. Tightness
closing around her throat, she counted the rows of
tubes. Fourteen rows, with ten in each row. One hundred forty people on the *Icarus*. About two-thirds of
the tubes were already filled.

On the near side of the chamber, below Anna's parapet, the egg sat in muddy light, a smooth, innocuous
shape, bloated, waiting. The top of it was only about
ten feet below the parapet. Movement below made
Anna duck her head back, and Anna's faceplate
knocked up against Morden's. His calm was gone
now, eyes wide, lips tight with fear, a mirror into her
soul. She found his hand, cold and clammy with
shock, took it, and they both looked over again. Three
aliens of humanoid shape stood beside the egg. Their
skin was a bluish gray, and they had ungainly large
heads. She couldn't make out their features from
above, but as one extended an arm, she saw long, thick
grasping fingers. These were not like the creature she
had seen in the nodule.

A ripple ran through the egg, and with a shift of the
thready light, the egg seemed to have been in a slightly
different position than she'd previously thought. Occu-
pying the space where the egg had been and now
wasn't, lay a human body in a breather and jumpsuit.

Anna recognized the coarse black ponytail, the comp-pad hanging from his belt: Razor.

The aliens seized him immediately.

"No, I won't!" Razor yelled. "No, I won't! No, I won't!" he repeated and repeated, struggling as they pulled him into a room below the parapet, one she couldn't see. After a minute or so the scream of the drill echoed out into the chamber, drowned out almost instantly by Razor's scream. Anna's gaze locked onto Scott lying peacefully in the tube, her head tilted slightly to one side as if she were sleeping. Something black shone at her temple against the short white of her hair, something metal-shiny extending from temple to forehead, and from temple to cheek, a metal band down the back of the head fastened to something black nestled in her hair just above the nape of her neck. It was an interface of some kind; something to link the brain—to something else. Razor's scream died.

Anna sank down against the parapet.

Donne shook her. "What are they doing?" she whispered. "Explain it."

At last she fully understood the mystery of the mouse, understood the behavior of this race toward them since they had landed, and the motivation behind it. "They use living creatures as part of their bi-omechanical technology, at the heart of their machines. They're preparing the crew to be wired in," Anna said. "They're using us as biological components in their machines."

As that answer registered on Donne's face, Anna realized that was why Donne had kept her alive: to explain how this race lived, how their technology worked, to clarify the threat. "And now that you have your mice and your answers, you'll kill us, right?"

Donne had already drawn her gun. "I'd be happy to

kill the largest mass destroyer of telepaths in our history. They'll probably give me a medal." Her eyes shifted to Morden. "And I've been dying to kill you, you sleazebag. If you'll just go back down the passage."

"There's no way off this planet." Morden's normally smooth voice now carried a slight vibration, probably from shock. "The captain is down there, and most of the crew. I've spotted techs from all three of our search parties. They've got almost everyone."

Anna's link chimed as someone linked in.

"What is this place?" As her head jerked up at the voice, a shape came out of the shadows, a white, waddling snowman shape, thighs brushing together.

"Churlstein, get down!" Anna waved him down with her hand. "Stay out of sight. Be quiet."

Donne had turned her gun on Churlstein. "How did you get away?"

Churlstein crawled onto the parapet, his bulk filling the space. He tried to sit back on his feet, his legs in the suit too restricted to bend. "I don't know. I remember climbing onto the egg and yelling to Chang. Then I was sleeping, and I woke up beside the egg. It had been . . . singing to me. I was trying to find my way back to the surface."

Anna heard movement below and peeked over, Donne and Morden joining her. A bluish-gray alien now stood beside one of the tubes, which held a tech who had been in Anna's group. The alien had opened the tube. It held a round device of some kind in its thick fingers, and it was wiring the device to the interface at the base of the tech's skull.

Some sort of preparation, Anna thought, or programming.

"What the hell are you doing?" Donne said.

Churlstein had his hand on Donne's PPG. She kicked him back, hard, and his helmet banged against the cave wall. Even though Donne had kept her gun, Churlstein had a gun in his other hand, which he now aimed back at them. Anna checked her jumpsuit pocket, found Churlstein had taken the PPG away from her. She wanted to scream. Didn't they understand what was going on right below them?

"There's no point in shooting me," Churlstein said. "I'm just the messenger." He took the PPG and, getting up on his knees, stuffed it into his pocket. "I just don't want you to hurt yourselves."

"That's not my plan," Donne said. And then her body convulsed inward as her hands clutched the sides of her helmet. She let out a tight, deep groan.

Churlstein climbed to his feet. "There's no reason to hide, either. Everyone knows you're here."

CHAPTER 17

In less than a minute, the image of the cruiser had grown to fill over seventy-five percent of the screen. Only the nose of the ship, with its huge fighter bay, and the belly were visible as it rushed toward the *Agamemnon*. It looked like a giant gun barrel pointed right down their throats. John had launched fighters, evacuated the outer levels of the ship, ordered pressure doors and blast doors sealed.

Things had grown quiet over the link. John seldom thought about dying, but as there was nothing much else he could do in the intervening moments, he thought of Anna, and the pain this would put her through. He wanted, more than anything, to see her one more time and tell her he loved her.

The cruiser filled the entire screen now. He could see every gun, transmitter, scanner, and sensor attached to the hull.

"Spano," Ross yelled over the link, "watch out!"

Then a jumble of static and sound squawked from the link, and Ross boomed, "Captain, I'm firing."

"Brace for impact," John yelled. The cruiser was nearly on top of them. When those explosives went, they could take out the *Agamemnon*.

The fore starboard cannon fired, the laser a line of

brilliance against the gunmetal-gray hull of the cruiser, momentarily connecting the two ships. John didn't know if the terrorists set off the explosives or the laser did. He saw two brilliant flares of light in succession, one in the belly of the cruiser, the second, blinding bright, in the fighter bay in the nose. He threw a hand over his eyes. Then, through the diminishing light, he saw the cruiser fly apart, and a huge fragment of hull from the nose flew straight at them. The *Agamemnon* lurched, and John felt the familiar falling sensation as the gravity lessened. A series of explosions ran through the ship like a shudder. John was thrown to the floor. He climbed to his hands and knees. Still the gravity seemed uncertain, his weight varying by the moment. "Damage report!" he yelled.

Ving had climbed to his feet and was clutching the console. "Several major hull breaches . . . sections of decks one through three. Fore starboard cannon destroyed."

John climbed to his feet next to Ving. "Casualties?"

Ving studied the data he was receiving. "Preliminary readings show the hull breaches limited to the evacuated areas."

They stood quiet for a few moments, waiting for further concussions. The gravity stabilized at its normal level. The crew of the command deck all watched John, their expressions gradually changing from fear to relief. Reports began coming in from the different sections to Ving.

John hit his link. "Lieutenant Ross."

"Ross here."

"What's your status, Lieutenant?"

"Fore starboard cannon destroyed, Captain. Other three cannons still operational. Lieutenant Spano has—

subdued Commander Corchoran. Minor injuries to them both. Security arrived soon after.''

John nodded. "Good shooting, Lieutenant."

"Thank you, sir," Ross boomed.

As soon as they had a clearer picture of the condition of the ship and the crew, and they were sure they had all systems under control, John put through a call from the command deck to General Lochschmanan. "The Homeguard cruiser has been destroyed, General."

"You had us worried, Captain. We'd been expecting to hear from you much sooner."

"We had some difficulties, sir." As he explained what had happened, John realized he'd never been prouder of a crew. Despite all the difficulties and divisions they'd begun with, they'd managed to come together into a crack operating team. "The entire crew performed admirably, General. I'd like to recommend Lieutenants Ross and Spano for commendations."

"You write them, I'll sign them," the general said. "It sounds like you need to layover for some repairs."

"Yes, sir."

"How would the *Agamemnon* like to be a part of the honor guard of ships at the dedication of Babylon 5? I believe you could make your repairs there and receive assistance in the treatment of your injured. The presence of the *Agamemnon* would serve as a dramatic sign to all interested parties of the strength of our commitment to Babylon 5."

The crew of the command deck looked excitedly at John. "That would be an honor, sir."

"One well deserved," Lochschmanan said. "Congratulations on a job well done, Captain."

John leaned back in his chair and smiled. "Thank you, sir."

* * *

"I've come to bring you their greetings." Churlstein stood, snowman white, against the darkness of the cave behind him. She'd never quite been conscious of the quality of desperate eagerness that hung around him until now, when it was gone. His arms hung at his sides, no longer working as if to draw out a specific response from someone. His shoulders were back, not hunched forward—in fact, with his head tilted up, he seemed to be striking a rather self-consciously noble pose. Behind the brownish reflection off the faceplate of his EVA helmet, his face was smooth, assured, not wrinkled up in frustration.

Anna stood, and with her Donne, one hand still pressing against the side of her helmet, the other holding the gun on Churlstein. Morden remained where he was, and she wondered if he had given up, or if he simply could no longer move. "Whose greetings?" Anna asked.

"The natives of this planet. The ones you've been trying to meet. They can't communicate in our language, so they sent me as an intermediary. Their name is too long to pronounce—ten thousand letters long, in fact, Dr. Morden. They are an ancient, noble race as far advanced from us as we are from the tree shrew. Their technology, as you well know Dr. Sheridan, is thousands of years ahead of ours. And they're willing to share it with us. Imagine limitless energy, biomechanical ships, an end to poverty—and us, the archaeologists to make the biggest discovery of all time. They've been in hibernation for almost a thousand years and are just now waking up. We woke them up, in fact. Their hibernation has made them very vulnerable; they need time to regain their strength before other races learn of their existence, other races who might covet their technology. They will teach us their secrets, if in turn we keep their secret. They want to work with us, learn from us about what's gone on for the last thousand years.''

"And what about them?" Anna said, pointing down at the crew.

"They didn't understand. They wouldn't have kept the secret, so they're being put asleep until it's safe to let them go.''

"Churlstein, you can't—"

"What did they promise you?" Morden asked, his smooth voice gone raw.

"Whatever I want," Churlstein said. " 'All that is desired.' And they'll give the same to you. You have only two choices: to serve willingly, and be rewarded with your greatest desires, or to serve unwillingly, like them.'' He inclined his head toward the crew below.

Morden touched her leg, pointed a finger down to the left. One of the bluish-gray aliens was making his way along the parapet toward them. Anna checked the other direction and found another approaching from there.

"Are these the ones you serve?" Anna asked. "Why don't they talk to us?"

"Them?" Churlstein brayed out a laugh. "They're servants.''

Anna sensed an opening and pressed it. This had been her original plan: to confront the creature in the nodule. It had hidden itself, had used distractions, deceptions, representatives. If only she could get through to it, perhaps there would be a way out. "Then where are they? Don't they talk to you?"

"They're talking to me right now. They're right here. They're all around you.''

The cave walls behind Churlstein, dark in shadow,

began, in vertical bands, to shift. The cave was no longer empty of light; it was filled with darkness. Anna recognized the solid, structural movement of bodies. They were bodies of darkness, darkness as a positive presence. The darkness gathered, in its shifting, fibrous movement, a shape momentarily suggesting a limb, another a head. Ghosts of constellations followed her eyes like afterimages.

Reality was fraying apart. Through the gaps radiated a furnace of desire, malice cutting straight into her, a hole opening up inside her just as Donne had said, a hole into which she was falling, a hole which needed to be filled.

She thought she was screaming, but then she realized it was Donne screaming, jerking back and forth, hands clasped to her helmet. The scream cutting a notch louder, Donne jerked her hands down from her head and brought the PPG to bear.

Churlstein flew back with the first blast, his chest blossoming with a black flower. Donne hit the roof of the passage next, to block out the shifting darkness, and a huge ledge of rock dropped—oddly fast in the higher gravity—and triggered a cascade. Anna ducked down against the parapet and felt Morden press against her back, shielding her. The bluish-gray alien who was reaching out long, meaty fingers for him jerked back with another blast. Then a torrent of rock spilled out over the parapet, slammed into them, and Donne's scream stopped.

When the cave-in finally subsided, Anna brought her head out from her arms. Her battered arms shook, their movements halting, painful. She was having trouble breathing. Beside her Morden used his good hand to push a heavy rock away. They'd been buried up to shoulder height, the parapet around them filled with rock.

"I can't see Donne," Morden said, breathless also. "Did she fall over?"

As Anna pushed herself onto her knees, she felt a flash of pain in her hip. She looked over the parapet, saw some rocks that had fallen around the egg. If any had fallen on top, they had been absorbed. As Donne would have been, if she had fallen onto it. Otherwise everything looked the same. "I don't see her."

They pulled themselves up, onto the rubble, their movements shaky, weak. On his knees, Morden braced his good hand on his thigh and bent forward, as if he were about to pass out. Anna crawled over the rocks, looking for any sign of Donne. In the gap between two rocks a white sleeve shone through. Anna guessed at the location of the head and began to clear away the rocks. Morden came to help.

Donne's face had finally lost its clenched, sullen look. Her jaw hung loose, and there was a softness to her skin that made Anna realize that the woman was not much older than her. Strands of dirty-blond hair had fallen free down over her face, one grazing the small D-shaped scar on her cheek. Donne's helmet hung propped against one shoulder. Her neck had been broken.

"Anna," Morden said.

In the muddy light all around them, the shadows were moving, moving out from the darkness on the far side of the chamber, moving on the walls, moving along the parapet, all moving toward them.

The full truth hit her then, the truth she'd been avoiding ever since Morden had said it: there was no escape.

But she wasn't about to accept one of the two choices Churlstein had offered.

"The gun," Anna said. "Look for the gun."

She could see Morden read the realization on her face, and the intention, and his mouth rose in a small, resigned smile. "I'm sorry."

They have no interest in the dead.

They dug with intensity now, scraping hands and arms raw as they cleared the area around Donne. Anna realized she was earning calluses for a lifetime, if only they had a chance to form. She saw the glint of metal and burrowed down toward it, revealing the top of the isocase with the mice inside.

The shadows were all around them, the air thick with their movement, their presence. All around her the universe rippled and frayed, Morden the one solid presence beside her. The hole opened again inside Anna. The dark well that needed to be filled.

Anna followed the edge of the isocase, found the latch, opened it. Inside, the husk with the mouse, a hint of warmth, a slightly fishy smell. She broke open the husk, her hands shaking. The mouse looked nearly identical to the one she had destroyed. "Morden, the mouse. I think together we might be able to activate it."

It was a desperate, unsubstantiated idea. Her thoughts had not been strong enough to fully activate the mouse. Who knew if two people might combine their strength to bring it to full activation? But if they could, the explosion, which had destroyed the isolab, would be more than sufficient to kill both of them.

Morden nodded, and she crawled close to him. "Hold on to it and focus on it as much as you can." He had to lift his right hand with his left to position it beside the mouse. Both hands were bloody, as were hers, and she realized he'd finally ruined the smooth skin of his palms.

They clasped their hands around the mouse, their fingers intertwining. His were as cold as death. The top of Anna's faceplate came to rest against Morden's as they both focused down on the mouse, on the object grasped in their four hands.

Then the darkness, which had hovered so close, seeped down into her brain and seized it like a claw. The vast, cold well expanded, swallowing her, unbearable emptiness and burning need. She plummeted downward at the speed of screams.

But the falling could stop, the well could be filled, light and warmth brought into the shadow within her. John could be beside her twenty-four hours a day, proclaiming his love, listing her virtues, his love providing everything he needed, everything she needed. Every archaeological theory of hers could be brilliant, and correct, her discoveries could change the world, end suffering, bring her peace, recognition, and fulfillment. She could bring people only happiness, no pain. Or the simplest dream, all the worse because she had believed it would come true, and now knew that it wouldn't: she could live to a ripe old age with John, their love only stronger with the passage of time, comfortable yet still passionate, sitting on a pair of rockers on a porch in Iowa. She felt each of these with the pain of a life lived in an instant and then taken away, the dark presence in her mind shuffling through her dreams, animating them with more vividness than Anna ever could.

Any of these could fill the emptiness within her, fill it with a light borne of darkness, a light that would contaminate everything it touched.

None of them would. Not if it was her choice.

The emptiness inside her ached for John as she realized she would never see him again.

She focused on the mouse, only the mouse, its elastic skin, its grayish blocks of shading, its devotion to the machine. And she searched deeper, for the creature at the heart of the mouse, the one that had once made a warm nest of shavings in the dark, and had now been trapped for countless years in a life that was not life. The shades of gray were shifting in block segments. Anna moved her fingers to the side. Lines of charcoal proceeded down the mouse's back, not as quickly as when Terrence had made contact with the mouse, but faster than when Anna had done it alone. Excited, she closed her eyes and focused more deeply on it. She visualized its elegant, complex skeleton, the heart beating at its center, and what she realized now must be the brain. She concentrated on it, feeling a sleepy stirring of awareness.

Wake up! Wake up!

She sensed Morden there, inside the mouse with her, his emotions startlingly intense. His careful control had deceived even her. Most immediate was the fear, which mirrored her own, of the shadows and what they would do. Unlike Anna, he seemed to have little fear of dying; it seemed almost to be desired. Below the fear was a surging tide of pain and exhaustion held back with crumbling barriers. He was ready to collapse. And then at the heart of him she found the excitement at the mental connection to the mouse, at sensing its stirring, at finding Anna there with him. The contact between them was intimate, undeniable.

Together they focused on the mouse's brain, urging it to wakefulness. Anna reminded it of its duty to the machine, telling it the machine needed to be activated, now, the machine needed its service. She felt a surge of heat from it, opened her eyes to see the charcoal moving in a wave, pulsing from head to tail.

An image formed in her mind then, an image of a woman and a girl, dark-haired, smiling, sitting on a commercial transport, looking out the window at the jump gate that would take them on an exciting journey. As the transport approached the jump-gate vortex, the mother took her little girl's hand and exchanged smiles with her. The little girl swung her feet. Just as the undulating red of hyperspace seized them, its currents exploded into a cataract, compressing the waves of space before them, propelling the transport ahead into wave upon wave of nonplace and nontime. Space folded in upon space, the particles of the transport burrowing into a wormhole within a wormhole within a wormhole, a crushing darkness, the cold of absolute zero, an energy well from which there was no escape, no life, but consciousness. And pain. Eternal.

Their cries tore a hole through Morden, a hole which could not be endured. Anna shrank from it.

"Stop it! Stop it!" he cried. "End their suffering. Please. I'll do whatever you want. Please." He was shaking against her, his body racked with sobs.

She squeezed his hands, trying to recover the intimacy she had shrunk from. The hole within him was suffocating, terrifying, all-encompassing. How could she tell him to endure it? How had she ever thought she could heal it? She reached into the maelstrom. *How do you know what they're showing you is true? Or that they'll do anything about it?*

The response came with Morden's careful calm, and she could almost see his fixed smile, the bandage over the abyss. *How do I know it isn't, and they won't? I have to do whatever I can. D'Vech creor chol.*

She had never heard the words of the dead language

pronounced before, so it took her a moment to understand. *Love abides no borders.*

They were in the wormhole, time crushed to an infinite standstill, a moment, frozen, perpetual, a mother and child dying, compressed beyond recognition, the shock of pain holding them together for this last, and eternal, cry to the one they loved. *Every light carries a shadow*, the pillars read. And this was Morden's shadow, the one he couldn't escape.

"Free them," Morden said. "I'll serve you willingly, happily, with all the skills at my command."

The image in her mind changed then, and she saw at last the ship Morden had described, wavering black and spiky against the red currents of hyperspace like a nightmare come to life. The ship shrieked out a beam of energy. The force of it spread in red ripples from its central core, propagating a subtle change through the geography of hyperspace and hypertime, entering, an echo of an echo of an echo, the invisible nonplace and nontime that held a mother and daughter. And with an undulation like a breath, the wormhole dissolved, the frozen moment passed into the future, faded, died. The cries sighed into stillness. The undulation resonated through the hole at the heart of Morden, the gentle lap of waves filling it with blackness, a lake in the darkness, water of peace and forgetfulness. Morden's hands pulled free of hers.

Anna opened her eyes. The pulsing of the mouse slowed, stopped. Morden's back rose, moved away from her. The space between them was immediately filled with shadows. Living darkness surrounded her.

Anna would become the mouse, caught in a cage of sinew and bone, hardwired into a machine, no more than a cog or a chip, a lost bit of organic tissue with a faint memory of nuzzling into warm shavings, lost as much to herself as to others, as trapped as Morden's wife and daughter had been.

In love with the machine.

Serving the machine.

Serving them.

The creature's eyes cut into her, distant stars of icy fire, reminding her of the emptiness she was to face. Would it be so bad to serve them willingly? To serve their hunger, their need, their fire and destruction? Was she willing to put a border between her and John, a border that could never be crossed? Was she willing to desert him?

She had to. If she served them willingly, she would lose herself as surely as if she melded with the machine.

She had failed the team. She didn't want to fail herself.

No excavations.

No friendships.

No life with John.

No life as she knew it.

This border would have to be abided.

She reached a bloody hand into the darkness, seized a chitin-hard limb. It flowed like liquid shadow through her fingers, and in that instant, in that unguarded moment of contact, she finally understood them perfectly. They were older than the oldest artifact she had ever found; they knew the ancient secrets of galaxies, and of the races who populated them, whom they used and manipulated with ravenous malice. They walked in the spaces between stars, in the spaces between molecules. They moved behind the scenes, in shadow, their presence everywhere, their influence in everything. They reveled in chaos, in conflict, in hate, in pain, in suffering. It called to them like music, and they orchestrated it like music. And they would not rest until the universe played them a symphony in fire.

They were the past the universe could not escape. They were the answer to *Where did we come from?* and *Where are we going?* And she was one of the first to be swept up in the currents of this past and future history. To the final question—*What significance can my life possibly have?*—she had no answer, except that she had loved, and learned, and fought, all with passion and all to the best of her abilities, and perhaps those who came after would learn from what had happened to her and the crew of the *Icarus*. But in any case, she would never give up. No matter what they did, no matter how deeply they buried her inside of a machine, she would hold tight to the core of herself. And she would not go quietly.

Her cry was hard. "So be it."

CHAPTER 18

THE ship's singing had grown impatient, eager for activity. Kosh didn't know why he remained. Delenn had failed to have the Earth vessel recalled. The humans had violated the ancient home of the shadows. Their message had barely had the strength to penetrate the atmosphere and reach his ship, a short distance away. None of the humans' vessels would have had the ability to detect it.

He had seen the woman, heard the fear in her voice, the anger at lies. The humans consumed themselves with lies. This woman even lied to herself, sending a message she knew would not reach Earth, knew would not bring help.

He should leave, before his ship was detected. And yet he remained. Waiting. As he had waited for three years. For what must happen.

The ship's song quickened. It perceived movement. The Earth vessel was rising clear of the atmosphere. Crude and ill-proportioned, it blasted its way out of the gravity well and took a course away from the planet and the rim. The ship ceased its singing to play a message it perceived from the Earth vessel. A computer voice said, "This is a distress call from the Earth science vessel *Icarus*. Our engines have reached critical parameters. Please respond with aid.'' The automatic message repeated.

Kosh directed the ship to look inside the Earth vessel. It was empty of life. The ship was quiet, puzzled. Kosh waited. The vessel continued a short distance, then, with a series of bright sparks, exploded in the silence of space. Fragments tumbled away into the darkness.

He broke the silence. ''The avalanche begins.''

Kosh directed the ship onto a new course, and with a joyful song it spread its petals and sped ahead.

Now he could leave. Now he could go to Babylon 5.

Jeff felt the muscles at the back of his neck relax as Ambassador Delenn approached the reception line. Since Ambassador Kosh had sent word that he would not make it in time for the dedication ceremony, Jeff had begun to worry that the whole ceremony would disintegrate before his eyes. Delenn's ship had not been expected until the last moment, and even though he'd been informed of her arrival a few minutes ago, he hadn't known whether she would come to the ceremony or not, considering their last conversation. Without her or Kosh, the ceremony would be little more than empty posturing. With her, it might truly mean something.

He, Garibaldi, and the rest of the security staff had finally, for one precious moment, gotten everything and everyone in order. All ambassadors and representatives had been lined up in the anteroom in a sequence acceptable, if not pleasing, to all of them. All malfunctions were repaired. All criminals were detained. All chaos was eliminated. All crises were resolved. Except one.

Jeff went to meet her. ''Ambassador, I'm so glad

you could make it. The dedication ceremony would be meaningless without you.''

"I do support the purpose of this station, Commander, though the Earth Government has given me reason to question its commitment."

Jeff showed her to her place at the head of the line, beside him. "I look forward to the opportunity to prove that commitment."

She looked up at him, and for a moment he thought, perhaps, that he had made a connection. "I look forward to that also, Commander."

Then the door beside him slid open, and the press secretary came through at the head of her party. She announced to the room, "The President of the Earth Alliance, Luis Santiago."

The president shook Jeff's hand. "Congratulations on putting this all together, Commander. You've done a terrific job. We're counting on you."

"Thank you, Mr. President."

As the First Lady took Jeff's hand, the president moved on to Ambassador Delenn. Steepling his fingers at chest level, President Santiago bowed in the Minbari fashion. "It is truly an honor to meet you, Ambassador."

She reciprocated. "We have come a long way to this moment," she said. "Perhaps we can go a long way farther." She extended her hand to shake his, and they did.

"I hope that we can," the president said.

Jeff realized that he was witnessing the birth of a totally new type of interaction between the races, without threats, without fear. Babylon 5 would be the place for this interaction. It would foster understanding, compassion. It was the dawn of a new age for mankind.

* * *

Outside the *Agamemnon* hung Babylon 5, a shining jewel in the night. Surrounding it were ships from every major race, save the Vorlons, arrayed in proud formation. John felt that he was present at a key moment in history, a turning point. Despite the failure of the previous four Babylon stations, despite the threat to this one, it had survived, and perhaps it could now fulfill its promise.

He'd invited Ross and Spano to the command deck for the ceremonies, and as he studied their profiles, the pride he saw there made him believe that they, too, would fulfill their promise.

The ceremonies were being piped through the com system throughout the ship, and as President Santiago took his turn as the final speaker, they all listened. "This has been a historic day, and I am honored to close these ceremonies with the dedication of Babylon 5. *Dedication* is an interesting word. We have faced many adversities in the building of this place. Forces surround us in opposition to this cause: forces within the universe, and forces within ourselves; forces from the past, and forces of the future. But we have not given up. We have remained dedicated to its cause. And it is this dedication, I believe, that has created this shining beacon in space, and this dedication that will lead to the fulfillment of its cause. We cannot allow this dedication to falter, even for a moment to lose sight of our better natures, for we stand at a crossroads in history, and our actions now will light us down in honor or dishonor to the last generation. We must remain dedicated to this station and its promise, for Babylon 5 is our last, best hope for peace."

John gave an astonished smile as he recognized the quote from Lincoln, his favorite president.

"It is with this belief that I hereby dedicate this station, this hope, Babylon 5, to peace."

The crew broke out in applause. John felt so proud to be a part of this, to be a part of Earthforce. The moment seemed infinitely precious, and momentous. He wished Anna were here to be a part of this, a part of history with him.

"Captain," the communications officer said. "General Lochschmanan on Gold Channel."

Odd that he would call now, John thought. The *Agamemnon* was scheduled for repairs. "Put him through."

The moment he appeared, John knew something was wrong. The general's normally impeccable posture was slightly off. His torso hung slightly forward over his desk, anxious. John's mind raced to think what it might be, unable to come up with anything.

"I'm sorry, John, I have some bad news. I think you may want to take this in private."

It almost sounded like the calls he made to the families of servicemen who had died. "What is it?" he said, finding himself breathless. The answer became irrelevant, because in the moment between his question and the answer, John knew the only answer it could be. It was an answer he had never imagined to hear as long as he lived, an answer that would end his life as he knew it and turn him into someone else, someone incomplete, someone he passionately did not want to be, someone without her. He gulped back a sob, the truth catching in his throat. It couldn't be. It couldn't be. It couldn't be. Had he saved all of these useless people, only to let her die?

"There's been a terrible accident, John."

* * *

Out of the cold and dark, it spoke to her. It explained the secret life of circuits, the joys of circulation and cleansing, the elegance of neurons firing in perfect harmony. It showed her the sublime beauty of itself, a machine vast, elegant, the upsweep of its bones towering dark in the vault of the universe, the subtle shifting patterns on its skin, the perfection of its internal pathways, form and function integrated into the circuitry of the unbroken loop. It taught her the dizzying delight of movement, the grace of flexion, the tight, precise focus of the beam, the joy of the war shriek. All the systems of the machine would pass through her; she would be its heart; she would be the machine. She would keep the systems coordinated, keep the complex, multileveled machine operating in synch, the beat of the song of its life a march that must never miss a note. The skin of the machine would be her skin; its bones and blood, her bones and blood.

And yet here, still, she could feel her body, a limp, useless thing, crude and primitive, yet cold, and longing for touch, longing to be enveloped in his touch—John, the one who held her in the dark and made her warm. The one she would never see again. He would love the machine.

She loved the machine. It was ageless, mighty, never tiring, never slowing. Unified in purpose, efficient in function, it was the perfect mechanism, a closed universe, an integrated loop whose life beat out again and again, a repeated pattern that would never end. It explained the secret life of circuits, the joys of circulation and cleansing, the elegance of neurons firing in perfect harmony. It towered dark in the vault of the sky. It was the machine, and the machine was the universe.

**Based on Original Outlines by
J. Michael Straczynski**

*Don't miss these thrilling
books set in the world of
Babylon 5!*

The Psi Corps Trilogy
by J. Gregory Keyes
**Dark Genesis: The Birth of the Psi Corps
Deadly Relations: Bester Ascendant
Final Reckoning: The Fate of Bester**

Legions of Fire
by Peter David
**The Long Night of Centauri Prime
Armies of Light and Dark
Out of the Darkness**

The Passing of the Techno-Mages
by Jeanne Cavelos
**Casting Shadows
Summoning Light
Invoking Darkness**

Published by Del Rey Books.
Available wherever Books are sold.